A Whisker of a Doubt

A Whisker of a Doubt

CATE CONTE

St. Martin's Paperbacks

This is a work of fiction. All of the characters, organizations, and events portrayed in this novel are either products of the author's imagination or are used fictitiously.

First published in the United States by St. Martin's Paperbacks, an imprint of St. Martin's Publishing Group.

A WHISKER OF A DOUBT

For information, address St. Martin's Publishing Group, 120 Broadway, New York, NY 10271.

www.stmartins.com

ISBN: 978-1-250-76153-8

Our books may be purchased in bulk for promotional, educational, or business use. Please contact your local bookseller or the Macmillan Corporate and Premium Sales Department at 1-800-221-7945, ext. 5442, or by email at MacmillanSpecialMarkets@macmillan.com.

Printed in the United States of America

10 9 8 7 6 5 4 3 2 1

To all the feral cat warriors out there saving lives every day. You are heroes.

Acknowledgments

Cat rescuers, especially those who work with feral cats, are special kinds of angels. People who care for ferals are outside late at night, early in the morning, in all kinds of weather, dealing with all kinds of people—all to make sure these cats have food, water, vaccines, and everything else they need to live their safest, most comfortable lives possible. The cats depend on their caretakers, even if they often can't show it. There are so many dedicated feral cat caretakers I could mention, but the two I want to call out most are Journey Ewell and Joni Nelson. Journey, for everything you taught me and the adventures we had together, and Joni, for your dedication and commitment and all that you do. The cats need more people like you in the world.

Thanks to my agent, John Talbot, and my team at St. Martin's beginning with Nettie Finn, for bringing this book to life. And special thanks to Jason Allen-Forrest for reading this book and making it better; I so appreciate you!

Of course, I wouldn't be here without the rest of the Wickeds: Sherry Harris, Jessica Ellicott, JA Hennrikus/Julia Henry, Edith Maxwell/Maddie Day, and Barbara

Ross. All these years later, the journey is still way better with all of you. Thanks for being my besties.

For all the readers out there: thank you for supporting all us authors. We would be nowhere if it wasn't for you.

And finally, thank you to Aime, my partner in crime and the most patient person I know. This was your first experience with me and my deadlines, and you're still around—and that's saying something! Love you, babe.

Chapter 1

"Maddie, are you sure you don't want me to come with you?" Ethan Birdsong, my business partner and probably soon-to-be brother-in-law, asked. "It seems kind of crazy out there. And I'm not just talking about the snow." Usually nothing much bothered Ethan—it was that chill, West Coast upbringing—but tonight worry lines creased his forehead.

"It's okay," I said, gently moving my chunky orange cat JJ off my lap and setting him down on the couch. He gave a squeak of displeasure and went back to sleep, wrapping his tail around his eyes. I knew exactly how he felt. I dragged myself up and off the couch and deposited my empty tea mug on the coffee table. "I'll be fast."

"But it's late. And dark. And snowing," my sister Val pointed out, snuggling up closer to Ethan under the fleecy blanket they were sharing. Ethan's long legs stuck out from the bottom. Not surprising, given his six-foot-three frame. "We could both come. Just to make sure you're okay, you know?" She didn't actually look like she wanted to go anywhere, but I didn't bother pointing that out.

My sister and my business partner had gotten together last summer, after Val's crappy marriage to her high-school boyfriend officially fell apart. They were perfect for each other and, for people who weren't jaded about their own failed relationship status like I was, adorable together. And since I was currently jaded, the last thing I wanted tonight was to be a third wheel in their cuteness even if it was only for a bad-weather outing—and a non-romantic one at that.

"Honestly, I'm good," I said. "It's not like it's a bad neighborhood or anything."

That was actually an understatement. The Sea Spray Lane community in Turtle Point, where I was headed to feed a feral cat colony, was probably the most exclusive neighborhood in the entirety of Daybreak Island, which consisted of five towns. Most of the residents in Turtle Point were either generational Daybreakers from very old money, or people who had summered here for most of their lives and decided to retire in style. There were a couple of younger families, people who'd made a fortune on Wall Street or in Silicon Valley or something like that, but mostly the demographic was over sixty, and crime was pretty much nonexistent in Turtle Point. The island itself was usually light on crime anyway, but the biggest issue I could remember in Turtle Point was when seventy-year-old Henny Wilheim threatened to run her husband over with her car because he had, in her words, "oogled the waitress" when they'd gone out for their anniversary dinner.

All of which accounted for the small police force—a fact my retired police chief grandfather used to gleefully point out often when he ran the Daybreak Harbor force, a much larger operation.

That was the other thing about our island. Each town had its own police force, which gave all the residents an added feeling of comfort. In the winters when the island was at a quarter of its normal capacity it seemed like overkill, but when the population exploded during the summer season everyone was grateful for the extra oversight.

But I knew what Ethan meant. Things had been surprisingly contentious out in the Sea Spray neighborhood because of the feral cat colony that had come to our attention a few weeks ago. Many of the residents found it appalling that these poor cats had dared to choose "their" woods to live in. Which meant they were opposed to feeders traipsing around out there, setting up cat shelters and feeding stations. When Katrina Denning, my rescue counterpart and animal control officer of Daybreak Harbor first told me there was major resistance to helping the cats, I'd thought she was exaggerating. Rescue people—and as a longtime rescuer and a current cat café owner I could say this—sometimes tended to inflate these types of situations if we felt the people weren't doing enough to help. But I'd seen with my own eyes over the past couple of weeks how much the situation had declined. Someone had even vandalized one of the little shelters some kids from a local school had made us. I couldn't be sure it was someone from the neighborhood, but it seemed pretty coincidental.

Residents had gone from lamenting about the "filthy stray cats" living in their neighborhood to flat out refusing us access through a lot of our entry points to the woods. Lack of education—and a lot of snobbery—in my opinion. But we'd gritted our teeth, pasted on smiles, and attempted to educate, inform, and engage. And with the kindness of a couple of the neighbors with hearts, we had permission to get to the feeding stations through certain yards.

It didn't help that there had been a rash of thefts in the neighborhood—Christmas decorations, for heaven's sake, so probably a bunch of bored rich kids doing the stealing—but the cat feeders were taking the blame. Some of these crazies were even talking about "removing" the cats through extreme measures. Unfortunately, when Katrina had heard about this last week it had sent her into a frenzy. She'd threatened some of the residents with animal cruelty charges, which ultimately resulted in her boss—the new police chief who had replaced Grandpa—banning her from caring for the colony. "At least until things settled down," she'd told me, almost spitting the words, clearly offended at Chief McAuliffe's approach.

So, it wasn't exactly a stable situation. Although I still highly doubted anyone was going to attack me.

It wasn't even my night to feed, but since Katrina had gotten herself banned and most of our other volunteers had quit because of all the turmoil, there was really no one else to do it. The only remaining volunteers were Adele Barrows, this guy Jonathan who couldn't care less about the drama, and me. Adele was one of my volunteers at my cat café, JJ's House of Purrs, and a quintessential crazy cat lady. She had more energy and spunk at sixty than pretty much anyone half her age—like me—especially when it came to cats. Jonathan worked with Katrina at the animal control office. He had covered last night, and Adele this morning, so it was my turn. So off I went: Maddie James, cat rescue superhero—who needed an extra cape because it looked pretty darn cold out.

"Are you really sure you have to go?" Val asked doubtfully, looking out the window. I followed her gaze. The snow had started coming down harder. I reminded myself that I was the cats' only hope of eating tonight and sucked it up. I was a rescuer. We were kind of like the U.S. Postal Service—neither rain, nor sleet, nor snow could stop us.

"I do. And it won't take long. They need food and I have to make sure their water isn't frozen." We'd placed heated water bowls in a shed with electricity that one kind resident let us use as a feeding station. But not all the cats went there, so we had to keep putting water out in the other shelters. Of course since it was freezing out, the water tended to ice over.

Honestly, I did wish someone would go with me. I just didn't want it to be Val. She'd complain the whole time about being cold and wet. And I didn't want to interrupt her evening by taking Ethan up on his offer. Too bad my friend Damian was around. Damian Shaw owned and operated the Lobstah Shack down the street. Usually he was up for anything, but he'd closed up shop for the month to visit his family in Ohio for the holidays. I grabbed my heavy sweatshirt off the back of the couch and pulled it over my long-sleeved tee, then donned an extra pair of socks, my giant puffy jacket, and a scarf.

"Your hat," Val said, tossing it to me.

"Thanks." I pulled it on and tucked the rest of my hair inside my jacket. "Back soon." I headed into the kitchen to fetch my boots and gloves and almost bumped into Grandpa Leo, who was heating up hot water for more tea.

"Where you headed, doll?" Grandpa asked.

"To feed the cats," I said.

"Roads aren't great," Grandpa said. "You want me to drive you? You're a California girl now, after all." He winked at me to show he was teasing, but I knew he would totally drive me if I asked him to.

"Aww, come on, Grandpa," I said, brushing his comment aside. "Once a New England driver, always a New England driver. I can handle a little snow." I hoped. I hadn't driven in snow in a long time. Like ten years.

"Take my truck, not the car," he said.

I nodded. "Thanks." I looked around for JJ and found him snuggled with one of the new cat café residents, Abe.

Abe was a gray kitty with white paws who needed a friend. Found scrounging near a dumpster, he had been very sad and scared when he arrived. After a few days and a lot of loving from JJ and some of the other cats—and the rest of us, of course—he was slowly coming around.

That was one of the things I loved the most about my café. It got kitties out of the stressful shelter environment and gave them a comfy home to live in while they waited for an adopter. People could come and visit with them here and see them in a more relaxed environment, which gave them more of a head start in the adoption process. And the fact that we got to use Grandpa Leo's house for this endeavor and that I got to live with him again was just the icing on the cake.

I gave JJ and Abe each a quick pet, then headed out.

The driving was a little hairy, but not the worst snow I'd ever driven in. It was actually the good kind of snow. Light and fluffy, and the air wasn't as terribly cold as it could've been, so the roads weren't freezing as fast. I took my time, enjoying the quiet. If luck was on my side, I could be in and out of here in half an hour, and back home in my flannel jammies sipping hot tea in front of the Christmas tree and chatting with Grandpa by nine.

I'd always loved being home for Christmas, although this year without Grandma would be really strange. And hard for everyone, especially Grandpa. But it would make the rest of us being together even more sweet, especially now that Val was finally happy.

The thought depressed me a little. I was happy Val was happy, of course. I'd just thought that it was my turn too. My budding relationship with local hottie dog groomer Lucas Davenport had been going so well—until that stupid trip he took off-island last month. Thinking about it made me mad all over again. Who just takes a ferry and promises to be back in a few days, then doesn't come back at all? I still couldn't quite believe it. Lucas had gone to Boston for a gig with his band, the Scurvy Elephants, which happened to coincide with a dog-grooming conference. It had been right before Thanksgiving, and he was supposed to be gone four days max. Then a bad storm shut down the ferry services for a couple of days.

But when they got back up and running, Lucas didn't return on one. All I got was a voice mail the night they began ferry service again that said he had something to take care of and needed to be away for a while.

And then nothing else. Like, *nothing*. He didn't call, didn't text, didn't answer my calls or texts. For a while I was freaking out thinking something had happened to him. It took me a while to come to grips with the fact that he'd blown me off. Pure and simple. Without even bothering to tell me he didn't want to see me anymore.

Since we'd never made our relationship "official" or declared ourselves a couple, I wasn't sure how mad I could be. But then, after agonizing about it for three weeks, I'd finally decided anyone who could do something like that was basically a terrible human, and I couldn't waste any more energy on it. No more wondering, no more worrying, and definitely no more contact—*if* he ever bothered to try to get back in touch.

At this rate, I'd be surprised if he came back at all, although he did have a business here. Which made the whole thing make even less sense. But he wasn't from here, so he'd probably decided that he didn't want to deal with another Daybreak Island winter. It could get kind of miserable for sure, especially if you weren't used to the isolation. And if you were a business owner, the lack of customers could easily shock you—both mentally and financially. But he'd left the business up and running. I'd taken a few casual trips by to confirm that his groomers were still there working.

I knew for a fact that Lucas had taken a few plumbing jobs to plump up his bank account in the off-season. I also knew that he had no desire to ever do plumbing again, so he was probably regretting having to do that. His dad had taught him in the hopes that he'd take over the family business. Instead, Lucas had left Virginia without a backward glance, joined a band, went to grooming school, and ended up here on a little island off the coast of Massachusetts, where he'd claimed to be happy.

I thought he'd been perfect. Perfect for me, at least.

"No such thing, Mads," I said aloud to myself, putting my blinker on and peering through the swirling snow as I prepared to turn onto Sea Spray Lane. "He's just a guy. Actually, he's a jerk." What other word was there for someone who'd ghosted me like that?

As I made the right turn, a car coming way too fast out of the cul-de-sac nearly slid into me. "Hey! What's *wrong* with you?" I smacked my horn. Then realized the car looked a lot like Katrina's dark gray Honda Accord. I squinted at my rearview mirror, trying to see for sure, but the car had already fishtailed off the street and was hurtling away, going way too fast for the weather conditions.

It couldn't be Katrina. She'd been banned, with the subtle threat of losing her job. Katrina knew that her being here would just cause trouble. Plus, Honda Accords were a dime a dozen.

But not all of them had a sticker on the rear window that read ADOPT, DON'T SHOP, like hers did. Like this one did.

I grabbed my cell and scrolled to her number, keeping one eye on the snowy road. If she'd been out here and fed, even undercover, she could've at least told me so I didn't make the trip. But her phone went directly to voice mail.

Weird. She was never out of touch. Especially now, with the situation so precarious.

Tossing my phone back into my bag, I pushed her and the car out of my mind as I parked on the side of the road and prepared to go out into the snow. I prayed it would be an uneventful night.

Chapter 2

The Christmas lights were off at the Prousts' house.

I'm not sure exactly why I noticed this in the middle of the snowstorm, which had picked up in the last few minutes. I was trying to make sure I didn't stray from the Hacketts' property on my way into the woods, and I should've been more focused on how my hands and feet were already freezing and I hadn't even started my job yet. But I'd been in this neighborhood enough over the past few weeks that I could tell you everyone's Christmas decoration story. Especially given the decoration theft scandal.

The Prousts, by contrast to some of the other homes, hadn't had anything stolen—at least that I'd heard—and they kind of flaunted it by lighting up every night. Virgil, the husband, had spent many a day out here tweaking and adjusting their decorations while his creepy wife, June, watched from some window. And their lights were plentiful: lining the roof, dripping down over the top-floor windows, winding around the giant pine tree in their front yard. And they were all white, of course. The only outlier was a small tree out front that sported multicolored, twinkling lights. White candles burned in every window. A classy, white-lighted Frosty the Snowman stood on their farmer's porch, waving his lit-up broom at visitors. But tonight, Frosty was as dull and dark as everything else.

I paused for a moment, hefting my giant bag of cat food to my other arm, and blinked through the snow swirling at me. I would've thought there was a power outage, but the two houses on either side of the Prousts' blazed brightly—the Barneses' and the Hacketts'. The Hacketts had the only house on the cul-de-sac with multicolored lights—a selection that rivaled the Prousts'. I also knew from hanging around here way too much that multicolored lights were quite frowned upon in the neighborhood. They were considered *crass*. Lilah Gilmore, our most prolific island gossip who lived at the top of the street, would tell me that colored lights meant the Hacketts were "new money." Apparently people with old money considered white lights much more respectable. Which made me wonder if Virgil Proust had run out of white lights for his little tree out front, or if he was making some kind of statement.

The Barneses' giant mansion, on the other hand, had the most decorations and lights out of the entire street. All white ("neighborhood-issued," as Katrina and I joked). They also had a giant handmade wooden Christmas sleigh with poinsettias and piles of fake wrapped gifts smack in the middle of the lawn. There were many days I'd seen Trey Barnes, one of the younger residents, out there perfecting things while his much-older wife, Edie, supervised. Apparently, it took quite a bit of time to get this light show to her liking. Trey hadn't appeared to be as interested in the job, but clearly had no choice. I'd wondered if there was some kind of competition between the Barneses and the Prousts.

Directly across from the Prousts, Whitney Piasecki's lights also blazed, though her selection was much smaller.

She'd only managed to get lights on her trees in the front yard and around her porch before her leg injury made it impossible to do anything else. There might not have been many, but they were turned on.

So with the entire neighborhood competing in some kind of silent best-of-Christmas challenge, the Prousts' dark home stuck out like a sore thumb.

"Maddie. Seriously," I muttered to myself. "They probably went out and forgot to set the timer." Which I also knew was a thing, because all the lights turning on at once had nearly given me a heart attack one night as I was heading through the Hacketts' yard next door. "Or blew a fuse. Anyway, what do you care? Let's get this done."

I hadn't always been The Girl Who Talked to Herself. Just lately. And usually in private. But tonight here I was creeping through a stranger's yard in a snowstorm, about to sneak through a snow-covered hedge to get into the woods while dragging a forty-pound bag of cat food. All while talking to myself. I really had become the crazy cat lady.

Gritting my teeth, I kept moving, staying close to the Hacketts' side of the shrubs. They had already given me permission to be in their yard anytime. The Prousts were less understanding about our volunteer contingency coming through to feed the cats.

Not that I was too worried. Even for those who weren't cool, they weren't likely to call the cops on me since I was not only former Daybreak Harbor police chief Leopold Mancini's granddaughter, but the daughter of Brian James, CEO of Daybreak Hospital. And all of these people knew my parents pretty well. Plus, given the ages of some of them, no one wanted to feel like they could be denied a stay in the hospital if they needed it. Not that my dad could actually do that, but the irrational fear was apparently enough to keep them from giving me any grief.

I kept my flashlight pointed at the ground to attract less attention as I moved into the woods. Katrina had given me my own Maglite for the night runs—good not only for its light output, she said, but also a good weapon in case anyone messed with me. She'd said it jokingly at the time, before we knew what we were getting into.

It wasn't that I was naive. It wasn't uncommon for feral cat feeders to get hassled. We'd all heard stories of people getting threatened, and in extreme cases, there had been attacks. But that was usually somewhere in a city, likely a low-income area where crime also ran rampant. Not in rich, fancy neighborhoods like this one. I truly didn't worry coming out here. Except I didn't love prowling around in the dark alone. Especially in the woods. I was definitely more of a city girl.

I was almost at the end of the fence. I paused and turned the flashlight beam ahead of me. I could see the first little makeshift cat shelter not far away, just past the edge of the tree line. And a couple of pairs of eyes, illuminated under my beam. They were waiting. That made it all worth it. I hoped Gus was out here. I hadn't seen my favorite tiger cat in a few days, and I was worried about him. The winter was so hard on these guys.

I shifted my flashlight to my other hand so I could adjust the bag of food. As I did so, it cast a wide beam over the Prousts' yard on my left. There was a gap in the shrubs here, and out of the corner of my eye I caught sight of a dark splotch on the snow. I turned to look, curious, then flicked my flashlight to a brighter setting.

It was a big spot, I could see now. I stepped forward to take a cautious look, hoping with all my heart it wasn't one of the cats, frozen or hurt in some other awful way. It was always a concern about the ferals in the winter. New England winters weren't kind to beings that lived outside. And even when they had caretakers like me and the other volunteers, we couldn't always keep them safe from the elements.

But when I inched closer, I realized with some relief that it was too big to be one of our cats, even the chunky black cat we'd named Toby. Upon closer perusal, it looked like a jacket. Or a duffel bag. Weird. Maybe one of the Hackett kids had been playing in the Prousts' yard, which they'd been known to do much to June Proust's displeasure, and left his jacket outside. Which seemed odd to do in the middle of winter, but those boys were a little nuts so who knew. I'd been witness to a scene when the younger Hackett kid had tried to light a bonfire in the Prousts' backyard, allegedly to practice for his Boy Scout trip, and June had marched over and let Monica have it. Monica, in turn, had grounded the poor kid on the spot, likely so she wouldn't have to listen to the wicked witch of the west side of the street anymore.

Maybe I should grab the jacket and leave it on their front porch. It seemed like the right thing to do. Then maybe the kid wouldn't get in trouble again. And Monica Hackett wouldn't have to listen to June blather on about how she needed to discipline her kids better. Plus, the Prousts clearly weren't home, so I didn't need to worry about getting caught trespassing myself.

Decision made, I stepped through the shrubs and strode toward the jacket. But when I leaned over to grab it, I gasped and stumbled back.

It was a jacket. But not just a jacket. It was also a pair of pants. And shoes. With a body inside them.

A body facedown in the snow. And it wasn't moving. And a few feet away from the body, right near my foot, was one of those scary-looking Christmas gnomes, also lying in the snow.

Trying to process what I was looking at, I crept closer despite everything in my body screaming at me not to.

I was my Grandpa Leo's granddaughter, after all, and I couldn't curb my quest for information. The flashlight fell out of my shaking hand, disappearing into the snow, and I had to root around for it, which got me a snowy hand and a wet glove. Cursing, I grabbed it, then shined it on the gnome. I toed it out of its icy coffin, rolling it over and lifting it to an angle with my foot. His red, pointy hat was broken off at the tip.

I let it fall back into the snow, then refocused on the still form, kneeling so I could see better. The snow immediately soaked into my jeans, making my knees freeze, but I didn't even notice. My entire body had gone numb, and it wasn't from the weather. It was a man, and he was completely still. The snow falling down around him painted a macabre picture of a perfect winter scene gone awry.

But even worse, I recognized the long ponytail crusted with snow and the small diamond earring in his right ear, which was visible with the way his head was angled. There was also a different color to his hair—a reddish tint that I realized with horror was blood.

It was Virgil Proust, the man of the house. No doubt about it.

And it didn't look like he would be turning his Christmas lights on anytime soon.

Chapter 3

"Maddie, when can we order the new stove?" Ethan asked. He looked like a little kid asking when Santa was coming. A really tall little kid with a beard.

We stood in the doorway of Grandpa's formerly un-attached garage watching the contractor crew measure the walls and examine the current flooring, which was basically a concrete slab that Grandpa had painted bright red—his favorite color—a few years ago. To give it its own personality, he'd said.

Ethan had successfully talked us all into transforming the garage into the new and expanded café portion of our cat café, JJ's House of Purrs. We had been operating the café out of Grandpa's kitchen since we opened last May, which obviously hadn't been ideal but was the best we could do at the time. We'd begun the renovation process shortly after the summer season had shut down, and it had been quite the endeavor. But along with a headache that lasted four months, we'd also gotten a much better floor plan for the first floor, one that allowed the cats to have their own wing and us to have an actual living room again. We'd given up our dining room for the cats and opened up the space by taking down the walls between

Grandma's former sewing room and another small room that had gone through many different uses, and created one big open space. The café now had its own entrance—formerly our mud room—and our customers weren't traipsing through our actual living space, which admittedly had been kind of weird. But I was never one to turn down a good tourist season, so I'd opened as soon as I had cats and worked with what I had. While it was a lot slower in the winter months, we still had visitors every week—many were locals and friends—and I'd been using their feedback to tweak the design of the place this whole time.

It was working out well for all of us. And once the garage-turned-café was done, we'd have our kitchen back as well.

I'd always wondered what my grandma thought about this odd turn of events as she watched us from her new all-seeing seat above us. Her beloved house was now home to at least eleven cats at any given time—ten shelter cats plus JJ—although lately that number had been creeping up since we'd seemed to have a record number of strays this year for a fairly small island. Either that or word had gotten around the cat world about the café, and every feline wanted to live here.

Her house was also home to me, which would've surprised her—she'd long ago abandoned any hope that I'd move back to Daybreak Island, especially once I'd moved out West—as well as Ethan, Val, and of course Grandpa, who was in his glory at having such a full house.

I guessed Grandma would find the whole thing delightful. She was the catalyst for all of this, really. I'd met JJ at her gravestone after her funeral. He'd followed me home, and had really begun this whole chain of events that led to the café opening last spring.

But the kitchen. That had been her special place, the

center of the house and despite the large dining room, the place where we all congregated most to eat. These days, if it wasn't for Ethan baking yummy muffins and brewing amazing coffee, it was really a place to store our takeout boxes. But now, Ethan's vision was coming to life and we were moving the café operations to a separate area. Once we got a stove. And that meant we might actually all think about cooking for ourselves again. Well, everyone but me. Cooking wasn't really my thing.

"Did you pick it out yet?" I tried to stall him, because I'd been slacking on getting the new budget reconciled. The renovations had been covered by our "anonymous" donor who had saved the house for Grandpa last summer, but retrofitting the new digs was still costing me more money than I'd planned at this point. The cat café hadn't been open long, and although we'd had a successful first season I wanted to be careful we weren't operating completely in the red from the get-go. But I understood this new space would have a lot of business benefits. It would offer us more seating areas, for one, which meant that any drop-ins could hang in the café while they waited for a slot to open up. I didn't like too many people to be in the cats' space at once. Some of the cats got overwhelmed easily. Without the separate seating in the café, I'd have to turn away anyone who hadn't scheduled their visit online, unless it was a slow day.

Ethan gave me a look that said he knew exactly what I was doing. "I had it picked out before we opened in May," he said.

I sighed. "Okay, fine. Order the stove. I'm adding new items to the store anyway. And my project this week is to get all the items online in Shopify." Since we now had space, I had brought my idea of a little gift shop featuring— but not limited to—JJ-branded items to fruition. I'd been having a blast getting all kinds of stuff made with JJ's adorable face on it, from tote bags to shirts to journals to stuffed toys in his likeness. Also I'd been picking out other items I wanted to stock, all animal related, most of which supported animal charities.

My phone started to ring in my pocket. I pulled it out and glanced at the number. I didn't recognize it, but answered it anyway.

The voice on the other end was vaguely familiar and largely hysterical. "Maddie! They're arresting me and I can't get hold of Katrina and I need someone to come help me *now*!" The last word ended on a shriek.

I frantically racked my brain for the caller's name. I knew it had to be one of our volunteers—dropping Katrina's name had been a dead giveaway—but for a second I blanked on whose shift it was to feed the Turtle Point cats. "Avery?" I asked, crossing my fingers that I had it right.

"Of course it's Avery! Who else would it be? Can you help me or not? Hold on." I heard a man's voice in the background, then Avery's high-pitched squeal. "Hey, back off!"

"Avery." I stepped out of the garage, holding up a finger to Ethan. "What on earth is going on? Where are you? Who is arresting you?"

"I'm feeding the cats and they called the cops on me." Her voice shook. "Katrina said if there were ever any problems and I couldn't get her I should call you. So I did."

Shoot. "Who called the police? Never mind, I'm on my way. Don't do anything until I get there." I disconnected and raced inside, grabbed my bag and Grandpa's car keys from the hook next to the door, and headed to the car, dialing Katrina as I slid behind the wheel. Her phone went straight to voice mail. I gritted my teeth. These were the days I didn't love being her backup.

Katrina was my former babysitter. Once I'd gotten over that, she'd become a friend. We hadn't stayed in touch much in the ten years I'd been off-island, but when I came home last spring—and ended up staying—we'd picked up right where we'd left off. It helped that we were both animal freaks and worked in rescue. Katrina had been a huge influence on me when I was deciding to stay and open the cat café with Grandpa Leo. Since the only other nonprofit rescue group on the island had closed its operations last year, she had been overwhelmed with too many animals, especially cats, when I showed up. Having the cat café as a safe place for some of the island strays was a godsend for her operations, especially since she was one of the few animal control officers—ACOs for short—I knew who actually cared enough to go the extra mile for the animals. It also meant she had a partner in crime for other animal-related adventures, like caring for this colony.

So much for our educate/inform/engage campaign. Apparently we hadn't been as successful as we'd hoped, if one of our feeding volunteers was about to get arrested.

I wondered if Katrina was purposely avoiding this phone call. "Call me," I barked into the phone, then disconnected and tossed it into the center console. I made it to Sea Spray Lane in fifteen minutes. As soon as I pulled onto the street I saw the police cruiser parked outside the Prousts' giant house. And a pair of feet clad in fuzzy boots sticking out of the open back door. As I rolled up, I could see Avery slumped against the front seat fiddling with her long nails.

Well, at least she wasn't handcuffed.

I wasn't quite sure where Katrina had found Avery Evans, although my guess is she was someone's kid home from college for winter break who had gotten tapped with doing some kind of good deed, whether to keep her out of trouble or add to her résumé. And since we were so low on volunteers, as the saying goes, beggars can't be choosers. She was a nice enough kid, but the couple of times I'd met her I'd gotten the sense that she was a drama queen, which made me wonder how much of whatever had happened today was totally innocent on her part.

Then again, she was at the Proust residence, and June Proust was not a fan of the cats—or any of us.

I pulled up behind the police car and got out. The cop standing next to the car looked bored to death. I pegged him as younger than me and wondered how much of a rookie he was. Virgil Proust stood in his yard, slightly away from the cop and his car. His hands were jammed deep into his pockets and he wore a miserable look on his face. When he saw me, he stood up straighter and did his best to put on a blank expression.

Virgil was an interesting character. I'd had the chance to meet a lot of these neighbors over the past couple of months, and he definitely stood out to me as not the typical Turtle-Pointer. He looked like an aging rock star with his long gray ponytail, diamond earring, and five-o'clock shadow. I'd heard he was a retired Harvard professor. I wondered what he'd taught. And while his wife was very vocal about everything (translation: a real pain in the butt), Virgil didn't say much at all. I had assumed he had the same outlook on life as his wife, though, which made me steer clear of him—and it appeared I was right.

"Hi there. What's going on?" I asked, walking over to the young, disinterested-looking cop, offering him my best slightly-puzzled-but-still-so-friendly smile.

Avery saw me and vaulted out of the car, like a spring that had just been uncoiled. "What took you so long?" she exclaimed, tossing her waist-length black hair—extensions, for sure—over her shoulder.

I ignored her and focused on the cop, waiting expectantly for an answer. I could feel my smile slipping a bit in the face of his disdainful gaze.

He observed me with what I imagine he assumed was his perfected cop stare. I didn't have the heart to tell him it still needed some work. These were the types of observations a granddaughter of a former police chief made. "Who are you?" he asked.

"I'm the person I assume you're waiting for," I said. "Maddie James. I'm helping run this volunteer operation. Avery is one of my volunteers."

"Not for long," Avery muttered.

I shot her a look that clearly instructed her to shut up and turned back to the cop. "Officer . . ."

"Patno," he supplied.

"Officer Patno. So is something wrong? What can I help with?"

"This gentleman"—he waved vaguely in Virgil Proust's direction—"called us to report someone trespassing on their property. He agreed to wait while we called you to apparently vouch for her. Not sure what you'd be vouching. If she was trespassing there's not much to vouch for."

Virgil walked over to us. Before he could say a word, the front door opened behind him and his wife, June, leaned out. She was scrawny, with giant glasses and short brown hair streaked with silver. For someone her size, she had a booming voice. "That's right! She was trespassing! You should arrest her now and get it over with."

Virgil paused where he was and visibly winced. "Go back inside, June," he called without turning around. "I've got it under control."

The door slammed shut. He squared his shoulders and focused on me. "Ms. James." His voice was soft. "My apologies. My wife spotted . . . what she thought was an intruder and panicked."

Avery bristled. "Intruder, my—"

"Mr. Proust. So nice to see you again," I said warmly. Sometimes I could be my pillar-of-the-community father's daughter so well I surprised myself. "I'm sorry for the mis-understanding and for alarming your wife, but I'm quite sure Avery didn't trespass intentionally. All our volun-teers have a good understanding of the yards where we have some . . . leeway and those we don't. If she happened to be near your property I'm sure she thought it was still the Hacketts'. Right, Avery?" I stared at her, willing her to agree with me.

Avery kicked at a chunk of ice on the sidewalk. "Yeah," she said. "Right. The Hacketts." Then she threw up her hands and faced the cop. "Dude, I just want to feed the cats. I have stuff to do. Seriously?"

The cop heaved a giant sigh, letting all of us know how he felt about answering this call, and turned to Virgil. "Your call, Mr. Proust. If you want to press charges, we'll bring her to the station."

Avery burst into tears.

"Hold on a second. Press charges? Really? Mr. Proust—" I started, but Virgil cut me off.

"I'm not going to press charges," he said quietly. "Please just stay out of our yard, okay?"

The cop shrugged. "Okay," he said. "Ms. Evans. Stay out of their yard. And any other yard you don't have authorized access to. Got it?" His stern glance moved to me. "That goes for you too," he added, for good measure.

I resisted the urge to roll my eyes.

"Oh, I got it," Avery said. Her voice still shook, but she sounded more angry than upset now. "I won't be in any-one else's yard around here, today or ever. I quit!"

"No. Avery, hold on," I said. "Let's talk about this." She was a drama queen for sure, but we needed her. We had scant volunteers right now, and losing another one would mean I may as well move out here because I'd have to take on pretty much every shift.

"I'm not talking about anything. I'm gone." With another defiant toss of her hair, she stormed off down the street and slammed into a beat-up Hyundai Accent that didn't look very winter-worthy.

The cop gave me one last look, got in his car, and drove away. The Prousts' front door opened again and June stuck her head out. "What is going on? Where is she going? Virgil!"

Virgil Proust met my eyes. "I'm sorry," he said. "You'd better go."

And he turned and walked up to his front porch, leaving me alone on the sidewalk.

Chapter 4

"This is all very interesting, but what exactly would you like me to do to help your cats?"

The man in the doorway of number nineteen Sea Spray Lane wore a pleasant but vague expression on his face as he peered through the crack in his storm door at me and my mom. He held the trifold brochure my mom had handed him between his thumb and index finger as if it might bite him, and leaned slightly away from us as if he were afraid we were criminals who had concocted an elaborate scheme involving cats to try to get inside his fancy house. I didn't recognize him from any of the prior clashes, so he was probably one of the few who actually had a life and minded his own business.

Which was positive, because he could likely be swayed our way—if he cared enough to show up at the meetings and voice his opinion. Which I was kind of guessing he didn't. And that made me start to feel impatient, like we were wasting our time.

My mother, however, was infinitely patient. And enchanting, as usual. "That's the beauty of it," she said, beaming a smile through the door at him that even in his vagueness he couldn't resist. Sophie James had a gift. Charm was her specialty. And she had a knack for making people feel like they were the only person on earth when she was speaking to them. "You don't need to do anything! Just let the kindhearted volunteers access the feeding stations, and help us educate the rest of the neighbors so they understand how important it is. They aren't exactly *my* cats, per se . . . but they are very important to me." She leaned in closer to the door, conspiratorially. "Some people just aren't as understanding and enlightened as you, Mr . . ."

"Barbagallo," the man supplied. "Curtis Barbagallo." He blushed a little under her praise. "I do try to be enlightened," he added modestly.

"That's right. Mr. Barbagallo. Of course you do, and it shows."

"Well, thank you. And you can call me Curtis," he said with a shy smile.

Behind her, I let out a loud sigh.

My mother ignored me. "So you'll be a voice for the cats?"

Curtis nodded eagerly. "I would be happy to. To whom do you need me to speak?"

"Well," my mother said, "there are a couple of neighborhood association meetings coming up. There's one in a couple of days, where my daughter"—here she motioned at me—"will speak to all of you. I don't recall seeing you at the last one?"

"I'm sorry, I couldn't make it." Curtis looked like he now felt guilty about that.

"That's no problem, but we really need you at this one. You see, some people want to—"

"Do you want to come in?" Curtis interrupted.

"No thank you," I broke in smoothly. "It's awfully kind of you but we have a few more stops to make."

"Ah." Curtis looked crestfallen. "I understand." He looked adoringly at my mother. "Please, continue."

"So this association meeting is a special one," my mother went on. "A few of your neighbors have decided to put on the January agenda a vote to take drastic measures to stop the poor feral cats from coming around. It's really not the answer. We'd like to use the special meeting next week to present some facts and opinions on why this shouldn't go forward. We need as many allies as possible to make sure this doesn't happen."

Curtis frowned. "What kind of drastic measures?"

My mother waited a beat for dramatic effect. "Poison," she stage-whispered.

Curtis's eyes nearly popped out. "My goodness!"

I knew how he felt.

"I know," my mother agreed. "It's unconscionable, right? To think of poisoning some helpless animals just because they want to live in a spot they're familiar with."

"No, that doesn't seem like the best option," Curtis said, and I was glad to note his eyes had lost that glossy, adoring look and were more focused on what my mother was saying. "I'm happy to speak up wherever you need. And certainly vote against those kinds of measures."

"Wonderful! Thank you." My mother handed him some of the literature we'd been passing out. "You can read more about the best ways to care for feral cats here. And I look forward to seeing you at the meeting on Monday at six p.m. at the Turtle Point Senior Center!"

"You bet," Curtis said, waving the literature at her. "I'll see you then!"

I leaned over and poked my mother. "Great. Ready to go?"

She frowned at me, then turned back to Mr. Barbagallo. "Please excuse my daughter. She lived in California for too long and now she's cold all the time."

I rolled my eyes as we hurried down the steps back to her car. "Really, Mom?"

"What? I got him on our side, Maddie. Isn't that what we wanted?" She beeped the Lexus open. She'd left the car running so the heat was blasting, and the heated seats warmed my butt as soon as I jumped in.

"Of course it's what we wanted. *If* he shows up. Also he was looking at you like he was a puppy dog and you had a steak. I didn't want him to follow you home." I pulled my scarf higher around my neck and huddled into my coat. "Dad might object."

"Oh, Madalyn." My mother tsked at me as she pulled away from the curb. "You've been so crabby ever since . . . well." She cleared her throat.

I whipped my head around to look at her. "Since what? And besides, you don't know the effect you have on people," I said, positioning the heater so it blasted into my face. "Ask Dad. He'll tell you."

My mother threw back her head and laughed, the sound like tinkling bells. She knew exactly what was up. She glanced over at me, still laughing, and I couldn't help but smile back. My mother's good nature was infectious, no matter what my mood was.

"So what were you saying about me being crabby?" I asked, but the bite was gone from my words.

"Honey." She reached over and squeezed my hand, creeping along down the road now slick with rapidly falling snow. "Whatever it was that happened with Lucas around Thanksgiving. You know you've been a little . . . off since then."

I let my gaze drift back out the window. She was right. My mom was usually right, but this time it was obvious. "A little off" was an understatement. I'd been in a huge funk for the last month since the infamous ghosting.

"So where do we need to stop next?" I asked, keeping my gaze focused at the winter wonderland outside.

I could hear my mother sigh again next to me. I knew

she wanted me to talk to her about Lucas, but the truth was, I was tired of talking about Lucas. Even if most of that talking was happening in my own head.

"We need to stop at the Prousts'," she said.

Now I couldn't help but look at her. "You're kidding, right? They haven't exactly made it a secret that they want the cats gone. Including trying to get one of our volunteers arrested. They don't want anything to do with our spiel. I'm sure they started the petition. They probably already bought the poison." I slumped miserably against the door.

"Of course I know that, honey. Well, not that they've bought poison. I hope they haven't." She looked worried about that. "But it just reinforces that they need to be *educated*." She peered ahead through the snow, flicking her windshield wipers to HIGH. "I think they're very active in the Audubon Society. Sometimes those people have a skewed view of the poor feral cats because they just think about it from the perspective of the birds. Which are very important too, but there's room for everyone. And if we can talk to them about why it's important people feed the cats so they have a consistent food supply, maybe they'll understand."

She looked so determined. I felt a rush of love for my mother, taking time out from her nights—many of them—to help with this effort simply because I'd asked her to, and because she thought she could help, given her and my dad's status in the community. And she really took it seriously too, including doing most of the talking, which I was incredibly grateful for. I knew this effort was cutting into her book-writing time—my mother was an aspiring mystery writer, a new venture in a long string of creative ventures.

"Here we go." She let the car roll to a stop on the street in front of the Prousts' house, skidding a bit as she braked. She peered anxiously at the sky. "It's really coming down. You should probably stay over tonight instead of driving back home, honey."

"I have the truck. I need to get home for the cats," I said.

She gave me a stern look. "Your grandpa is home. Isn't he? And Val and Ethan?"

"They are, but I need to get back."

My mother didn't look convinced. "We'll see."

I hid a smile as I got out of the car and pulled my hood over my head. I followed my mother as she strode purposefully through the snow up to the front door. I couldn't help but admire the lights, even though almost every other house on this street had white lights too. Personally, I liked a little color at Christmas.

My mother was at the door already, her finger poised over the bell, when she turned to see where I was. I hurried the rest of the way. But before she could push the bell, I heard shouting from somewhere around the corner. The two of us froze in place, shamelessly listening.

It was a woman's voice. I recognized it immediately—Whitney Piasecki, who lived across the street. She was so sweet and bought us food for the cats every week. And she was at the side door shouting at June Proust.

"You're just mean, June. And you know what? You're crazy too! How about you mind your own business and stop worrying about what everyone else is doing? You should be ashamed of yourself."

I couldn't make out June's response, but it didn't sound pleasant. But then I heard a male voice say, "That's enough. I think you should leave now."

My mother's mouth dropped. She met my eyes with a *Can you believe this?* look on her face. I peered around the side of the porch in time to see Whitney shake her cane at the open side door. "You are going to be really sorry about all this. Trust me."

Ooh. I leaned over farther, hoping to hear exactly what the Prousts were going to be sorry about. The cats, or something else? I was dying to know. But at that moment June Proust's beady little eyes behind her giant glasses shifted away from Whitney and over to me. Red-faced, I ducked back around. "We should go," I muttered to my mother.

"Too late," she said. "I already rang the bell."

"Great." I blew out a breath. "She's not going to be—" June yanked the door open and glared at us. "What?"

". . . in the best of moods," I finished under my breath.

My mother ignored me. "Hi, June! You remember me, I hope. Sophie James." She held out a hand.

June took it with the enthusiasm of someone being handed a dead fish.

"And my daughter Maddie," my mom continued, as if she'd gotten a warm welcome. "Hello, Virgil," she added when June's husband stepped up behind her at the door, his face solemn. "We wanted to stop by to talk to you both about feral cats, since there seems to be a lot of misconceptions about them. Could we come in for a few minutes?"

"Don't bother!" Whitney shouted at us from the walkway, where she was limping back to her own house. "You'll have a better response from that fence over there!" I could see her chest heaving even through her shiny gold parka, she was so mad.

"Get off my property!" June screamed, almost rupturing my eardrum in the process.

Virgil stepped in front of her. "It's not the best time," he started to say to my mother, but his wife cut him off, her head popping up over his shoulder like one of those annoying bobblehead dolls.

"Cats! You want to talk about cats?" She leaned forward, looking maniacal, her glasses sliding down her nose. "Since when did this become the most pressing matter in town? And why does it have to involve all of us? This is a *private* neighborhood. With private *property*!" Her voice went up on the last word, making her sound unhinged. *"And you're all trespassing!"*

Virgil leaned over and placed a hand calmly on her shoulder. "June, please."

She turned, wrenching away from his touch, and stormed away.

He caught the door before it slammed, shooting my mother an apologetic look. "I'm sorry. Like I said, now isn't the best time."

"Don't worry about it," my always-unruffled mother assured him, pressing a pamphlet into his hand. Katrina had ordered a bunch of literature from Alley Cat Allies, a national organization that helped feral cats. They had a lot of educational materials available. "We're happy to come back when it's more convenient."

Virgil took the pamphlet and glanced at it. I couldn't tell if the look on his face was disdain or something else, but when he looked back up, the facade was back on. "Thank you," he said. "I apologize again. I know it's cold outside."

"If you read that, I'll be happy." My mother beamed at him. "And let us know if you have any questions!" Without waiting for an answer, she took my arm and pulled me down the stairs with her.

Once we were back in the car we looked at each other, wide-eyed. I didn't know whether to burst out laughing or what.

"She's nuts," I said finally.

"She does seem a little . . . off," my mother agreed.

"We should go ask Whitney what that was about," I said.

"We should leave it alone," my mother said firmly. "It's none of our business." Before I could argue any further, she put the car in DRIVE and headed out of Sea Spray Lane, back to the real world full of colored lights and non–cat haters.

Chapter 5

My phone had been blowing up with text messages since I'd stepped my first UGG-clad foot into the Turtle Point Senior Center, where the Sea Spray Neighborhood Association had called a special meeting in the little assembly hall.

"Technically, she's not on Sea Spray Lane so she shouldn't get in trouble if she just comes in," my mother said helpfully, reading over my shoulder.

Katrina was outside texting me question after question, trying to gauge if she'd lose her job if she came to the meeting. I'd told her that if she came in quietly, sat in the back, and kept her mouth shut she'd be fine. My mother seemed to think so too.

I fired off a text telling her to come in with a hat on and be nondescript, then put my phone on Do Not Disturb. If she had any other questions she'd need to come in and ask me in person.

My mom and I were sitting in the front row where Edie Wright Barnes had graciously led us as their "special guests." Edie was heavily on the "no cats" side of the fence, but she knew better than to be rude to my mother. Despite the fact that my mother dressed like a gypsy, free-spirited herself all over the island, and advocated for the "filthy creatures" currently invading Edie's precious neighborhood, she was still Brian James's wife and, therefore, would always command respect.

"I told her," I said, sticking my phone in my bag. "But you know Katrina. She's really worried about all this. As much as she cares about the cats, she needs her job."

The drama with Avery a few days ago hadn't helped matters either. June Proust had called the Daybreak Harbor PD—Katrina's employer—to lodge a complaint because she'd been mad that Avery hadn't been arrested. Tensions were already high since Katrina had been banned from Sea Spray Lane, and he wasn't happy to hear more complaints from that neighborhood. She'd kind of shot herself in the foot when she'd gotten (anonymous) word that someone had started a petition looking to poison the cats. She'd gone straight to the neighborhood and started knocking on doors, demanding to know what kind of soulless individual could even think of such a thing. Needless to say, her approach had not worked in her favor.

Except for a very short stint when she'd left the island for college, Katrina had lived here forever. She cared about the island and the animals on it, especially the ones who needed help. She did the best she could for the animals in need with very little funding and often used her own money. I knew for a fact she personally supplied food for some of the feral colonies around the island, even the ones for which she'd found feeders. Usually people were grateful for the help, and most people felt sorry for the cats. But the Sea Spray people were causing so many problems, it was shocking.

And tonight I had to sit here and listen to them being all fake with my mother and me, and it made me really cranky. But then, most things made me really cranky these days.

The door opened in the back. I turned to see Katrina slinking in, her black knit cap pulled low over her forehead, covering her dark blond hair. She also had glasses on, which was interesting because Katrina didn't wear glasses. I watched, trying to keep the grin off my face as she slid into a seat in the back and pulled her giant puffy coat up around her face. She ignored me.

"Welcome!" Edie Barnes clapped her small, bird-like hands together to get the small crowd's attention, causing me to jerk my attention away from Katrina. I risked another glance around the room to see if any of our allies had come. Monica Hackett was here, and Whitney Piasecki. They sat together in the second row. Monica winked at me. Whitney blew me a kiss. Trey Barnes sat a few rows behind me, arms crossed over his chest. When Edie sent a semi-withering stare in his direction, he sat up straight and pasted an interested smile on his pretty face. I had no idea what his position on the cats was. He didn't seem to have much of a position on anything, although he was, admittedly, nice to look at. Along with being at least twenty-five years younger than Edie—maybe more—I hadn't seen many indications of large amounts of brain cells.

The rest of the crowd, unfortunately, was of the "no" camp. June and Virgil Proust were in the front row. June Proust was practically vibrating with negative energy. Her husband stared at his phone, looking completely checked out. They didn't even acknowledge each other's presence, though they sat next to each other. Elaine Deasy, another neighbor, was a straight-up "no." My mother and I had been to her house recently to offer some education, and she'd basically shut the door in our faces. No sign of a Mr. Deasy, though she wore a ring, so maybe he'd distanced himself from all this. It didn't look like any of them had noticed Katrina yet.

Then there was Lilah Gilmore. She wasn't so much a

no as she was all about the drama. In her unofficial role as town—or really island—crier, she soaked up these things like a sponge and got the news around town faster than the *Daybreak Island Chronicle*.

And speaking of the *Chronicle*, where was the reporter? My best friend Becky Walsh was the editor-in-chief of the paper, and I'd asked her to cover this story. I was hoping that if it got some publicity—slanted toward the cats, of course—that it would make these guys back down. I didn't see anyone who looked reporterish. I hoped she hadn't forgotten.

My mother elbowed me. I turned around and faced front again as Edie waited for everyone to sit and give her their unwavering attention.

"Thank you for making time for this special meeting. We've got some guests here with us today," she went on. "Sophie James and her daughter, Madalyn. They're here to speak about why they feel the . . . critters that live in the woods need to be fed by humans."

I covered up my snort with a cough. My mother sent me a warning look. I got it. *Don't rock the boat.*

But man, these people.

My mom got up and approached Edie with outstretched arms, air-kissing her like the best of them. "Thank you so much for having us," she said, and beckoned me to the front of the room while Edie hurried to her seat next to Trey. I noticed that although there were seats still in the front row next to the Prousts, Edie didn't sit there. Odd, because she and June were usually inseparable.

I joined my mother, feeling stiff next to her. My mom flowed through life like a river no matter what the situation. Her long skirts and giant, colorful scarfs perpetuated the image, and tonight was no different, although she had tried to tone it down just a tad to ensure these uptight New Englanders took her seriously.

"Good evening everyone," she beamed. "Maddie and I are delighted to be here to talk about the feral cats, which I know has become a sensitive topic for your neighborhood." She paused, looking around the room, gauging the response. A few people nodded. The opponents looked even more stiff than I felt. Monica Hackett looked amused. I could tell she thought the whole thing was just stupid. I noticed Curtis Barbagallo standing in the back, like he'd come in late and didn't want to disrupt the class. He gave my mother a little wave, then sat down next to Katrina.

"My daughter is actually the expert here," she said, squeezing my arm. "I'm going to let her tell you the real story about these cats. But first, I want to address some concerns right off the bat." She stepped away from the podium, closer to the crowd, like a lawyer about to deliver what she hoped was an impactful opening statement. "I know there have been a lot of upsets in your neighborhood. Bickering, new people coming in and out—"

"Don't forget the thefts!" This from a guy in the back row whom I didn't recognize.

My mother fixed him with a stare that wasn't exactly withering, but made him squirm all the same. Once he'd quieted down and the silence had dragged on for a beat long enough to make it uncomfortable, she continued. "And some unfortunate acts of theft and vandalism. I want to be clear that my daughter and her fellow volunteers are professionals. They have one purpose only for being in your neighborhood—to help the poor animals who can't help themselves. They are living beings, and the only reason they are outside living in the woods is because somewhere along the way, an uncaring human tossed a cat or two out to fend for themselves. If those cats weren't fixed, they reproduced—and *those* cats reproduced—and before you know it, you have a line of innocent cats who never had the benefit of a warm house or a human touch." She paused and looked around, making eye contact with each member of the fifteen or so people in the audience. "These people—or cats, for that matter—aren't coming around to be a nuisance to you, or to negatively impact your quality of life. So my ask of you all is to have some compassion for the cats and some patience for the volunteers."

A few people shuffled in their seats. Virgil Proust stared at his phone. June shot him daggers out of the corners of her eyes. My mother ignored all of this and looked at me expectantly.

Showtime. Ugh. I hated public speaking. Especially to a room full of unfriendlies. I cleared my throat, trying not to appear as stiff as I felt. "Thanks," I said. "So really, I just wanted to give you some facts about feral cats." I felt like I should have a slide presentation or something. "The most important thing to remember is that they aren't socialized, like my mother said. Which means they don't want to interact with you. They either haven't ever been in contact with humans, or it's been a really long time."

"So they're vicious," June Proust said, nodding so emphatically I feared her giant glasses would fall off her face. "I told you. They could spread rabies." She poked the woman next to her, who yanked her arm away from June's offending finger.

I could see Katrina sit up straight in her seat in the back, and sent her a look. "Not at all," I said loudly, over the hum that had started in the crowd. "It's actually the opposite. They're afraid of you."

"Hmmpf." June didn't sound like she agreed.

"Then why can't they just be moved to a place where they're not bothering anyone?" Edie Barnes chimed in. "Why do they have to live in our woods?"

Katrina literally twitched trying to stay quiet.

Whitney Piasecki slowly pushed herself to her feet,

favoring her bad leg. She reminded me of a younger Bette Midler, with wild red curls and bold makeup. "They aren't bothering anyone," she said, looking straight at Edie. "At least, not anyone who has better things to do."

A snicker went through the crowd. Katrina applauded. Edie shot Whitney a death stare, then turned it on Katrina. I could see her trying to figure out why she looked familiar.

"She has a point, Edie dear," Lilah said from her seat where she was inspecting her manicure. "They're just cats. You'd never see them if you didn't go looking for them." She winked at me and my mother, then met Edie's eyes and shrugged. "I'm just saying."

"It's never ideal to try to move a colony," I said, trying to get their attention back to me. "Especially now that they have feeders." I didn't mention that the long-term plan with feeders was to try to get the people in the actual neighborhood to take responsibility, not just assume the volunteers were going to traipse over there twice a day forever. "It's a last resort. The cats are bonded to their neighborhood. They're used to it. They feel safe there. They might even try to return if they're taken away. And even if this colony was successfully relocated, it can create what's known as a 'vacuum effect.' Meaning other cats will move in to take advantage of the resources."

Edie made a face. I hoped her face froze that way.

"We're also holding clinics where we can vaccinate them for things like rabies"—this with a side glance at June—"as part of our trap-neuter-return efforts so they don't continue to reproduce," I went on, trying to ignore the haters.

"What on earth does that mean?" June snapped. "And how much is it costing us taxpayers?"

Virgil Proust heaved a sigh, then leaned over and said

something into her ear. She frowned at him. He got up and walked into the hallway, pressing his phone to his ear.

I gritted my teeth and refocused on June. "It's not costing *you* anything. It's costing the rescue people money, but not you."

But she had stopped listening to me and was staring after her husband. I could legit see her anger—red rising up her neck and face, making me think of those old Looney Tunes cartoons where one of them—Elmer Fudd, I think?—got so mad at Bugs Bunny that his blood boiled all the way up his body until his head exploded.

"I really don't see what the problem is," Monica Hackett cut in. She stood too, pushing the sleeves of her sleek cashmere sweater up on her forearms. "Who cares if a bunch of cats live in the woods? How is it affecting your lives at all? This whole thing is ridiculous. Christmas is right around the corner, and we should all be focused on being kind, not causing trouble and taking it out on a bunch of harmless animals."

I wanted to applaud her but managed to resist.

Edie turned to her with a saccharine-sweet smile. "My dear, I'm afraid it *is* affecting us. It's bringing our property values down. We have strangers traipsing around our properties. And we've had a *plethora* of valuable items stolen from people's yards."

I had to roll my eyes at this. Apparently some light-up Santas were now valuable items.

"And I'm afraid that's only the start of it. Wait until people's houses actually start getting broken into." Edie crossed her arms and faced front again, daring someone to disagree with her.

My mother accepted the dare. "Hold on a moment," she said sternly. "My daughter is running this operation, and I do take offense at the insinuation that she has brought in undesirable people who are stealing from you all. They are there to do a job. And like I said, they are professionals."

A sudden movement in the back of the room caught my attention. I watched in slow-motion horror as Katrina jumped up and strode up to where my mom and I stood. I wanted to jump in front of her and stop her from doing this to herself, but I couldn't actually move.

She stepped up next to us and faced the group. "I'm sure some of you have no desire to hear from me, but I need to say my piece," she said, pulling the fake glasses off.

I watched Edie Barnes's mouth turn into a giant O. She sat up straighter, as if she was about to say something, but Katrina ignored her and plowed on.

"I'm Katrina Denning and I'm the ACO for Daybreak Island. All we want to do is help these cats. We didn't mean to cause any problems in the neighborhood and we certainly have no interest in stealing anyone's stuff. Yes, I did get upset when I heard that someone wanted to poison the cats—"

"Terrible idea," Curtis pointed out from the back of the room.

"It is," Katrina said. "Thank you. We just want to feed the cats, get them fixed, and let them live their lives. Please just let us do that."

I held my breath. I think my mom did too; certainly Whitney did. Everyone waited in suspended animation to see what would happen next.

But actually, it was nothing that any of us could have imagined.

At that moment June, who had been laser-focused on her husband since he'd left the room to make a call, shot out of her seat and into the hallway after him. From my vantage point at the front of the room, I was at the perfect angle to witness what happened next. Virgil's back was to the door so he didn't see her coming. I watched in fascination as she reached over his shoulder, yanked the phone out of his hand, catching him by surprise, and hurled it against the wall. All heads in the room whipped around at the noise it made as it hit the wall then fell to the floor, shattered.

I held my breath as Virgil turned slowly around to stare at his wife, wondering what he'd do. Shout at her? Worse? But he didn't do anything. Just stared at her, like he'd never seen her before.

June turned around and returned to her seat. "Well?" she demanded. "What else?"

Chapter 6

"So sweet of Whitney to get us all that food," I said, shoving a snow-covered branch aside as we plowed through the woods to our destination.

"Yeah, she's awesome. Too bad more of them aren't like that." Adele Barrows said, huffing a little as she lugged her bag of food and a gallon of water. I worried about Adele. Aside from volunteering regularly at my café, she also worked as a crossing guard, drove a taxi, did all kinds of other rescue work including feeding the feral colony, and smoked like a fiend.

I wished Adele would quit smoking. And drinking boxes of wine. But it was hardly my business. We were on our way to check traps and do the morning feeding. Adele had come to the café early and gotten things cleaned in record time, so we figured it would be easier to just go together and get it done. When we arrived, Whitney must have been watching for us. She had come out to greet us and pointed us toward her garage, where we found two giant bags of dry cat food and two cases of wet food.

"A little something to help out," she said, giving me a kiss on the cheek. "I wish I could get in there and feed for you."

"Eventually," I told her. "You need to get all the way better first."

She rubbed her leg and grimaced. "Seems like this is taking forever."

I supposed I should ask her what had happened to her leg at some point, but that also wasn't my business and honestly, I just wanted to feed and get out of there. I thanked her and grabbed one of the cases of wet food.

Armed with it and two traps, I headed off, walking slightly ahead of Adele. The first thing I noticed were all the footprints. I frowned. None of our people—well, the one person we had left besides us two—would've come out here already. We were tightly coordinated, and with so few of us it was hard to get in each other's way. Also it hadn't snowed for the past two days, so everything was pretty tamped down and starting to melt in some places with the fluctuating temps. But it looked like there had been a lot of people running around out here. Literally. The prints went in circles in some spots, like people were chasing each other.

Weird. I figured it was a bunch of kids messing around, though. What else was there to do out here in the winter?

"At least there are a couple of good neighbors," I said over my shoulder to Adele. "We have enough dry food for the next two weeks at least. And the wet food should last about that long too." Finding people to physically do the feeding would be our number-one win, but people who bought us food were close seconds. Even buying cheaper food, feeding a whole feral colony was expensive. And if you were feeding more than one colony at a time, well, the food bill alone could be insurmountable, never mind vet care to get them all fixed and up to date on vaccines even at the heavily-discounted clinic rates. And since Katrina wasn't allowed to collect donations in her official capacity as animal control officer, the donations had to be given to me through the cat café. Semantics, sure, but that meant on paper that this colony was my responsibility.

Katrina certainly didn't have the funds to support the effort for a long time, although she told me she'd gotten a bunch of anonymous cash donations and had been buying the food that way since we started caring for this colony. The money had been left in her home mailbox every week, which led her to believe it was the person who had alerted her to the colony. Between that and Whitney's donations we were set for a while.

Katrina had gotten an anonymous call about the cats three weeks ago. She'd mobilized her core crew immediately—which was basically Adele and me—and we jumped into action. After assessing the colony over a few days, we estimated about fifteen adult cats and a couple of young kittens. One of Katrina's first acts was to reach out to Dr. Kelly, the island vet who had officially retired over the summer but had unofficially gone back into business when a series of unfortunate events took the new island vet off the scene. Dr. Kelly had been a huge help to Katrina over his many years in business by providing discounted vet care for her rescues. He agreed to vet the cats for his usual discount, and we'd managed to trap five cats and one of the kittens for a mini-clinic last week. The kitten was young enough to be socialized. We'd named him Gimley and he was now at my café. We were going to set traps this morning to try to catch more.

I wondered if the anonymous tipper and donor was Leopard Man, our quirky island character. As his name suggested, he dressed head to toe in leopard-print garb. He also spoke almost completely in Shakespearean phrases, loved cats more than anything, and had a sixth sense for cats in trouble. He always did what he could to help. He never liked taking credit for anything, so it would be just like him to do it that way. I wasn't about to voice that suspicion, though, since talking about his own generosity made him uncomfortable.

Katrina hadn't actually had a feral colony to care for in a while—she, along with the island's former rescue group, had managed to reduce the feral population drastically, and the ones that were left had their own ongoing feeders. We had no idea how or when this situation started out in Turtle Point, but it was even harder to accept given the status of the neighborhood. The last couple of colonies she'd been managing were out on the other side of the island, in more rural communities where people didn't really have the means to care for them. Or know better in the first place not to turn unfixed cats loose outside where they could repopulate.

But this fancy-schmancy neighborhood . . . that was different.

"So where do you want to put the traps?" Adele asked, pausing to look around.

"Over behind the shelters," I said, pointing ahead. Although I must've been a little directionally off today because I couldn't actually get a visual on the shelters. I was hopeless in the woods, even though these woods couldn't have been more than two blocks deep. Good thing too, because otherwise there was a chance I'd get lost when I was here on my own and never make it out. A Girl Scout I was not.

A group of local high school students had built some shelters for the cats, which meant we had more places to store their food, and we could put blankets inside the little houses for them. Before now, we had a makeshift house that Grandpa had tried to make. His effort was valiant, but the house itself was a little iffy. Other than that, Whitney let us use her heated shed. She'd made it a real room with heat and electricity, her attempt at a "girl cave," she'd told us jokingly, but never used it. Which had never really made sense to me since Whitney lived alone in a giant house. The entire thing could be one big girl cave, in my opinion.

Adele was not so patiently waiting for me to get my bearings. "Did you move the houses since I've been out here?"

"No. They're way too heavy. I thought we had put it closer than this."

I took one more slow spin around. We weren't that far into the woods, directly behind the Hacketts' house, which was friendly territory. We'd tried to strategically place the three houses behind homes we knew did not object to the cats or their feeders, so at least one of the houses should be somewhere around where we were standing.

"Thought so," Adele said. "I mean, I know I'm a crazy old bat, but I didn't think I was that crazy." She squinted into the tree line. Then she pointed to the left. "What's that?"

I peered in the direction of her finger. Deeper into the woods, I could see a speck of green, which was the color of the feral houses. "I don't know. Did someone move our house?"

Adele's eyes darkened. "Who would do that? Jonathan's even scrawnier than you." Jonathan was our other remaining volunteer. "If you can't move it, he sure can't." She started toward it.

I had to smile—*Should I consider that a compliment?*—as I dropped the traps and food and followed her. She reached the house a few steps before I did. But the way she just stopped and stared, I assumed there was a problem. I pulled up beside her and surveyed the damage.

This, I wasn't anticipating. Someone had taken one of our shelters and destroyed it. The little shingles had been ripped off and one of the sides had been completely caved in. I had a moment of panic that a cat or two had been inside at the time, but a quick peek in the door with the flashlight on my cell phone put those fears to rest.

"What the . . ." I murmured. "Who would do this?" I circled around it, trying to figure out if there was some way to make it usable again. I couldn't ask the class to make another one.

"Well," Adele said, waving in the direction of the houses behind us. "Plenty of choices, I suppose." She shook her head, disgust sharpening her features. "Though I got a real hard time seeing how they think this'll solve anything. But I guess the rich just don't care."

Adele was even less a fan of the island's upper class than Katrina was. She had her reasons, but the constant reminder of the haves versus what she and Katrina considered the have-nots was a big part of the problem out here. "Yeah, but most of these people are older. You think *I* don't have the strength to move that house? If *I* don't, they sure don't. It weighs a freakin' ton." I'd been surprised at how heavy they were when the teacher and kids delivered them. That had been a banner day. I thought June Proust would lose her mind. She'd stood on her deck glaring at the kids the whole time.

"Not all of them," Adele reminded me. "That Trey Barnes is, what, your age, even though he's married to that nasty old Edie? I mean, man, she's older than *me*." Adele shook her head, no doubt thinking about the injustice of rich old women snagging young hot men. "He's big and strong. Probably had his drunken friends over and they all drank a case of beer and came out here to wreak havoc. Maybe Edie even gave him an extra allowance to do it."

She had a point. Trey Barnes—although not quite as young as me—always seemed to be hanging around, in the yard or on the street, but it was never obvious what he was actually doing. And I had seen him with his group of friends a few times, usually when Edie was off at her charity luncheons or whatever it was she did all day.

Still, it seemed like such a childish thing to do. I tried to shrug it off, even though it made me super sad. "Could've been anyone. There's probably tons of kids with nothing to do who come into the woods to smoke pot or whatever. Maybe they did it just to be jerks." I wasn't sure if I believed that either, but I was having a harder time imagining any of these prissy people taking the time to come out here and figure out how to haul a cat house deep into the woods and destroy it. Their hands would get dirty, for one thing. And the last thing I wanted was for more trouble out here if we all went off half-cocked and started accusing them of doing this. "Look." I pointed to my right. "That house is fine."

Adele sniffed. "For now." She headed over there with her food. I went back to retrieve my stuff, but before I walked over to join Adele I pulled out my phone and pressed the button next to Katrina's name.

"Someone wrecked one of the feral houses," I said when she answered.

"What?" Her shriek nearly went right through my eardrum.

I grimaced and held the phone away until I was sure she was done.

"Yeah. Adele and I just found it."

"Oh, screw this. I'm calling the police."

"I wouldn't do that," I said. "That will cause all kinds of trouble. Chaos in the neighborhood, more police lights, more reasons to complain about us. Plus, what are we going to tell them? That this isn't our property, but we dropped off some cat shelters and someone who does live here vandalized them?"

"So you want to let them win? They have every right to mess with us and keep messing with us because this is their property? It's the woods! No one *owns* the woods." I could feel her anger vibrating through the phone.

"I know. It's crappy and awful and I don't think they should get away with it either. But I don't see a way to get this sorted out without making everything worse. And if they ban us all from being out here, the cats will suffer, no one else. I just wanted you to know, I didn't want to you to fly off the handle."

She didn't answer.

"Well?" I pressed. "Promise you're not going to call?"

The silence stretched so long I thought she'd hung up, but finally she sighed. "Fine. Whatever. We'll just let them wreck all the houses. Maybe they'll kill some of the cats too."

I sighed. "Katrina—"

"It doesn't matter, Maddie. I know you don't want to hear it, but someone's going to pay for this. Mark my words."

Three beeps from my phone, signaling she'd hung up.

"Okay, Godfather," I muttered.

My cell phone rang again before I could return it to my pocket. But it wasn't Katrina calling back to yell again. It was Becky.

"I need a quote," she said by way of greeting.

"About what? It's not the best time," I said.

"Where are you?"

"In the woods."

I could hear her snort a little. "Then it actually *is* a good time. We're doing a story on the thefts in the Sea Spray development. We got a call from . . ." I heard papers rustling as she flipped through a notebook. "Someone named June Proust. She's saying the volunteers are bringing bad influences into the neighborhood."

I felt a flare of anger. June was not only a bully, but she was clearly determined to slander everyone who had a heart along the way. I should've let Katrina call the cops. I was being a wuss trying to keep the peace. They didn't deserve it.

"Yeah? Well I have another angle to your story."

"Oh yeah? Do tell."

"Someone vandalized one of the cat shelters. Adele and I just found it. So I guess it's an eye for an eye, or at least we can make the accusations right back at them."

She whistled under her breath. "Cat fight, eh? Come by the paper. I'm here until six tonight."

I hung up and joined Adele, who had finished filling up dry-food bowls in the first house and was impatiently waiting for my wet food.

"Hey," I said. "You think Gabe will build us some new feral houses?" Gabe, my contractor, was Adele's nephew and an awesome guy.

Adele broke into a smile. "You bet your booty, if I tell him to. I'll call him when we leave. Now get over here with that food. I'm freezing my tush off."

Chapter 7

I dropped Adele back off at the café and ran inside to make sure everything was under control. Val was sitting at the kitchen table, surrounded by a sea of notes, her laptop and, oddly enough, strings of blinking Christmas lights. At least they weren't white. Ethan had something in the crockpot and was perusing a cookbook. There was coffee in the pot. They looked like some backward scene from a fifties sitcom.

"Do I even want to know what you're doing?" I asked Val.

She didn't even glance up. "Working on this Christmas party I'm running tomorrow night. I need lights for every table and I can't decide between the big ones or the little ones." She held up two strings. "What do you think?"

In addition to getting divorced and moving in with me and Grandpa, Val had also started her own business over the last few months. She was now a party planner extraordinaire, running small and large affairs for the island residents including holiday events, birthday parties, and anything else they wanted to celebrate. She loved it and was completely in her element.

"The little ones," Ethan and I said in unison, then

looked at each other and burst out laughing. We'd always been on the same wavelength. It's why we did so well in business together.

Val rolled her eyes and tossed the lights back on the table. "I'll go with the big ones," she said.

"Whose party is this, anyway?" I asked.

"It's for the senior center. In Turtle Point. Dad referred me to the director."

"Aww. That's cute," I said.

"It's going to be fun," Val agreed. "We're doing Secret Santas and everything."

"Adorable." I grabbed a travel mug and poured coffee into it. "I have to run over to Becky's. Can you guys man the café if anyone comes in?"

"I can," Ethan said.

"Thanks. Back in a bit."

I found a parking space right in front of the *Chronicle* and hopped out of the car. I rang the buzzer out front and Becky let me in immediately.

"This just keeps getting better and better," she called down from the top of the staircase that led to the newsroom.

"What does?" I began the trek up, wishing I'd been working out more.

"The Evans family is suing the Prousts. Did you know this?"

"*What?*" I rushed up the rest of the way, winded by the time I reached the top. "As in Avery Evans? Our former volunteer?"

"Yeah. Mr. Evans just called me. Poor baby Avery was traumatized by her recent experience nearly being arrested while she tried to do a good deed." She grinned. "Did they really almost arrest her?"

"Yep." I could only imagine what the Prousts would do when they heard about this. Or maybe they already had, and that was why they'd called the paper in the first place with the news about bad influences infiltrating their neighborhood. So much for trying to keep the peace.

"Come on in," Becky said, leading me to her office. The newsroom was dead, with only one reporter banging away on his computer, and a lone copyeditor yawning as she waited for the final story to plug into the layout. The fast-paced life of a newspaper on an island in the winter. "Thanks for helping me with the story. Coffee?"

"Sure. Are you writing it, or one of the reporters?"

She turned to the little Keurig she kept on a table behind her desk and brewed me a cup. "I am. We've got a bunch of people on vacation. I don't mind." Becky had been editor for a year now—her dream job—but I knew she missed actual reporting a lot of the time. She usually jumped at the chance to do things like this.

I dropped into the chair in front of her desk. "So you're writing a story on this *rash of thefts* in the charming Turtle Point Sea Spray neighborhood?" I used air quotes around the offending phrase. It seemed like a betrayal that Becky was giving them any of her precious inches. Unless the news was that slow and she was desperate. But even then I'd be hard pressed to get behind it.

"Well, yeah." Becky shrugged and handed me my coffee. "It's definitely worth a story. And it *is* slow this time of year."

"Ah, come on, Bec." I put my mug down on her desk maybe with a little more force than was necessary, the coffee sloshing a bit over the sides. I grabbed a tissue to mop it up. "You know it's all nonsense. I wouldn't be surprised if they hid the stuff away somewhere just so they could accuse us of something."

"Maddie." Becky fixed me with her best "you're joking" stare. "That's nuts. Not to mention illegal."

"I know, but I wouldn't put it past them." I still couldn't

believe the chutzpah of those people. I didn't actually blame Mr. Evans for being mad. A lawsuit seemed like a stretch, but I appreciated the sentiment.

"You said someone destroyed your shelter." Becky sat back, winding a blond curl around her finger. "Do you know who?"

"I don't, but it seems pretty likely it's someone from the neighborhood."

"I can't print it because it's likely. Did you see anyone? Get a tip?"

I shook my head. "No. But they didn't see anyone or get a tip that it was me or Katrina or any of our volunteers stealing their stupid Christmas decorations, and you're still writing a story."

Becky thought about that. "Okay. You have a point. We can counterpoint that there's been other acts of vandalism in the area that clearly aren't you guys. You wouldn't destroy your own shelters."

"They'll still try to say we brought *undesirables* to the neighborhood so it's no wonder they're vandalizing everything in sight," I said bitterly.

"Eh, that's weak. The shelters are in the middle of the woods, right?"

I nodded.

She picked up a pen, tapped it against her desk. "I don't have a lot to say about either thing, honestly. Just what was in the police reports, and a quote from Proust and you." She waited expectantly.

I leveled a steady gaze at her. "It's disappointing that anyone would destroy a shelter that a bunch of students made out of concern for the well-being of some poor feral cats who are just looking for a little warmth and food this holiday season," I said.

She grinned. "You're good at that."

"Of course I am."

"What students?"

I gave her the name of the school and the teacher. "Maybe get a quote from him? Or one of the kids?" I suggested helpfully.

Becky thought about that. "That's not a bad idea. I know the principal over there. I'll call her." She jotted down a note on a pink sticky pad and glanced at her watch. "I need to run this story in tomorrow's paper so hopefully I can track someone down."

"So for the rest of the story. Are you going to make it sound like we're a bunch of crazy cat ladies?" I leaned over and riffled through Becky's ever-present candy jar, pulling a Dove milk chocolate caramel out and unwrapping it. "Because that would be wrong. And traitorous." I pointed the candy at her. "And you're my best friend so you shouldn't do that anyway."

Becky regarded me with her big blue eyes. Anyone who didn't know Becky could get the idea that she was the passive, agreeable all-American girl next door. She was tiny, maybe five one, and exuded sunshine and warmth. But Becky wielded her keyboard like a giant sword and didn't take crap from anyone. I've watched her cut down mighty men with one fifteen-inch article, smiling all the way to the printing press. She was sharp, ruthless in her quest for truth, and never gave up on anything that mattered to her.

Especially a story. And the people she loved. Now she frowned at me. "Of course I'm not doing that."

"But I'm sure June's quote is all about pointing the finger at Katrina and the volunteers," I said.

"Maddie. I can't help the quotes. We're reporting the story fairly and objectively. How do you know what she said anyway?"

I gave her a look. "I can make a pretty good guess based on what they say to my face. And it's all crap."

"Well, I don't report crap," Becky said.

"I know, I know." I sat back and popped the candy into my mouth before it melted in my hand. "I still wouldn't be surprised if it's a set up."

"Why do you say that?" she asked.

"Because they really want us to go away. And if they can get people to think we're there to scope out their fancy mansions and to steal things instead of to feed the cats, they can get rid of us *and* turn people against us."

"Sounds like a lot of work," she said doubtfully.

I spread my arms wide. "They don't have much to do. Does June Proust know about the lawsuit?"

Becky shook her head. "If she does, she didn't mention it. It hasn't actually been filed yet. And I'm not putting it in the story for that reason."

"I wonder if Katrina knows about it." I slumped lower in my chair. "This whole thing is such a stupid mess."

"For real," Becky said. "It does seem silly. They really dislike cats that much?"

"It's the *optics*. They think it makes their neighborhood look dirty and brings down property values. Someone actually said that to my mother." I stood and pulled on my jacket. "I have no idea how people can be so cruel. But hey, maybe add a line in the story about how we're accepting donations for the ferals? Money or food?" I winked.

Becky smiled. "Maybe I can add in a sidebar," she said.

As I clattered down the stairs from the second-floor newsroom, I thought about Avery Evans' family suing the Prousts. I actually thought it was kind of funny now, after seeing what someone had done to our shelter. It probably wouldn't go anywhere, but at least the optics would look bad for the Prousts for a while.

Chapter 8

I hadn't trapped any cats yesterday. I'd pulled up my traps at night—it wasn't smart to leave them set if no one could check on them for so many hours—and figured Adele could set them up again in the morning if she'd be around to check on them. She'd volunteered for the morning duty, which left me free to spend the day in the cat café.

JJ, as usual, was my little shadow. He walked around like he owned the place, making sure that everything was in order, that the cats were okay, and that any visitors gave him treats. We had three customers, a record for this time of year. He charmed them all. Usually at least once a day I had to tell someone he was not one of the cats up for adoption, and today was no different. Instead, I pointed the woman to Gimley, and she filled out an application. Then I sold her a JJ coffee mug.

I spent the rest of the time organizing the area we were going to use as our gift shop. Along with my current offerings of JJ-branded items, I'd ordered new tote bags, notepads, journals, and even some fun branded sweatpants and I couldn't wait to start offering them. Thanks to some awesome opening-day publicity, the café was gaining interest not just on the island but beyond, and I'd started to get requests to sell animal-related items.

Always a businesswoman, I'd quickly realized a gift shop was an opportunity to raise my profit margins. The fees to visit with the cats were low by design—we wanted this to be a place where anyone could come and enjoy a few minutes with the furbabies. And ultimately, the goal was to get them adopted, so if a visit turned into a forever home, it was better than making a few dollars. But people loved to buy things, especially in a tourist town. And they loved to buy things from specialty places. So if someone went home with a JJ mug and another trinket or two, all the better.

The house was quiet. Val was planning our Christmas Eve menu and doing some last-minute stuff for her party that night. Ethan was out somewhere, and Grandpa had gone Christmas shopping. So I basically had the house to myself. It was actually peaceful and productive and I was feeling good when Adele called to tell me the traps were indeed set and at last check she hadn't caught any cats, and could I check them tonight when I went to feed?

I told her I would, and figured I'd wrap up work for the day. It was dinnertime and I hadn't stopped to eat lunch. And I had to feed JJ, which was probably why he'd been squeaking at me for the past half hour. "Sorry, bud," I told him. "I'm coming."

He gave me a reproachful look, then stalked to the kitchen with his tail high to wait for me.

I followed him and found the *Chronicle* strewn on the table. I remembered Becky's article and flipped through until I found it in the local news section, page seven. After I put JJ's food in his bowl and as he was attacking it, I read the article while I heated up some leftover chili I found in the fridge. It was short and to the point.

RASH OF THEFTS, VANDALISM HAS
TURTLE POINT COMMUNITY ON EDGE
BY BECKY WALSH

Residents in Turtle Point's exclusive Sea Spray Lane development are struggling to keep their holiday spirit despite a string of thefts that have left many missing Christmas decorations.

"It's really terrible that someone has to try and ruin what should be such a beautiful season," said June Proust, one of the residents. While the Prousts haven't personally had anything stolen, she said it's left her feeling unsafe.

I made a face. What was really terrible was that people could want to try to poison innocent cats, but I guess she couldn't mention that part. I skimmed the rest of the piece while I ate. It was pretty generic: how the police were investigating, that they had instituted more frequent drive-bys, and that residents should install motion detectors in their yards. Near the end there was a brief mention of the feral house that had been vandalized in the woods where some "local animal rescuers were caring for a feral colony." The piece closed with a quote from an Officer McDonald about how they were taking the incidents very seriously. Nothing about the lawsuit, so I guessed it hadn't been filed yet. I still hadn't mentioned that to Katrina. I should tell her. She'd say it was karma.

I tossed the paper back on the table as Val raced into the kitchen, a look of sheer panic on her face. "My car won't start."

"Really? Your fancy car? It's practically brand new," I said. Val had a Lexus, one of the leftovers from her marriage to Cole Tanner. Sometimes I had to remind her that she used to be considered part of Turtle Point's elite.

"It doesn't matter how old the stupid thing is. It won't start and I need to get to the senior center!"

"Well, where's Ethan?" I asked. "Isn't he home yet?"

"He's out at a Tai Chi class with Cass."

I felt a rush of guilt—and a little jealousy—at hearing that. One of the reasons I'd been excited to move home was to get to spend more time with Cass Hendricks, one of my best friends and longtime mentors. Cass owned and operated Jasper's Tall Tales, a spiritual self-help center, tea room, bookstore, and all-around refuge. But now it seemed Ethan was spending way more time with him than I was. I'd been so busy with the remodel, the café, and the colony. And it showed. Ethan was way more Zen than I was these days. I also figured part of me was avoiding Cass because he'd want to get to the bottom of this Lucas thing, and I wasn't ready to talk about it with him yet.

"Well, I need to go feed the cats and check the traps, so you can't take Grandma's car. Grandpa's out too with his truck."

"Then you have to drive me."

I sighed. "Seriously, Val?"

"Yes, seriously! How am I supposed to get there?" She moved past me to grab a Christmas cookie from one of Ethan's early batches off the counter.

"Have you heard of Uber?"

She shot me a haughty look. "*You* might be fine riding around with complete strangers in the dark, but I surely am not."

I resisted an eye roll. "Well, I can drive you but then you have to come with me to feed the cats when you're done."

She shook her head. "I'm managing the party."

"How long is the party?"

"Ends at eight."

I smiled. "Perfect."

We eyed each other, neither of us willing to give in until we got what we wanted.

"Maybe Craig will go with you."

"That's the best you can come up with? Why would I ask Craig when you're right here?"

"Because he's right here too. Behind you." She pointed.

I whirled around to find Officer Craig Tomlin standing at the kitchen door. "When did you get here?"

"Just now," he said.

"Oh. Well, I didn't mean why would I ask you generally. I just mean why would I call and drag you away from whatever you were doing. You know. To come all the way over here." I was babbling. Val watched me with barely concealed amusement.

"No problem," Craig said dryly. "What was it that you wouldn't ask me to do?"

This wasn't awkward at all. I mentally cursed Val. Craig had been my high school boyfriend, and when I'd returned to the island he'd tried to rekindle our old flame. I had to admit I'd given it some thought. Craig had grown up well, for sure. But I'd been interested in Lucas, and even though Craig hadn't been happy with that, we'd settled into a cautious friendship. But he kept tabs on things with Lucas, and I knew he knew that there were some problems. Problems I didn't want to discuss with him.

"I have to go feed and check the traps out in Turtle Point. Adele set them up a couple of hours ago. Dr. Kelly is available for surgeries this week and I have no cats yet."

"And I need the car," Val chimed in. "Something's wrong with mine."

"And she's a big baby and won't take an Uber," I added, for good measure.

He looked from me to Val and back with barely concealed amusement. "Reminds me of high school," he said dryly. "Sure, I'll take you."

I blinked. "You will?"

"Yeah. Give Val the car and let's go."

"But don't you have something else to do? Why did you come over, anyway?" I flushed, realizing how that sounded.

He didn't look fazed by my comment. "I actually came because the chief wanted to make a donation to your party," he said to Val. "We've been donating to all the senior centers on the island for Christmas. Keeping up with Grandpa Leo's tradition," he added with a sideways glance at me. Grandpa had been very generous as the police chief, and every year he would do something for all the senior centers. "Anyway, we have some stuff for you to bring."

"That's so sweet! Thank you," Val said. "I'll get the car."

"That is really sweet. And I didn't mean—oh, never mind." I muttered, ignoring Val's laughter as she left the room.

We swapped out Craig's giant fruit basket and a tray of cookies and brownies for a bag of cat food. I waited while he brought the goodies over to Grandma's car and loaded them in for Val, then we headed out.

"Thank you for taking me," I said.

"No problem. So where am I going?"

"Sea Spray Lane in Turtle Point."

"Oh, this is the colony you guys have been having trouble with. You're trapping cats out there?"

I nodded. "Dr. Kelly offered to fix the ones we could get to try to get that population stabilized. We've gotten six of the cats done. One of them is that cute kitten I have now—Gimley. You know, the little black and white one?"

Craig nodded. He'd been playing with Gimley the other day when he was over to see Grandpa. I keep telling him he should adopt a cat, but so far he hadn't bitten.

"So what will you do if you catch some?"

"We'll bring them to the animal control center. Katrina has a spot for them." I hoped. She'd mentioned the shelter was full right now. She had more dogs than planned. One of the reasons the cat café was so important to the island was because the cats had a hard time in the small facility with the dogs, and if they were overrun with dogs it cut back on the already sparse spaces they had for the cats. This way, they could live in a nice home while they waited to be adopted. I wished we could do the same for the dogs, but that might be a bit much to take on just yet. "If we can get them tonight, Dr. Kelly will spay or neuter them, give them their shots and a flea-and-tick treatment. And tip their ear."

"Tip their ear?"

I nodded. "So they can be identified as being fixed."

"Huh." He thought about that. "And then what happens after that?"

"They recover for a couple of days—longer for the girls—then we put them back."

"So maybe you should tell these clowns out there that you're removing them for good when you trap them," Craig suggested. "Since they want them gone anyway. How will they know the difference?"

"Because we'll have to keep coming back to feed them?"

He thought about that. "Good point."

"Yeah. Maybe you should leave the cat planning to us."

He smiled a little. We pulled onto Sea Spray a few minutes later. "So where should I park?" he asked.

I directed him to the Hacketts' driveway.

Craig obliged. "You have a flashlight?"

I nodded. "You?"

He gave me a look. "Course."

"Cool. You carrying the food?"

"I guess I am," he said with a chuckle.

I waited until he'd hefted the bag, then led the way down the Hacketts' yard. I stuck close to the fence until we got to the tree line, then shined the light ahead. "Ready?" I said over my shoulder. "Let's do this."

Chapter 9

He stepped up next to me, shining his flashlight in tandem with mine. His was better. "Ready as I'll ever be. You really come here and do this alone?" he asked as we moved deeper into the woods.

I laughed. "You act like it's a black ops mission in enemy territory." Although, come to think of it, the enemy territory concept wasn't too far off. "It's Turtle Point. Nothing much happens in Turtle Point, even in the woods."

Craig grunted. "You don't know that. You'd be surprised."

That didn't make me feel much better. I focused on the Havahart traps, which I could now see just ahead. And one of them had a cat. Score!

"Yay," I said quietly, poking Craig and pointing.

He shone his light straight onto the poor cat, who had seen us coming and was now cowering in the back of the trap. I recognized the cat—the fluffy black cat I'd started calling Toby. Katrina had said he was pretty smart about the traps. Thus far he'd evaded capture—I think he'd figured out a way to eat the food without getting trapped.

Cats are so smart. "You mind an extra stop on the way home?"

Craig laughed. "I left myself open for this, huh?"

I smiled innocently at him. "Hey, you never know where rescue work will take you."

"I guess not," Craig said, but he didn't look like he minded all that much. Actually, he was kind of looking at me in a weird way.

I cleared my throat. "So, we should go fill up the food bowls," I said, shining my flashlight on one of the little cat shelters stationed a few feet away.

"Okay. Just food? What about water?"

"We have to go to the shed over there." I used my thumb to point behind us, toward Whitney's house across the street. "There are heated water bowls in there. We'll hit that on the way out." I led the way to the first little shack and peered inside. Empty. I took the bowls out and Craig poured food into them. I returned them to their spots, then shined my light around until I spotted my other shelter. The one that someone had trashed.

"Can you help me with something?" I asked.

"You mean something *else*? Sure thing."

I led the way over to the house.

"What happened to *this*?" Craig asked, circling it.

"No idea. Some kids being jerks, probably."

"Kids? What kids live around here?"

I thought of Monica's boys, but I didn't think they'd do this. They were much more interested in playing Star Wars video games and killing people with light sabers or whatever it was they did in the other dimension. "I'm sure there are kids on surrounding streets," I said. "Anyway, I'd like to see if I can still use it until we get another one built."

Craig knelt to inspect it more closely. "I can probably take this busted wall off. That way you could still put food in there," he said.

I thought about that. Normally I'd worry that with a big

opening, a larger animal could trap a cat in there. But here on the island, there were no predators—like coyotes—like there were out on the mainland. "Can we move it closer to the other one? I'll help."

"Yeah. Let me see how heavy it is." He started to move it alone. I'd forgotten how strong he'd gotten since we'd dated as kids. But still, it was heavy, so I got on the other side and pushed while he dragged.

Once we had it where we wanted it, Craig said, "I think I have something I can use to pry this off in the car."

"Okay. I'll go put the water in the shed while you get it."

He started to reply, but we both heard it at once. Something—or someone—crashing through the woods.

We both froze. Craig whirled around, hand automatically going to his waist. Looking for his weapon, but he wasn't on duty.

Even though my heart was pounding wildly, I managed a nervous laugh. "It's probably a deer. Relax."

But he held up a hand. I fell silent, hardly daring to breathe.

I heard it again. Unmistakable footsteps. Human, not a deer or another animal. And they sounded like they were getting closer. I hated how dark it was out here. I couldn't see anything in the pitch-black, and Craig had grabbed my flashlight and switched it off.

It felt like ages that we were suspended there, waiting to see who or what was coming. Who would be out here at this time of night? In this neighborhood? It wasn't exactly the kind of woods where people would go for a walk on a sunny summer day, never mind a below-zero winter evening with snow. I thought of the thefts I'd been hearing so much about and wondered if the culprit could be skulking around.

The footsteps picked up speed, and sounded like they were right behind us. Craig flashed his light on. "Who's there?" he called out, his voice commanding. No response. Then, suddenly, rapidly retreating footsteps. He started moving toward them, then stopped when he realized they were running in the other direction.

We waited until the sound had faded away, then I turned my flashlight beam up again and looked at Craig.

"Let's finish up and get out of here," he said.

I wondered if it was our decoration thief back to wreak more havoc. But wouldn't someone who was stealing stuff like that need a car? How on earth were they getting away with the stuff on foot?

He picked up the trap and we hurried out of the woods to his car. He put the cat in the backseat and rooted around in his trunk for a minute, then pulled out a small crowbar. "This'll work for the cat house. Wait for me here and we'll do the other thing together."

"I'll just go do it," I said. "It's in her backyard—"

"Maddie." He shot me a look. "You shouldn't be out here alone at this time of night."

I rolled my eyes. "So you gonna come out with me every night? Because the cats need to get fed."

He sent me a side-eye. "I'm serious."

"I am too."

"You don't know what's going on out here. Didn't I hear there's been a lot of thefts? That could've been the thief. If they're bold enough to steal from people's yards, they'd probably think nothing of robbing you blind in the middle of the woods."

I didn't mention that the same thought had gone through my mind. Still, I tried to keep up my confident act. "For what? My cat food?"

"Stay here."

I thought about arguing, but that meant we'd be out here all night and I was getting cold. "Fine," I grumbled.

"Lock the door," he said, then took off back to the woods.

I watched him jog through the Hacketts' yard then sighed and cranked the heat a bit higher. "Well, either way, I'm glad we got you," I said to Toby in the backseat, glancing behind me.

Toby didn't look super glad, but I was used to that. I'd sleep better knowing he was safe for at least a few days.

Craig was back in less than ten minutes with the cat food. "All set," he said. "I filled up the bowls. They were still inside. Now where's this shed?"

I started to get out but he said, "I'll do it. Just show me where."

"I thought we were going together?"

"Maddie. I'm offering to help. Just tell me where it is."

I pointed out my window. "That yard. Food and water." It was kind of nice to have help.

"Did you see any cats?" I asked when he returned.

He nodded. "There were a couple in the shed. They ran and hid when I came in." He locked the doors and put the car in DRIVE. "All set?"

I nodded. "Did you see Whitney?"

"No. But there was a guy who came out onto her back porch when he saw me. I told him I was with you."

"A guy?" I wondered who. "That's good. At least he didn't shoot you." I was kidding, but he looked grim.

"Don't joke. That'll be next. This doesn't seem like the friendliest community. So where to?"

"The animal care center," I said. "I'll call Katrina and tell her we're on our way."

Katrina didn't answer, though. I left her a message to call me back ASAP, that I had a cat to drop off, then sighed and looked at Craig. "I don't suppose you have a way to get in if she doesn't call me back."

He shook his head. "We don't all have access to the center. Only the chief and her backup."

"Who is her backup?"

He glanced at me. "Mick."

I made a face. Sergeant Mick Ellory and I had a bit of a history. Not an entirely favorable one, mostly due to the fact that I'd been his number-one suspect in a murder right after I'd moved back to the island. We were mostly okay now—especially since I didn't do it—but I didn't usually seek out his company.

"Great. I guess Toby is coming home with us." I needed a place to put him. Looks like Grandpa was getting an office mate for a few days.

But at that moment my phone rang. Katrina, thank goodness. "I have a cat," I said.

"Awesome. Which one?"

"Toby."

"Cool. I'll meet you at the Dunkin' over by the town line in less than ten minutes."

I frowned. "What town line?"

"Turtle Point and Daybreak."

"I can just drop him off at the center. I'm sure that's closer for you," I said. "Are you at home?"

"No, I'm out and about so it's fine. I'll see you there soon." She disconnected.

Odd. Why would she be over by the town line? She lived in downtown Daybreak and the center was five minutes from her house. I hoped she wasn't trying to do stuff on the down-low over here at Sea Spray. Or maybe she was just out Christmas shopping and I was totally overthinking it.

I pushed it out of my mind and directed Craig to the Dunkin' to deliver our cargo.

Chapter 10

I stood frozen, staring at the lifeless form in the snow in front of me, not quite knowing what to do. Was Virgil alive? Dead? My instinct told me the latter, given the bluish tint to his skin, but I couldn't be one hundred percent sure. It was cold out, after all. He was bundled up, making it hard to see if he was breathing or not. I didn't want to touch him since this looked . . . suspicious, especially with the broken gnome nearby. I wished the gnome could talk.

How long had he been like this? There were no footprints aside from mine nearby. Not his, or anyone else's. So whatever had happened had been before the snow had really started piling up, wiping away any of that evidence.

I stared at his back, trying to see if it was moving even slightly. I needed to call for help if there was a chance.

But I saw nothing. Everything in my body shouted at me to get out of there. I took a few steps backward, fumbling in my coat pocket for my phone. I should call 911 and get out. Wait by my car for the nice, safe police to come.

"Ah, come on," I muttered, coming up empty. I searched my other pocket. Nothing. I felt around my jeans pockets. Not there either.

Then I remembered I'd left it in my bag in the car. Mentally head-smacking myself, I turned and started to run back toward the street, then detoured back into the Hacketts' yard, slipping and sliding through the snow. I didn't want anyone to see me running away from Virgil Proust's body. That could only bring additional problems I didn't need right now.

But as I hit the Hacketts' driveway, snow exploding from around my boots, Harvey Hackett's car pulled in. He got out, looking at me curiously. "Maddie? What's going on?"

"Harvey!" I burst out. "I need help. A phone. It's Virgil Proust." I pointed behind me, noticing my finger was shaking.

"Virgil? What about him?" Harvey looked behind me, peering through the shrubs.

"He's hurt. Maybe . . ." I couldn't finish the sentence. "We need to call someone and I don't have my phone."

"Where is he?"

"There. In his backyard."

He started to follow my pointing finger. "Go to my door. Monica is home," he instructed.

"But—" I protested.

"Go!"

I ran up their front steps and pressed the bell, missing it the first time I tried. Monica Hackett opened the door a minute later. She looked like she was ready for bed, in a pair of comfy flannel jammies and a cup of tea in her hand. She smiled when she saw me, but her smile faded when she saw the look on my face.

"Maddie? What's happened?" she asked, opening the storm door and ushering me inside.

"Call an ambulance!" I burst out. "Harvey's going over—"

"Harvey? What happened to Harvey?" In a flash, she'd

deposited her mug on the hall table and leaned out the door, looking for her husband.

"Harvey's fine. He's checking on Virgil. Virgil needs an ambulance," I said, finally getting the words out.

Monica snapped into action. She moved into the kitchen and picked up her phone, moving out of earshot. I heard the TV in the other room and figured the kids were in there and she didn't want to call their attention to whatever was going on.

She was still in the kitchen when Harvey came in. It hadn't taken him very long to assess the situation. His face was white. He put his hand on my shoulder, but didn't speak. I understood what he was trying to say.

Virgil was dead.

Monica returned just as the boys realized their dad was home. They raced out of the living room to Harvey, chattering and reaching for him, giving me curious looks. Harvey bent down and gave them each a hug, then told them to go upstairs and he'd be up in a few minutes.

Monica took them up. Harvey and I stood in silence. Snow dripped off our boots onto the expensive hall carpet, but Harvey didn't seem to notice, much less care. By the time Monica returned, I could hear sirens in the distance.

"What happened?" she asked, looking from me to Harvey.

Harvey shook his head. "I don't know, but it doesn't look good."

"Where . . . ?"

"He's outside. In the yard. Maddie saw him when she was cutting through to go feed the cats." He looked at me for confirmation.

I nodded, realizing I'd forgotten all about the cats. I still needed to feed them. They had probably given up on me by now. I felt terrible.

The ambulance and police cars pulled up together. Harvey went outside to meet them. Monica turned to me.

"Would you like some tea?" she asked. "You look like you're freezing."

"No. I mean, I'm not freezing. Yes I'd love some tea. I'm just . . ." I looked outside again.

"Come into the kitchen." Monica slipped an arm around me and led me off. "You've had quite a shock." She flipped on an electric teapot to heat up the water, then pulled out a couple of tea bags. "Chamomile, mint, or rose?"

"Rose, please."

She reached for a mug. "When did you get here?"

"Just a few minutes before I came to your door. I was heading out through your yard when I noticed there were no Christmas lights on next door." I closed my eyes, remembering the sense of foreboding I'd gotten from the dark yard. "I thought about how weird that was. They love their Christmas lights. And then I saw this . . . lump in the snow. At first I thought it was a cat, but . . . it wasn't. I was glad it wasn't, but then I felt terrible." I wasn't aware I was shivering until Monica pressed the hot mug into my hands. I wrapped my fingers around it gratefully.

She kept going to the window and peering out. I could see the worry on her face, although she tried to mask it when she turned back to me.

The door opened and Harvey came in, followed by a police officer. Not the one who had almost arrested Avery, thank goodness, although this one didn't look friendly either. Harvey said something to the cop that I couldn't hear, and then led him into the kitchen. He went over and squeezed Monica's hand.

The cop nodded at Monica. "Ma'am. Sorry to disturb

your evening." Then he homed in on me. "Miss . . ." He glanced at his notes. "James?"

I nodded, still holding on to the mug.

"I'm Officer MacDonald. I need to ask you about what happened when you got here tonight."

I recognized the name from Becky's article. "Okay," I said.

Harvey and Monica exchanged a glance, then Monica said, "We're going to go check on our boys."

Officer MacDonald nodded, not even looking at them as they left the room. He didn't really care about them. I was the one he wanted to focus on. He indicated the table. "May I sit?"

I shrugged. "It's not my table."

Officer MacDonald frowned, but sat. "What's your full name?"

"Madalyn James. Maddie." I paused. "My grandfather is the former Daybreak Harbor police chief. Leo Mancini," I added for good measure.

He didn't look impressed. "You told Mr. Hackett you came across Mr. Proust this evening?"

"I did."

"Do you live in the area?"

I shook my head.

"Are you friends with the Hacketts? Or the Prousts?"

"No. Acquaintances with the Hacketts," I amended.

"So you were here visiting them?"

I shook my head again.

"Then why were you in the neighborhood? Specifically the Prousts' backyard?"

"I wasn't in the Prousts' backyard. At least not until I saw . . . I was here to feed the cats," I said, trying to stifle my impatience. I was pretty sure all the cops in Turtle Point knew about the situation here with the neighbors versus the cats, but clearly he was going to make me go through the whole story.

"The cats?" he repeated in a tone of disbelief.

"Yes," I said. "The cats. I'm sure you've heard all about it."

"Actually, I haven't. But now I can't wait." Officer McDonald sat back as if this was the most interesting story he'd ever anticipated hearing. "Can you tell me what happened? Starting from when you got here."

I took a sip of tea, trying to stop my hands from shaking. My brain kept flashing back to Virgil Proust in the snow with the broken Christmas gnome next to his head. "I got here about . . ." My eyes flicked to the clock on the Hacketts' microwave. It was almost nine. How could it be almost nine? My family would be looking for me soon. "About eight fifteen. I parked a little ways down the street." I jerked my finger behind me as if he could see Grandpa's truck from here. "And I came down to walk through the Hacketts' yard to get to the cat shelters out in the woods."

"So you drove the"—he studied a page in his notebook— "pickup truck?"

I nodded. "It's my grandpa's."

"And you were sneaking through their yard because . . . ?"

"I wasn't sneaking through their yard," I said. "They told me I could cut through their yard whenever I wanted. Some of the other neighbors aren't so . . . accommodating."

"What do you mean?"

"Some of the neighbors were not happy about the cats, and they weren't happy that there were people who wanted to feed them and take care of them."

"So these cats. Where, exactly, do they live?"

I sighed. I didn't mind explaining, but I didn't like this guy's condescending tone and I doubted he really cared about the cats and really, didn't we have more pressing matters to discuss right now? "They're feral. Meaning, they don't have experience with humans. They live outside. They usually stick to the woods behind this neighborhood. That's where their shelters are."

"You come take care of them?"

"I'm one of the feeders. We provide food and shelter to the extent we can."

"And you said the neighbors don't like it."

"I said some of them don't like it. Others, like the Hacketts, are really helpful."

"So did Virgil Proust not like it?"

I hesitated. "Not really. His wife definitely didn't. He wasn't as outspoken as she was, but I'm guessing he had the same opinions."

"So you weren't on good terms with Mr. Proust," Officer McDonald said.

"I didn't say that. I've barely had any contact with Mr. Proust."

He consulted his notes again. "There have been a few calls out to this area recently. One in particular was put in by Mr. Proust."

The Avery incident. I inclined my head in acknowledgment.

He regarded me as if he expected me to crack under his gaze and give him the real story. When I didn't, he said, "So how did you find Mr. Proust?"

"I noticed the Christmas lights were out." I couldn't stop picturing the blackness next door where there was usually bright white lights. "But I had my flashlight and I saw what looked like a jacket out in the snow. I went closer to look." I swallowed hard. "And I realized it was a person, not just a jacket. And I saw the gnome. And . . . blood."

"Blood. Where?"

"In his hair." In my peripheral vision I could see the

flashing lights of what I guessed was the ambulance out-side. I wondered if they were going to the hospital, or straight to the morgue.

"Any other footprints?"

I shook my head. "The snow had covered any tracks, even Mr. Proust's."

"Tell me about this gnome."

"A Christmas gnome." I wrinkled my nose, focusing on that instead of Virgil Proust's still body, his ponytail flat and wet, bloody, and plastered to his neck. "Ugly thing. It was in the snow near the . . . its head was broken off. That's what killed him, right? Someone hit him with it?"

Officer McDonald wrote something in his pad then looked at me. "The medical examiner will determine cause of death. What did you do next?"

"I checked to see if he was moving or breathing. I thought maybe he'd fallen. But he wasn't moving at all. So that's when I ran over here and bumped into Harvey just getting home. He told me to come inside and he went over to see what had happened. I came here and Monica called you."

McDonald narrowed his eyes at me. "You touch any-thing? The gnome, maybe? Or Mr. Proust himself?"

"I moved the gnome with my foot." I could tell he wanted to ask why I went closer to the body instead of running away screaming. I kind of wondered myself.

McDonald still watched me like one would a criminal he half expected to commit a crime right before his eyes. I was getting tired of this and I still needed to feed the cats. Then I wanted to go home and crawl into bed. "Is that all?" I asked.

He nodded. "For now. Please write down your contact information in case I have any other questions." He pushed his pad and pen toward me.

I scribbled my address and phone number and handed it back.

He pocketed it and rose to go, then paused. "Was there anyone else that you knew of who had problems with Mr. Proust? Anyone in the neighborhood, perhaps?"

I hesitated. I'd seen enough crazy stuff around this neighborhood in the last few weeks that I could offer up a few examples for sure. "It didn't seem like too many people were getting along around here," I said.

"What do you mean?"

"People felt differently about the cats and all. And I'd seen Mr. Proust a few times at various neighborhood . . . events, and he seemed to be having some issues."

"Issues with whom?"

"His wife," I said, remembering the neighborhood association meeting.

"They were fighting?"

"Something like that, yes."

"Anyone else?"

I thought of Whitney at their door, screaming at June. But June hadn't been killed. Although her husband had come to her defense. But Whitney? I shook my head slowly. "Not that comes to mind," I said.

"Okay. Call me if you think of anything else." He handed me his card.

I took it and turned it over and over in my hands. "Do you want me to get Harvey?" I asked.

He shook his head. "No need. He gave me his report outside. Thank you, Ms. James." He picked up his coat and walked down the hall. I heard the front door close softly behind him.

The Hacketts still hadn't returned. I needed to go, but I didn't really want to go into the woods alone. I finished my tea and put my mug in the sink, then went over to the bottom of the stairs where they had disappeared. I was going to call out, but I heard their voices, soft and furious at the same time.

"Come on, Harvey. I'm sure people have heard about you giving Virgil a hard time," Monica hissed. "It's going to come out."

"Don't worry about it," Harvey responded, and I could hear the impatience in his voice. "No one needs to know anything about that. So just keep quiet, okay?"

I backed away from the staircase, not sure exactly what I was listening to, but I didn't want them to know I was. I went back to the kitchen and grabbed my coat, pulling it on as I yanked the door open and hurried outside. I went straight to my car and called Ethan.

"Can you come help me feed the cats?" I asked when he answered. "I'll explain later."

Chapter 11

I waited in my car for Ethan to show up. Even though the heat was cranked, I was shivering. I didn't think it was the cold. I couldn't believe what had happened tonight. I felt like I was kind of in shock. Virgil was dead. And not only dead. *Murdered* dead. Someone had taken that creepy gnome and beamed him with it. The cops hadn't confirmed it, but it was obvious. A random act? Someone trying to rob rich people? A break-in gone wrong, like Edie Barnes predicted? Or had the killer targeted him?

I wasn't sure which one would make me feel better. If there was some random killer around here, it certainly wouldn't make me feel safe when I was in the woods, and the cats would still need to be fed. But if it was someone he knew . . .

I picked up my phone again with shaking hands and called Katrina. This time, she answered.

"Maddie? What's up? You okay?"

"I'm fine. But Katrina . . . someone killed Virgil Proust." I bit my lip, realizing I was about to cry.

I heard her gasp, then nothing but silence from the other end of the phone. I couldn't even hear breathing. "Katrina? Hello? You there?"

"I'm here," she said after a minute, but she sounded weird. Robotic. "What are you talking about, Maddie?"

"He's dead. Murdered. I found him in his backyard." I closed my eyes, immediately regretting it because Virgil's body and the gnome appeared behind my eyelids.

"You found him? When? How?" There was a strange hitch in her voice.

"Katrina. Were you on this street today?" I asked, ignoring her question.

"Was I . . . why are you asking me that?"

"Because I thought I saw your car."

Silence. Then, "How do you know he was murdered?"

"Someone hit him over the head. With a Christmas gnome." It sounded ridiculous even to my own ears, but there was nothing funny about it.

"With a . . . Do they know who did it?" she asked. "Do they know who killed him?"

"No, I—"

A fist rapped on my window, nearly giving me a heart attack. It was Ethan.

"I have to go. I'll call you tomorrow," I told her. I disconnected and opened the door, trying to calm my pounding heart. "Didn't mean to scare you," he said, giving me a curious look. "So what's going on? I see police cars. What did you do?"

He was kidding, but it didn't feel funny. "Someone's dead," I said, and watched the smile fade from his face.

"What? Maddie, that's not funny."

"I know it's not funny. One of the people who lives here is dead. I found him in his backyard."

"How did he die?" Ethan asked. "Please tell me it was of natural causes."

I didn't answer.

His face went even more pale, if that was possible. "There has to be a mistake."

I shook my head slowly. "I don't think it's a mistake, sadly. But listen. Ethan." I snapped my fingers in front of his face until he refocused on me. "I still need to feed the cats. Can you please help me so we can get out of here? I really don't want to hang around."

He looked dubiously at the dark woods behind the houses. "Out there?"

"Yes out there," I said impatiently. "Where else?" I really didn't need him freaking me out about going back out there. I had a job to do. I had to stay focused until it was done. End of story.

He looked like he'd rather walk home barefoot in the snow, but he sighed. "Let's go. You have a flashlight?"

I held up my Maglite and looked around for the cat food. Then I realized I'd dropped it somewhere on the ground near Virgil Proust's body. Shoot. I hoped the police would give it to me.

I pocketed my phone—I wasn't going without it this time—and grabbed the gallon of water I'd forgotten on my first, failed trip. I led the way down to where the police were gathered.

McDonald spotted me and came over. "Where are you going?"

"I have to go feed the cats. I didn't get to do it. And I think my bag of food is somewhere over there." I pointed vaguely in the direction of where they were all clustered. I figured it had to be pretty difficult to secure a crime scene in this weather. The snow was still coming down, wrecking any evidence that may have been left. I expected even *my* footprints were gone by now.

McDonald's eyes cut to Ethan. "Who's this?"

"My friend. I called him to help me. I don't really want to be out there alone."

He sighed. "Make it quick."

"Thank you. Can you see about my food?"

He gave me a look that said *I really don't have time for this right now*, but raised his walkie-talkie and spoke into it. It crackled, then another voice barked, "Yeah, there's a bag of food. Send her over."

I motioned to Ethan to follow me and we hurried through the Hacketts' yard. A cop handed Ethan the bag and we continued out to the woods. "You gonna tell me what happened?" Ethan asked finally, once we'd reached the first shelter.

"Later."

We worked in silence, filling up food and water in the two makeshift shelters. At the second, a couple of cats fled out the door as we approached. My heart leaped as I recognized one of them as my missing Gus. "Aww, at least one good thing came out of tonight," I murmured, more to myself.

When we were finished, I said, "We have to go across the street to the shed, then we're done."

Ethan nodded, and we headed back the way we'd come. As we emerged from the Hacketts' yard, I heard June Proust before I came around the corner and saw her. She was wailing, the sound ear piercing and desperate. One of the police officers was restraining her. I guessed she was trying to get through to see Virgil's body, though I had to assume they'd moved it by now. I almost felt sorry for her at that moment.

Then she saw me.

The cries stopped. She took a step forward, her movements jerky, as if her limbs weren't working right. She wore a long wool coat that dwarfed her small frame and a pair of snow boots. I wondered why Virgil hadn't been out with her, wherever she'd been. I grabbed Ethan's arm and started to move in a wide berth around her, but she wasn't letting me get by.

"You!" she screeched, the sound like fingernails on a chalkboard.

I stopped, feeling my frozen face creep toward red. The cops had all turned and were watching too. The one who'd been restraining her froze, arms still outstretched like he wanted a hug, as she advanced toward me.

Instinctively I stepped back, one hand going up in defense. "What?"

Her hand shook as she pointed a skinny finger at me. "You and your rotten friends. You killed my Virgil."

I stumbled backward, her words hitting me like a two-by-four. It was one thing for her to yell at us about trespassing, but to accuse us of murder? "It's horrible what happened, June, but we had nothing to do with it," I said, trying to stay calm even though everything in me wanted to scream back. But after all, she must've been in complete shock, so I tried to cut her some slack. I made a move to go around her, but she reached out with a claw-like grip and clamped on to my arm. I tried to wrench it free but she was surprisingly strong for such a scrawny, older woman. Probably all that yard work.

"I know what you and your friends are up to," she hissed. "Skulking around our neighborhood, stealing things, planning to rob us all blind. Is that what happened? You were trying to rob us and my Virgil stopped you?"

I was so stunned by her words and the venom behind them that I was actually speechless for a moment. But Ethan saved the day. He reached over and plucked her fingers from my wrist. "Officer, a little help?" he said to the cop standing closest.

June whirled on him, advancing with one hand raised as if to strike him. "I'll give you something to complain about—"

"Mrs. Proust!" The cop in charge of restraining her had

apparently gotten back the use of his limbs and stepped in between us. "That's enough. Is there someone I can call for you?" Glancing over at us, he said, "You'd better go."

Ethan grabbed my arm and pulled me away. "Wow," he said when we were out of earshot. "That lady is crazy."

"You're not kidding," I said, still shaken. "She really thinks we had something to do with Virgil's death."

We hurried across the street to Whitney's in silence. As I pulled open the shed, I heard my name being called. Whitney was on her back deck, waving at us.

"Who's that?" Ethan asked in a low voice.

"She owns this house. She's cool. Here." I handed him the water and pointed to the shed. "Can you do this?" I slogged through the rapidly piling snow over to the deck. "Hey, Whitney."

"You okay, honey? What's going on out there?" She jerked her thumb behind her toward the street and all the commotion.

I waited until I reached the deck stairs. "It's Virgil. Something . . . happened. He's dead."

She stared at me, her mouth moving, but no words forming. "He's . . . what?"

"Dead," I said grimly. "I found him in his backyard."

She stumbled back, her cane scrabbling for purchase, and I thought for a panicked moment she was going to fall. But she caught herself on the railing. "My God. What happened?"

"I don't know. The police are looking into it."

She stepped back, brushing snow out of her red curls. "You should go home, honey. Get yourself inside and away from this mess," she said in a strange voice, then yanked open her back slider and went inside.

Odd reaction, but everyone processes this stuff differently I guess.

Ethan joined me a minute later. "Everything okay?"

"Yeah. I just told her what happened."

He looked closely at me. "Are you okay to drive?"

I nodded. "Yeah, fine."

"Let's go." He took my arm and we headed back to our cars. "I'll be right behind you." He opened the door to my truck and waited until I got in and locked the door before heading to his own car.

I turned the engine on and waited for it to warm up while Ethan did the same, absentmindedly rubbing my wrist. I could still feel June's claws wrapping around me like a vise. I thought again how strong she was. How she'd pried the phone out of Virgil's hand and hurled it against the wall the other day, smashing it to bits.

Strong enough to brain her husband with a Christmas gnome and try to blame it on someone else?

Chapter 12

I lay awake in bed and watched the sun come up the next morning. I'd barely slept the whole night. When I did close my eyes all I could see was Virgil in the snow. Or that stupid gnome leering at me with its broken hat. The one time I did fall asleep, I had a nightmare that there was a Christmas gnome in my bedroom and it was coming to get me. Like something out of a Stephen King novel.

Grandpa and I had stayed up pretty late talking after Ethan and I had gotten home. I could tell he was itching to be part of the investigation, but of course he couldn't be. Officially, anyway. But more than that, he was concerned about me and advised me to stay out of the area. I appreciated his concern, but it wasn't an option. I was still the feeder in charge. And of course this happened to be a morning Adele couldn't do, because she was working one of her other jobs, so I was back on duty even though Sea Spray Lane was pretty much the last place I ever wanted to go again.

I dragged myself out of bed and threw on a sweatshirt and some fleecy leggings. JJ got up with me, hoping for an early breakfast. I was happy to oblige if it meant stalling for a bit before I had to leave. I thought of texting

Jonathan, but he was already doing tonight's run. And I wasn't one to push my responsibilities onto other people, so I abandoned the idea as soon as it arrived. Instead, I set about making coffee because Ethan wasn't up yet. Or else he'd gone out for a run to shake off last night's fiasco.

I put JJ's food out and was standing at the counter watching the coffee drip into the pot when Grandpa came into the kitchen. "Doll! What are you doing up?" he asked.

I glanced at the clock. "I'm usually up by now. Besides, I have to go feed the cats."

He frowned, his bushy white eyebrows knotting together. "Okay. I'll go with you."

I looked at him gratefully. "You will?"

"Course I will. I know you're just as stubborn as me and will go anyway, so I may as well come to keep an eye on you."

That made me feel much better. It would also give me a chance to talk to Grandpa about what happened. I poured us both some coffee into travel mugs and we bundled up, then headed out. I had a feeling Grandpa not only wanted to be supportive of me, but also to get his eyes on the crime scene. Both were fine with me.

I was even more than willing to let Grandpa drive. I sipped my coffee and stared out the window. Finally, he broke the silence.

"So what do you think happened to Virgil Proust?"

I took another sip and kept my gaze out the window. "Someone killed him."

"And your gut says . . ."

"I don't know," I said. "Do I want it to be a random, horrible crime? No. But that means someone he knew killed him, and you can't really ignore the timing with everything going on out here."

Grandpa acknowledged my assessment with a nod

as he turned onto Sea Spray Lane. But he didn't have a chance to respond. The dread had already been mounting in my chest as we got closer but my heart sank even further when it registered that there was a cop car in front of the Barneses' place. I had a moment of sheer panic that someone else was dead until I got a little closer and saw Edie standing outside, her arms wrapped around herself as she talked to the cop. Her husband, Trey, stood next to her looking concerned, hands shoved deep into the pockets of his North Face parka.

The rush of relief was overwhelming. I didn't much like them, but I was really glad they weren't dead. "What now?" I muttered.

Grandpa slowed down and I knew he was totally going to stop to see what was going on. I thought about encouraging him to drive past and try to stay out of it, although odds of that working out were about zero to none. It was more likely that he would take on the role of Chief Mancini—stop the car, be polite, and see what was going on and if we could help. Edie might throw a snowball at me anyway, but at least I could say we tried.

Grandpa pulled the truck over and rolled down the window. I took the lead, leaning past him to call out. "Hi there. Everything okay, Edie?"

Three heads swiveled around to look at us. The cop looked curious. Thankfully it wasn't McDonald from last night, or the one who had almost arrested Avery. Trey looked confused. Edie looked angry. Her eyes narrowed to slits when she looked past Grandpa and recognized me.

"I should say not," she said, her voice shrill with tension. "Ever since your friends came to town, they've brought nothing but trouble to all of us. Murders and burglaries! And now *we've* had a theft too! A family heirloom has been stolen!"

"Now hold on just a minute, ma'am," Grandpa said, shoving the truck into PARK. I recognized his uber-polite tone as the one he used right before he lost his temper.

I placed a hand on his arm and squeezed, a silent request to let me speak. "I'm sorry to hear you've had something stolen, Edie, but I can assure you it has nothing to do with me or my friends," I said coolly. "Besides, since most people have been chased away by the very warm welcome they've received from some of the neighbors here, I'm pretty much the only one at this point. So I hope you're not suggesting *I* stole anything." I stared her down. I could see Grandpa Leo smiling in my peripheral vision.

That shut her up. She actually stammered a bit when she responded. "Of course not. I just—we are devastated about our antique Christmas sleigh being stolen, that's all. It belonged to my father." She wiped a nonexistent tear away to heighten the drama. "And we've never, ever had such problems around here before. I mean, the Wilkies' light-up reindeers were stolen the other day too!" She gestured to the house across the street. "And it's completely ruining Christmas."

No mention of Virgil and how his death might put a bit more of a damper on the mood. Odd, given her relationship with the Prousts. I resisted the urge to tell her to revisit *How the Grinch Stole Christmas* for a reminder about the meaning of the season. "I'm sorry to hear that, Edie. I hope you find your sleigh soon."

I could tell she was trying to decide if I was being sincere. Finally she gave up on me and turned to Grandpa. "You look familiar. Do I know you?"

"Leo Mancini. Former police chief of Daybreak Harbor," he said, sticking his hand out the window to shake hers.

Edie gaped at him, the recognition dawning. So did

the cop, who had been watching this exchange with a smirk. He immediately stood at attention, looking like he was about to salute Grandpa.

"Sir. It's an honor to meet you," he said. "I've heard a lot about you. Officer Kevin Handy."

"As you were, Officer Handy," Grandpa said with an amused smile. "This is my granddaughter, Maddie. She's helping out with the neighborhood cat colony."

Handy frowned. "The what?"

Oh, come on, I wanted to say. Another one playing dumb. There was no way the entire force of what, five people, hadn't been briefed on this, likely multiple times. "The feral cat colony. Don't tell me you haven't heard of it. It's been the biggest news in this town since probably before I was born. Unless you count the multi-colored Christmas-lights scandal." I couldn't help myself. Sarcasm was, after all, a big part of my nature.

Edie huffed out an indignant breath but said nothing.

"White lights are classier," Trey said matter-of-factly, clearly missing his wife's cue to stay quiet. They were the first words I'd heard him utter.

I arched my eyebrows at him. He had the grace to look down at his boots and scuff his feet into the snow.

Handy, meanwhile, was still mulling over my comment. I feared he wasn't that bright. "Christmas-lights scandal?" he asked. "When was that?"

Grandpa took pity on him and jumped in. "How long have you been with the force, Officer?"

"Almost two years, sir."

Grandpa nodded. "I hear you boys just caught a big case."

"'Fraid so, sir."

"Well, always happy to help in an unofficial capacity," Grandpa said.

Edie looked like she was about to stomp her foot to

bring the attention back to herself. "Maybe you can help them figure out how to investigate the burglaries," she said to Grandpa. "Because it's been going on for weeks and nothing's happened!"

Grandpa cocked his head. "Well, on my force murders trumped anything, but you're saying houses have been broken into as well?"

"Not that we know of," Trey said. "Just stuff outside."

"Ah. Then it's a simple theft," Grandpa said. "Burglaries are, by definition, about entering a building."

Edie didn't look particularly grateful for the clarification.

Grandpa, clearly enjoying himself, glanced at me. "What do you think, doll? Should we get feeding?"

I nodded. "Yes, we should go."

"Do you, uh, need any help, sir?" Officer Handy asked.

I thought about making Officer Handy escort us into the woods. Maybe carrying the food. But I knew Grandpa wouldn't let me.

"No, thank you," Grandpa said. "Except maybe to make sure your force is treating my granddaughter and her friends with respect when they come out here. They're doing a community service helping these cats, and they've been given nothing but a hard time."

Officer Handy's face turned red. "I'm sorry about that, sir. And, ma'am," he added, peering in at me.

But Grandpa was on a roll. "I understand someone also vandalized one of the shelters that a bunch of school kids built for the cat food," he said, with a glance at Edie and Trey. "No one reported it because, well, frankly they thought it wouldn't be treated seriously. But I think any kind of theft or vandalism is serious, don't you agree, Officer?"

Out of the corner of my eye, I watched Trey's face redden as he stared studiously at the ground.

Handy nodded so vigorously I feared his hat would fly off. "Absolutely, sir. Would you like me to take a report on that now?" He fumbled for his pen and notebook, dropping both before he got himself together.

I could see Edie getting madder by the minute.

"No, Officer, we'll let it go this time," Grandpa said. "But like I said. I'd really like a promise from you that your force will be looking out for everyone in this neighborhood, even the visitors."

"Of course, sir. You have my word."

"Thank you, Officer," Grandpa said. "I'll be sure to put in a good word with Chief Dunn." Chief Dunn was Turtle Point's chief—Handy's boss.

"Thank you, sir."

I bit the inside of my cheek to keep from laughing, then turned to Edie and Trey with my best solemn look. "I'm very sorry for your loss," I said gravely. "I hope it's just a kid playing a prank and you get your property back soon."

Grandpa lifted his hand in a wave and we drove slowly down past the Prousts' house, where all that was left of last night's events was some yellow crime-scene tape strung across the lawn. I could feel the little group's eyes on us as we parked in front of the Hacketts' and unloaded our supplies. It wasn't until we were in the woods out of earshot that I turned to Grandpa with a big grin.

"I should've brought you out here from the start," I said. "That was awesome."

He waved me off. "Poor kid. He has no clue. But I was being serious. I am going to call Dunn. There was a murder out here, and I want that police force watching over all of you volunteers as much as they are their constituency."

"Thanks, Grandpa." As we got to work, my thoughts drifted back to Edie and Trey. Who would come back overnight after all that chaos and steal a giant Christmas sleigh? I'd seen Edie and Trey's sleigh. It was huge. I'm sure it was easy enough to pull away, but it seemed like a bold move right after a man was murdered. Whoever had done it had to be pretty set on their objective.

But what was the objective?

And why had Trey looked so guilty when Grandpa mentioned the vandalized cat shelter? I thought about Adele's assessment of him the other day. He was certainly strong enough. But what would he have to gain from it?

Chapter 13

I'd forgotten how much chaos went into a Mancini-James holiday. Especially a holiday as cherished as Christmas. Our family had always done Christmas Eve big. There was something magical about the night, long before it got to the hour when Santa's sleigh passed over all the houses. The coziness of it all—the fire in Grandpa's fireplace, Christmas carols playing, the giant tree standing proudly in the living room. While I'd loved my life out West, the holiday vibe just hadn't been the same for this transplanted New Englander. It wasn't Christmas if you weren't freezing your butt off and/or had at least a dusting of snow on the ground.

I'd worried about how Grandpa would do on his first Christmas without Grandma. He hadn't talked about it at all. Christmas had been his and Grandma's favorite, and it would be hard for him. Hard for all of us. My mom and I had already brought some lovely Christmas arrangements to her grave. But he'd surprised us a couple of weeks ago. Val and I had come home from grabbing lunch and found Grandpa and Ethan covered in pine needles, wrestling with one of the biggest trees I'd ever seen. Grandpa had looked up from under it, where he was securing the tree into the stand, and shook his head. "You girls weren't supposed to be home for hours. The lights were supposed to be on when you got here."

Later that night, my parents and my younger sister Sam came over and we all decorated it, like we used to do when we three girls were kids. While I'd come home for most Christmases while I lived away, I hadn't been part of the prep in a long time.

It felt good to be home.

Truth be told, I enjoyed the tree decorating much more than the cooking. As usual, there were way too many of us crammed in the kitchen, trying to make enough food to accommodate all the people who would ultimately visit. In my case, it wasn't because I was compelled to cook or felt especially useful trying to do so. It was more obligatory. Which meant I was in the way. My mother and Sam were making the fish and arguing over how much seasoning to add to each dish. Ethan was skillfully ducking between them and just doing it. Val was putting appetizer platters together, ignoring them all. Grandpa was hovering over the pot where his potatoes were theoretically boiling, although they would never get there if he kept taking the lid off. He was also in the way.

Finally, mercifully, I poured myself a glass of wine and ducked out to the living room where my dad was keeping out of the fray with some of our early bird guests—a couple of Grandpa's friends talking about cop days, and Anne Marie, Dad's longtime assistant at the hospital. Dad had the new kitten, Gimley, on his lap, while JJ lounged at his feet. JJ loved parties, especially when he could command all the attention. I didn't have the heart to tell them that Gimley would be going to his new home shortly after the holiday. I dropped into Grandpa's recliner and sipped my wine.

My dad regarded me with an amused smile. "Chaos in there?"

I nodded. "But it all smells good. I'm starving."

The bell rang. We all looked at each other. "I'll get it," I said, since no one else moved. And technically it was my house.

I pulled the front door open to find Cass smiling at me on the porch. I gasped and threw my arms around him for a hug. I hadn't realized how much I'd missed his hugs lately until that moment. He was a solid mass of muscle, and he gave really good, strong hugs that made you feel like you could hide there. I buried my face against his chest. As always, he smelled of sage and some other kind of herbs.

Cass could've been in his fifties, but really he was ageless. He hailed from Haiti, as was apparent by his thick accent. His hair hung in thin braids down to his waist and he wore thick silver rings on every finger. He was pretty much the coolest person I knew.

"My long-lost mentee," he said, stepping back to look me over. "You look tired."

"Exhausted," I said. "Come in." I'd no sooner shut the door behind him and accepted the bottle of fancy rum he always brought over on the holidays when the door opened again and Becky's curly blond hair popped in.

"Merry Christmas," she called.

Grandpa, who didn't miss a trick, stuck his head out from the kitchen. "Everyone go off the record!"

I had to laugh. It was his favorite joke whenever Becky was around. She took it like a good sport.

"Yeah, yeah. It's fine. I'm not above using anonymous sources," she said, ushering her mother in ahead of her. Donna Walsh was an older version of Becky—same blond curls, same baby blue eyes. She looked exactly the same as she had when Becky and I had been kids.

I tucked the rum under my arm and took the giant platter of cookies out of Becky's hands. My dad had already pulled Cass into a conversation, so I focused on Becky.

"Thank you for this. You didn't have to," I said. "Hi, Mrs. W. Can I get you some wine?" I kissed her cheek.

"That would be lovely, honey."

"Go, have a seat and chat with my dad," I said, waving at the chair I'd just vacated. JJ saw her coming and ran toward her, squeaking his signature squeak. The first time I'd heard it I'd cracked up—this big, tough cat with such a cute little sound—but he'd been offended and I'd had to make it up to him with lots of treats. And for the record, everyone who met him was utterly charmed by his squeak.

After she'd greeted JJ appropriately, Becky followed me to the dining room to find a spot for the cookies. A giant crash came from the kitchen. I winced. "So glad I'm not in there. It's a bit of a mess."

"I bet. Hey, speaking of mess. Have you heard from Lucas at all?" She blinked innocently at me. "You haven't mentioned him."

I shot her a look. "I'm trying not to be in a bad mood, thanks."

"So does that mean you haven't heard anything?" she persisted, like a true reporter.

I hadn't told her about my visit to the grooming salon last week. I hadn't told anyone except Val, and only because she'd happened upon me right after I returned from that little visit. I didn't necessarily want to tell anyone else.

"Nothing," I said. It wasn't entirely a lie. I hadn't heard directly *from* him. But I had heard that he was alive and well. I found a spot for the cookies between all the other sweets we'd already put out and deposited the tray. "I'll get you a drink."

"Bourbon, please," Becky said.

"Make it a double," I muttered and went to get the drinks.

The doorbell rang again. It would be like this all night—people were forever dropping in on Christmas Eve. The island was small, and we pretty much knew everyone. Grandpa had invited Leopard Man and his new girlfriend, Ellen the librarian, and I was expecting Katrina too. She usually spent Christmas Eve with us. She and her mom weren't super close, and we were like her family.

No one was moving to get the door, so I detoured from my drinks to do it myself. But it wasn't Leopard Man, or Katrina. It was Craig, who I wasn't expecting. And Jade Bennett. I knew they'd been dating, but didn't know it was Christmas Eve–serious dating. Jade held a bottle of wine and Craig had a gift bag and a platter of something.

"Hey," I said, not really sure what to say.

"Hey," Craig said back. He looked kind of uncomfortable.

"I think she means merry Christmas." My mother suddenly appeared next to me, gently pushing me out of the way, and took the platter from Craig's hands.

"Of course," I said. "Merry Christmas. I didn't know you were coming." I cocked my head at my mother, who clearly did. "Hey, Jade," I said as she stepped inside. "Nice to see you."

"You too." Jade gave me an awkward hug.

"Thanks for inviting us," Craig said to my mom, and handed her the gift bag.

"Thank you, dear." My mom took them. "I'll put them under the tree. Maddie, maybe you can get them drinks?"

Drinks. Shoot. I still hadn't gotten Becky's bourbon. Or mine, for that matter. "Yes. Of course. What can I get you?"

"Wine is fine for me," Jade said. "Red, please."

"I'll have the same," Craig said.

I gave him a funny look. He never drank wine. But

apparently his tastes had changed now that he was dating the bar owner.

"You got it. Be right back. You can hang out in there." I waved toward the living room, then went into the kitchen.

Val had two plates of appetizers in her hands, which I almost knocked over when I came through the door. "Sorry," I muttered, grabbing the nearest bottle of red and the bottle of Bulleit bourbon from the liquor stash on the far end of the counter.

I'd just finished filling all the glasses when my mother came in. "Let me help you," she said, picking up the wine glasses.

"Mom. What is that about?"

She paused on her way back to the door. "What?"

"Inviting Craig and Jade? It's kind of uncomfortable for them, no?"

"Uncomfortable for them? Maddie. Honey. Craig is just like Becky and Katrina. Old friends. Family, basically. Why wouldn't we invite him?"

So many reasons. He had always been kind of jealous of Lucas. And now that Lucas was out of the picture, I would have thought he might not want to make me uncomfortable by bringing his new girlfriend to my house so I could see how happy and in love they were.

On second thought, maybe it was me that was uncomfortable.

And of course I didn't have a good answer for my mother. "You could've at least let me know," I finally said, taking a sullen sip of my bourbon.

My mother leaned over and gave me a hands-free kiss on the cheek, balancing the wine glasses. "Honey. Everything is going to work out. Trust me." With a satisfied nod that it would be so, she left the room.

I took another sip and went to find Becky. She was with her mom. I handed her the drink and went over to where Val was arranging her platters. "How you doing?" I asked, spearing an olive with a toothpick. "Need help?"

"No, I'm good!" She beamed at me. I'd never seen Val so happy. Or in such a chronic good mood. Who would've thought my strong, silent business partner would be the one to completely turn things around for her. Well, that and her successful new business. "This party is great, isn't it?" She surveyed the room with her hands clasped under her chin. "It's so nice to have everyone here. I'm so excited for Christmas this year. I got Ethan new boots and a new coat. He doesn't dress warmly enough for New England. And a stereo system for the new café, since he likes to play music while he cooks. I can't wait to give it to him."

"That's awesome, Val. I'm really happy for you."

She looked up from fussing with the shrimp cocktail platter. "How are you doing?"

"I'm fine."

"Right."

"I am." I waved her off. "I'm used to being single anyway. What does it matter?"

"It matters a lot when you care about someone and things are uncertain."

"They aren't uncertain. They're over." I looked around for where I'd left my drink.

"You don't know that," Val said.

"Ah, but I do. I have no desire to date him anymore. I didn't sign up to date Houdini." I glanced up as the doorbell rang again. "Probably Katrina. I'll get it."

But once again, I was wrong.

Chapter 14

I paused outside the grooming-salon door, trying to appear nonchalant but peering inside like a stalker. I could see Caroline, Lucas's main groomer, inside. She was alone save for the husky on the table in front of her. I lurked for a few minutes, debating whether I should go in. On the one hand, Lucas could be hurt or something. If so, and someone called his family to tell them, maybe they had called his shop. It would make sense, if no one knew about me yet. Which they might not, depending on how close he was to his family and how he thought of us. I had no idea about either. We weren't *officially* official yet. At least, we'd never verbalized that.

So I figured before I completely wrote him off, I'd check here. If something had happened, at least then I would know. That is, if anyone here knew.

On the other hand, I could look like a pathetic stalker girl who'd been ghosted by a guy who wasn't even really her boyfriend yet and was having a hard time letting go.

Ugh. "I hate my life," I muttered, and turned to go.

I noticed Craig standing on the sidewalk, regarding me with an amused—or maybe pitying—smile. He was in uniform, so was clearly out on patrol. "What?" I snapped.

He shrugged. "Nothing. Did you get a dog?"

"They do cats too," I said defensively, not bothering to call attention to the fact that I had no cat with me, not even JJ, whom I usually took around town with me. He was welcome in all the shops and even most of the eating establishments. He was definitely an island fixture. But it was too cold out. He didn't like being outside in the winter.

"Still no word, huh?"

I wasn't in the mood for his pretend sympathy. And I really didn't want to talk about my abysmal love life with my ex-boyfriend. That was the problem with an island the size of a postage stamp. Everyone knew freakin' everything.

"I've gotta go," I said, pretending I hadn't heard him. "And it looks like you're working?"

He looked at me for a long moment, then nodded. "Yeah. I'm working. See you."

"Bye." I waited until he walked away then took a deep breath and yanked the door open.

Caroline looked up. If she was surprised to see me she didn't show it. But she had kind of a one-expression face anyway.

"Hey, Caro," I said, trying for cheery.

"Hi, Maddie. What's up?" Her hands didn't falter as she continued to clip her charge, but her eyes lingered on me.

"I'm sorry to bother you. . . . Should I come back?" I asked, jerking my thumb toward the door.

"No, it's good. What can I do for you?"

"I was just wondering"—I sighed and decided to just go for it—"if you've heard from Lucas at all."

She blinked at me. "Yeah, actually. I did. Like a week ago? Maybe a little more?"

I stared at her. "You did?"

"Yeah." She shrugged. "He asked if I could hold down the fort for a bit longer."

I waited, but she didn't say anything else. A woman of few words, Caroline was. "Did he say anything else? Like where he is? Is he okay?"

She placed her clippers on the metal tray next to her. The husky waited expectantly, his tail thumping slightly. When she looked up at me, there was a slight look of pity on her face. "He didn't. Honestly. It was a very short call and there was a lot of noise in the background. Like it was a public place? He was very apologetic about delegating all the appointments, but hey. It's the slow season so it's all good."

"Yeah," I said. "All good. Thanks, Caro."

"Anytime," she said.

As I turned to go, she called me back. "Maddie. Lucas is a good guy. I'm sure there's an explanation for all this, yeah?"

I wasn't so sure, but I didn't want to say that. "Sure," I said.

"If I hear from him again, I'll tell him to call you."

You shouldn't have to tell him, I wanted to say, but instead managed a smile. "Thanks."

By the time I got home, I'd gotten over the shock and upset that he'd been in touch with his groomer and not with me, and I'd graduated to angry. Like, really angry. Maybe I didn't have the right to be this mad, but I was. Just because we hadn't pledged our undying love for each other yet didn't mean we hadn't had something. He was always at my place, I was always at his. He'd spent time with my family. He'd been around through some really tough times. I'd started to depend on him. He had stuff at my place. And how did he respond? By disappearing without a word. Would a text kill him, for crying out loud?

But that one piece—the fact that I'd let my guard down and really started to care about him—made me angriest.

I pulled into the driveway on two wheels and stomped on the brake, bringing Grandpa's truck to a screeching halt. A couple of heads poked out from the garage—Gabe's contractor crew—curious about all the noise. I ignored them and charged inside. I was on a mission.

Slamming the door behind me, I raced upstairs to my room. Even though Lucas lived alone, we spent most of our time here because of my responsibilities with the cats. Plus I think he'd loved being around our house with all the activity—Grandpa's antics, Ethan's cooking, Val with her new business, and all the cats. Which meant he'd left a lot of stuff here.

And I needed it gone.

Shedding my coat and scarf as I went up the three flights, I ran into my bedroom and slammed the door so hard the house might've shaken. I started grabbing clothes out of the closet and throwing them into a pile on my floor, muttering the whole time. JJ, who'd been curled up on my bed, opened one eye, took in the situation, and disappeared, scrambling for cover under the bed.

I heard a tentative knock, then my door cracked open. "Maddie?" Val stuck her head in, looking alarmed. "What's wrong? What are you doing?"

"Nothing. Go away." I took the book Lucas had left on my nightstand and chucked that into the pile too.

"Seriously? You look possessed. What's up?" She took a tentative step into the room, then jerked back as another book—one he'd bought me when I told him how much I wanted to read it—went flying past to land on the floor with a thud.

"What's up? I'll tell you what's up." I turned around,

eyes blazing, a pile of hangers in my arms. "That . . . *jerk* is alive."

Val looked thoroughly confused. "What jerk?"

"Lucas!" I chucked more clothes onto the pile on the floor. Had he moved his whole apartment here, for crying out loud?

"Wait. You're angry because Lucas is alive? When did you talk to him? Isn't this good news?"

"Girls?" Grandpa's voice from downstairs. "What's all the ruckus up there?"

"Nothing, Grandpa," Val called back. "Sorry."

"Has anyone in this house ever heard of privacy?" I yelled. "Can't I have a meltdown in peace?"

"Maddie." Val stepped all the way in, tentatively at first, then closed the door behind her. "Take a breath and tell me what happened."

I didn't usually let either of my sisters see me in such a state—I was the oldest after all, and I had a reputation to uphold—and it made me even more upset that she was there to witness my meltdown. "I don't want to talk about it," I snapped. "I just want to get this stuff out of here."

"Okay. Let me help. What do you need, a bag?"

I nodded.

"I'll get one. Be right back." She slipped out of the room.

I shoved my hands on my hips and surveyed the room. I'd grabbed all his stuff out of the closet and anything he'd left out in the open. I yanked open the drawers of the nightstand I'd cleaned out on the side of the bed he liked and pulled out a few items—earbuds, Altoids, a day planner.

A day planner?

I snatched it up, flipping to the most recent entries. Not that I thought he might have written *Flee from Daybreak Island and never return* as an entry, but perhaps there was some clue.

But no, it was actually pretty boring. Grooming appointments; the gig his band, the Scurvy Elephants, had secured; and the conference that had taken him off-island in the first place. I flipped forward a few pages and frowned. He had entries in there for the past couple of weeks. Things that I knew were on the island. Like *plumbing job at the library*, and *pick up M's gift at Lee's*.

I frowned. "M" would be me, probably. And "Lee's" was an adorable little boutique with the best jewelry. So maybe he hadn't planned to never return?

I abruptly closed the book and threw it in the pile. So what if he hadn't planned it? That could even be worse. Spontaneous ghosting. Either way, he was gone and hadn't bothered to contact me. He'd contacted his coworker, but couldn't find the time to even send me a text. So what if he had entries in his planner? He didn't even like doing plumbing jobs. He probably was looking for somewhere else to live where you could have a steady stream of income all year round, not some stupid island where you worked your butt off for five months and twiddled your thumbs the rest of the time.

Val returned with some trash bags. She stepped in cautiously, checking to see if there was anything in my hands first. "All set," she said cheerfully, holding up the bags. "What am I packing up?"

"That." I pointed. "And what are you so happy about?"

"Just trying to be upbeat." She knelt next to the pile and started placing clothes neatly into the bag.

"Just throw them in so I can get them out of here." I grabbed some of the shirts and balled them up to toss them in the bag.

Val grabbed my arm. "Maddie. Stop. I've got it. Seriously, will you tell me what's going on please?"

I sighed and sank down on my bed. "Lucas called Caroline."

"Who's that?"

"His second in command at the grooming salon."

"How do you know?"

"I went by there. I just"—I lifted my shoulders and let them drop in a defeated shrug—"wanted to know."

Val sat back on her heels. "What did he say?"

"Asked her to hold down the fort a while longer. Apologized. That was it."

Val thought about that. "And you're sure he hasn't called or texted? Maybe from a number you don't recognize? He could've lost his phone."

"He didn't lose his phone. He doesn't want to talk to me. It's fine. I'm done thinking about this." I stood up abruptly again. "I'm going to go throw the bags in a dumpster."

"What dumpster?" Val wanted to know.

"I don't know. Whatever dumpster I can find." I was horrified to realize tears were filling my eyes.

Val came over and gave me a hug, then made me sit down on the bed with her. "Maddie. I know it sucks and it's kind of weird—"

"Kind of?" I interrupted. "Rational people don't just vanish. Not unless they're in witness protection or something." I dropped my head into my hands and pressed my fists against my eyes, willing myself not to cry. "I dated a guy out in Cali. We were serious—at least I thought we were. But he had this bad habit of ghosting me every so often when he got freaked out, or when we'd had a fight. Then he'd come crawling back and I was dumb enough to let it happen again. I'm not"—I swallowed as my voice betrayed me and broke—"I'm not doing that again."

Val was silent for a moment, then leaned over and hugged me. "I'm sorry. I didn't know that. And I get it. But there's got to be an explanation. Lucas isn't a bad guy. Look, I have that same intuition you do when it comes to this stuff. It works better on others than on myself," Val said dryly. "And I know he's not a bad guy."

"Whatever. I still want his stuff gone." I pulled away from her and crossed my arms stubbornly.

"Okay. Fine. I'll take care of it," Val said. "Is there more?"

I went into my bathroom and came back with all his stuff—shampoo, electric toothbrush, moisturizer—and threw it on the bed. "I should do it. It'll be therapeutic."

Val added the latest items to the bag, then hefted it up like Santa Claus. "I've got it. It's gone. See? No worries."

"Out of the house," I commanded. "In the trash."

She saluted. "You got it. I'll tell Grandpa everything's okay up here."

"Great," I muttered. "*You* can lie to him then."

Chapter 15

I had to blink to clear my vision. And then I still thought I was imagining things. Otherwise, it meant Lucas was real, standing on my doorstep holding a small gift bag—from Lee's, ironically—and wearing a nervous smile. I had no idea what to say. Or why he was here. Unless it was to properly dump me. Which I guess was better than just disappearing into thin air.

"Hey, Maddie," he said. "I hope it's okay I stopped by. I figured you guys would be . . ." he gestured at the party behind me, seemingly at a loss for words.

"Yeah," I said. "We're having a party."

Lucas nodded, his face sinking into a semi-miserable expression while he still tried to keep the smile pasted on.

He looked . . . off. Don't get me wrong, he was still gorgeous, but something was different. He looked thinner. Pale. His eyes were cloudy and troubled. I wondered if he'd been ill and that was why he hadn't been in touch, then shoved the thought out of my mind. If he'd been able to get back to the island and call his staff, he'd clearly had the ability to send a text or make a phone call somewhere along the way.

My heart started to pound, that awful feeling of facing

down the confrontation you'd almost hoped for but now dreaded. I didn't know what to say. I didn't know what I wanted. I did know that despite whatever was wrong, he looked . . . good. Like the guy I'd had a crush on immediately when I saw him last summer. The guy I'd subsequently fallen for.

He looked like Lucas. And it made me sad.

Which totally threw me off. "Wow. I guess they do have transportation back to the island," I said, trying for sarcasm. It would have been a lot more effective without my voice shaking. "What"—I cleared my throat—"what are you doing here?"

"I wanted to see you." He glanced behind me, wincing a bit at the crowd. "Can we talk?"

I leaned into the doorway, blocking the inside from his view. "Talk about what? The fact that you left for a three-day conference and have been gone for a month with no word? Or that you were able to get in touch with your employees but didn't even have the courtesy to text me once and let me know you were alive?"

"Maddie. I know how it looks—"

"Madalyn!" Grandpa's voice boomed in my ear. "You're letting all the cold air in. What are you—oh, hello, son! Come on in!"

"No, Grandpa, Lucas was just—" I began, but Grandpa ignored me and pushed the door open all the way for Lucas. "Leaving," I finished as Grandpa reached out a hand and pulled Lucas over the threshold into the room. I cringed inwardly. I felt like the whole room was staring at me. When I looked up, Cass's eyes met mine. I could read the concern there.

Conversation filtered off as the rest of the group in the living room realized we had company. Val turned from where she was fussing over the platters of food, and her mouth dropped open. Craig stared openly. My dad, sensing the weird vibe, immediately rose and came over to greet Lucas. His gesture cut off any awkwardness in its tracks.

"Merry Christmas, Lucas. Good to see you. Let me take your coat," he said.

Lucas shot me a look that was part apology, part plea for help, then obliged, shifting the bag from hand to hand while he wrangled his coat off. "Thank you. Good to see you too. And merry Christmas to you too," he added.

My dad looked at me. "Maddie, maybe you can get Lucas—"

"A drink?" I finished. "Sure. Happy to. What'll you have?" I turned to him with a too-bright smile.

He half shrugged. "Scotch?"

"Great. Coming right up." I headed into the kitchen, seriously considering detouring to my room and hiding for the rest of the night.

Val followed me into the kitchen, nearly walking into me she was so close. "See? I told you it wasn't over!" She squealed, clapped her hands gleefully. "It's like we conjured him up! Isn't it great? What an awesome Christmas gift!" She shook my arm, trying to elicit a response from me. I resisted the urge to slug her. Last year, if faced with this same scenario, she would've thrown him out herself. Amazing what a little romance could do for the cold-hearted.

"Conjured who up?" my mother inquired, looking up from her green bean casserole.

"Lucas," Val chirped when it became clear I wasn't going to answer. "He's here!"

My mother's head snapped up. "Really! How lovely." She looked at me anxiously. "Isn't it lovely?"

"It's grand," I snapped, grabbing the scotch.

"Hmm. I should go say hello." My mother dropped her

spoon and swept out of the room, her long red velvet skirt sweeping the floor behind her.

Ethan turned from the stove, assessing me with those knowing eyes. "Mads? You okay?"

Thank God, someone sane. "No! What am I supposed to say to him when I haven't spoken to him in a month and Grandpa just invited him to Christmas Eve dinner?"

"Ouch." Ethan winced. "Do you want me to do something?"

"No." I plucked a glass off the rack and poured. "I'll handle it."

"Did he say where he was?" Ethan asked.

"He didn't have a chance. I'd barely opened the door and Grandpa popped up over my shoulder, inviting him in."

"He's staying for dinner? Before you've even talked?" Ethan asked.

Val opened her mouth to butt in, but Ethan shot her a look. Clearly, he'd learned from our longstanding business relationship how to handle me and my issues better than my sister had.

"No idea. I guess we'll find out." I tried for a smile that came out like a grimace, then headed back to the living room with the glass of scotch. My hand shook so much I was surprised I didn't spill it on the way.

Lucas had moved to the couch—likely my father's doing—and was pretending to be engaged in whatever conversation they were having while Craig gave him the side-eye. Cass was talking to Craig, trying to keep him occupied, I assumed. I could tell Lucas was totally uncomfortable. I walked over and shoved the glass at him, then turned to walk away.

"Maddie." Lucas rose from the couch, glancing apologetically at my dad, and ushered me to the corner of the room out of earshot of the little crowd. "Can I just talk to you for a minute?" He asked in a low voice. "I'm not going to stay."

"Probably a good idea if you don't." I crossed my arms and waited.

"Can we go somewhere quiet?" he asked.

I opened my mouth to protest and he cut me off. "Please, Maddie. I know you're trying to spend time with your family and it's Christmas and you're probably pretty angry at me—"

"Angry? Why would I be angry?" I crossed my arms and stared at him. "We weren't, like, *together* or anything, right? So why would I be mad?"

He winced. "That's not true. We were. Are."

"No, we're not. And you have a funny way of showing it. . . . Five minutes." I turned on my heel and led him down the hall to the cat café area. He followed, and I waited until he stepped inside before closing the door behind us. The cats that didn't want to be out at the party were lounging in here. They'd all gotten new beds for Christmas— fluffy, stress-reducing beds. Gifts from Leopard Man, their other primary benefactor.

Lucas looked around, forgetting for a moment that we weren't having a friendly conversation. "Wow. The place looks great. Is it done?"

"Mostly. We're in the process of redoing the garage now. Ethan is getting his separate café space." I wanted to tell him more. I wanted to share all the adventures with the contractors over the past month, like the time two of the cats had gotten into the giant vents they'd put in for the new heating system and we'd all almost had a heart attack until they walked right out again like nothing had happened, but then I remembered that it didn't matter. He probably didn't want to hear my dumb stories anyway.

Silence usually meant one thing—that someone was done with you. And even if they had a momentary lapse of conscience and came back around, it has highly likely they'd do the same thing again. I wasn't about to give him that chance. "So what did you want to talk about?"

He took a breath. "I wanted to explain. And I wanted to give this to you." He handed me the bag. Reluctantly, I took it but didn't open it. "Maddie. I'm so sorry I was out of touch. Trust me, I didn't want to be, but things got a little out of control."

"Out of control? Like what, a party gets out of control? What does that even mean? A house fell on you? Someone kidnapped you? There was no cell service in . . . wherever you ended up? Come on, Lucas." I stalked the room, then turned back to face him. "Were you sick? In a hospital?"

He shook his head.

"Well, that would've been one of the only reasonable explanations. Look. I felt like things were on a good path. If I was wrong, I wish you would've just told me, but I didn't get there by myself."

"You weren't wrong. We were—are—on a good path. That's why I want to explain." Lucas stepped forward, his expression earnest, and reached for my hand. "Maddie. Please. It's kind of a long story, but I think you'd—"

"Maddie!" The door flew open and Val rushed in, looking stressed. "Sorry," she said, skidding to a stop. "I really hate to interrupt. But there's kind of an emergency. Grandpa just got a call from the Turtle Point police."

I immediately went on alert. "What happened?" *Please don't let anyone else be dead.*

"It was a courtesy call. Because they know him. But they made an arrest in the Proust case."

Lucas looked from Val to me. "What's the Proust case?"

"Someone got killed," I said impatiently, brushing him off, then turned back to Val. "Who did they arrest?"

She hesitated, nervously tugging on her left index finger with her right hand. "Katrina."

Chapter 16

Thursday, December 24, Christmas Eve: two days after the murder
9:10 p.m.

Christmas Eve came to a screeching halt. Lucas and I completely forgot about our conversation. Once the shock wore off enough that I could actually move my legs again, I rushed out to Grandpa. He was still on the phone. Becky, who can sniff out a story better than a bloodhound can track a scent, was blatantly eavesdropping on the conversation.

I went up to him and tugged at his arm, like I used to do when I was five and needed his attention. He held up a finger.

"Can you get down there right away?" he was saying. "I'll cover the cost. Fine. Thank you." He hung up and looked at me. "Doll. Take a breath."

"What happened? Are they crazy? They can't arrest Katrina!" I thought for a panicked moment that I couldn't actually breathe, then forced myself to take a few slow, deep breaths. Between this and Lucas, this night wasn't really shaping up to be what I'd expected for my first real Christmas home in a decade.

"Come on. Let's go down there and find out what's going on," he said, putting his arm around me. "I asked Jack Gaffney to represent her."

Jack Gaffney was one of Grandpa's old friends and a hardcore defense attorney. He was basically retired now and had moved back to the island, but he still took on special cases. He was good. I was glad to hear this, anyway. And thankful for my grandpa's generosity. There was no way Katrina could afford a lawyer like that on her salary.

"Okay," I said. "Let's go."

"Sophie!" he hollered in the direction of the kitchen. "We'll have to delay dinner. Maddie and I have to run an errand."

Craig stood. "I'm coming too." He glanced at Jade, clearly hoping she wouldn't mind.

"Go," she said, motioning toward the door. "I'll be here when you get back."

"Can I come?" Becky asked.

"Rebecca!" Donna Walsh wagged a finger at her daughter. "It's Christmas, for heaven's sake."

Becky ignored her mother and fixed an imploring gaze on me.

"Katrina will freak out. Are you going to report this?" I asked.

She looked grim. "If it's official I'll have to."

I looked at Grandpa. He nodded. "She should come. Talk to the cops in person. Let's go."

"But why would they arrest her?" I asked Grandpa as he led me over to the door and handed me my coat.

"I don't know, doll. They have evidence, they said. Grab your shoes."

I barely noticed that Lucas had returned to the living room. As I pulled my shoes on and Grandpa hustled me and Becky out the door, it occurred to me I should've said something to him. But the moment had passed. We had to go. I wished I could bring Cass, but four of us descending on the police station was already a lot of people.

We piled into Craig's car, Grandpa in the passenger

seat and me and Becky in the back. Craig glanced at Grandpa. "What's the address again?"

Grandpa rattled it off as I sank into my seat, trying to separate all the thoughts swirling in my head. Lucas had been about to give me an explanation about his vanishing act. One of my best friends had been arrested. Craig had brought Jade to my house for Christmas.

Really, Universe?

"So what happened?" Craig asked when we were almost through town.

"Not sure yet," Grandpa said. "Dunn told me they had 'overwhelming evidence' that Katrina had been involved in Virgil Proust's death."

I leaned forward. "Overwhelming evidence? What does that mean?"

"Not sure," Grandpa said. "He didn't elaborate."

Becky was on her phone already. I didn't want her to print this story. Then again it wasn't Becky's fault Katrina had been arrested. She hung up and glanced at me, reading my mind. "It's just the facts, Maddie. But the more publicity, the more chance we have to flesh out the real killer. Right?"

I hadn't thought of it that way. "Right," I said.

She reached over and squeezed my hand. None of us spoke for the rest of the drive. There wasn't much to say until we heard the whole story. I was stressed, though. What on earth was going on? Why would they arrest Katrina? She hadn't even been in that neighborhood for the last week or two.

Or had she? I remembered pulling onto Sea Spray that fateful night and thinking I'd seen Katrina's car speeding in the other direction. Of course I'd been wrong.

Hadn't I?

The Turtle Point Police Department was quiet tonight. It was also festive, with lights strung up around the outside of the building. Grandpa humphed from the back-seat when he saw that. "They always had to be showier than the rest of us," he muttered.

Craig hid a smile at that. "I heard there was always a bit of a competition going between him and Chief Dunn," he said in a low voice to me.

"Just because I'm retired doesn't mean I'm deaf," Grandpa said.

"Sorry, Chief." Craig pulled into a parking space near the front of the building.

Grandpa scanned the parking lot. "I don't see Jack's car," he said.

"Well, they can't question her until he gets here, right?" I asked.

"Depends on if she's agreed to answer their questions or not. Let's go." He shoved open his door and got out. Craig and I scrambled to keep up with him as he strode to the front door.

We burst into the building behind Grandpa, who went right up to the desk. "Officer. I'm former Daybreak Harbor Chief Leo Mancini. You're holding a woman, Katrina Denning?" He didn't bother to wait for an answer. "Is her attorney present yet?"

I loved these glimpses of Grandpa as a formidable law enforcement officer. Like most kids, I'd taken for granted his career and his stories when I was younger, and then being gone for the last ten years hadn't helped. Now I found myself craving his tales from life in the PD, from the days when he was a beat cop all the way up through the ranks to leading the department. And when I got to see him back in action, it was all the better. He was only seventy-four and I knew that he wasn't going anywhere anytime soon if he had something to say about it, but I also knew that life could be short. I wanted to grab and hold on to all the moments I could.

But right now, I had a friend in a jail cell, so I couldn't get all mushy. The officer jumped out of his seat. He started to salute Grandpa—a dead giveaway of former military—then remembered where he was. "I'll find out right away, sir," he said, and disappeared down the hallway.

Craig and I sat in the waiting area. I looked around. It was definitely more festive than I ever remembered the Daybreak Harbor PD being. They even had some Christmas decos up for the poor rookies who had to work the holiday shifts. Grandpa was totally judging, I could tell.

We sat there for what seemed like an hour until the door to the inner sanctum opened and a silver-haired man came out. Grandpa grinned when he saw him. "Jack! You must've gotten a new car. I didn't see yours out there."

"Oh, I got a few new ones since the last time I saw you," Jack Gaffney said with a wink. He and Grandpa did the man-hug/pat-on-the-back thing for a moment or two, then he looked around. "They with you?"

Grandpa nodded. "My granddaughter Maddie. She's friends with Katrina. Becky Walsh, *Daybreak Island Chronicle* editor. And Craig Tomlin. With the Daybreak Harbor department."

"*Chronicle*?" Jack asked incredulously. "You serious?"

"She's doing her job," Grandpa said.

Jack tilted his head toward the door, indicating we should follow him outside. Becky said she was going to stay to try to get a statement from the department.

Once we got outside, Grandpa said, "So what's the story?"

"The usual," Jack said. "They have enough evidence to make the arrest. I told her to stay quiet no matter what they say. She likes to talk though. Protest, actually."

"Because she didn't do it," I broke in.

Jack regarded me curiously. "That's not my concern,

whether she did or didn't. I just need to keep her out of jail." He looked back at Grandpa. "The part that's . . . troubling for her is there won't be arraignments until after the holiday. So unfortunately she's stuck here."

"She's got to spend Christmas in jail? Are you *kidding* me? Grandpa, there's got to be something we can do!"

He looked grim. "I'm afraid not, doll. She can't post bail until it's set."

I looked at Craig, who also looked grim at this news, but he didn't speak.

Clearly they weren't coming up with any solutions. "So we have to convince them they have the wrong person, then. Grandpa. Can't you talk to the chief? He has to listen to you. Professional courtesy and all that. Right?" I was grasping, and even as I said the words I knew it wouldn't fly. Grandpa would've bristled at someone else coming in and telling him how to run an investigation when he was in charge, and so he certainly wouldn't want to do that himself.

Grandpa shook his head. "He wouldn't have to listen to me even if I were still the Daybreak chief—which I'm not. I can go talk to him, see if he's receptive at all, but it's highly unlikely. They have to have something to have arrested her in the first place."

"What could they possibly have?" I asked, incredulous. "Grandpa. You've known Katrina as long as I have. She used to babysit me, for goodness' sake. She's not a killer."

"Maddie. I agree with you," Grandpa said. "But there's nothing we can do."

"Can we at least see her?" I asked. My voice cracked. I hated this. My friend was a good person who was trying to help a bunch of poor, outdoor cats. And suddenly she was arrested for murder? It smelled bad to me. The cops were biased against her—clearly they were going to pander to the rich people in their town who paid their salary rather than the outsider who no one wanted here in the first place.

"We can ask," Jack said, doubtfully. "I'm not sure they'll let anyone but me see her. Maybe your grandfather."

"Well, let's go find out," I said, swallowing my tears and marching back to the door. I yanked it open and waited for them all to file inside, then brought up the rear of our little parade.

Jack approached the cop behind the desk again, who was taking a stern stance with Becky. "You're going to have to wait for the press release," he kept saying. I could tell she wanted to reach through the little hole and poke him in the eye.

Finally she stepped aside and Jack spoke. The cop looked hesitant, but he picked up the phone and said something. A minute later, the door opened and another cop came out. Jack and Grandpa went over to him. They spoke in low tones. Craig and I couldn't hear what they were saying. Craig sensed my frustration and reached over to squeeze my hand. I glanced down at my hand in his, then up at him. He quickly let it go.

Grandpa looked over his shoulder at me and shook his head, then he and Jack vanished into the inner sanctum behind the other cop.

"Great," I said, throwing up my hands. "I can't even see her and she has to spend Christmas in here? What is going on, Craig?"

"I don't know, Mads," he said. "But . . ."

"But what?" I glared at him.

"But cops don't go around arresting people just for the heck of it. Good cops, anyway."

"Well, who said they were good cops?" I shot back.

The cop behind the glass looked up and glared at me. I guess bulletproof didn't mean soundproof.

"I can't believe they won't even give me the official statement," Becky said. "I have to literally take it from the call log." She looked miffed and wandered away to call someone else, probably her web editor.

We remained silent for the next agonizing twenty minutes until Grandpa returned. When he did, he didn't speak and ushered us outside. Once we were in the car, I couldn't stand it.

"How is she? What happened? What's going on?"

"She's okay. She says she didn't do it."

"Well, no kidding," I said. "Of course she didn't do it."

But Grandpa didn't echo my declaration. Didn't say anything, actually. Under the parking lot lights I caught a glimpse of his face. His expression was somber. Thoughtful. "What?"

"She says she didn't do it," he repeated. "But she admits to being at Virgil's house that night." He pointed at Becky. "And that is off the record."

Chapter 17

I wasn't feeling very festive the next day, but Christmas was Christmas and we had a big day ahead of us at my parents' house. Last night, we'd gone back to our house for a very subdued Christmas Eve feast after Grandpa and I returned from the trip to the Turtle Point Police Department. Lucas had left right after we did, Val told me, and he'd asked her to have me call him.

I hadn't.

My parents had been just as concerned about Katrina—they considered her another daughter, really, and like I'd reminded Grandpa earlier, she'd babysat us. They would've known a future killer if they'd seen one. The parent vibe and all that. I didn't believe for one second she had done anything, and I knew they wouldn't either.

So we'd all pretended to go back to celebrating, but none of us were in the mood. I noticed Grandpa pushing the food around on his plate and I knew he was lost in thought about this mess too. I couldn't imagine what he was thinking. Katrina had been part of his department, so he knew her from that perspective as well. He didn't believe this either.

But then there was the elephant in the room: Katrina had been at Virgil Proust's house. She'd admitted to it. Which was crazy. She had completely avoided the question when I'd asked her if she'd been in the neighborhood that night. Which meant she hadn't wanted me to know if it was true.

There was always the possibility that she'd gone there to confront the Prousts, despite her boss's wishes, about the things that had been happening—calling the cops on her other volunteer, the shelter vandalism, the threats about poisoning the cats. She'd said the day before the murder that someone was going to pay. I'd laughed it off at the time, chalked it up to her being dramatic, but maybe something had happened. An altercation. Maybe Virgil had tried to do something to her. She could've tried to fight back and it had gone wrong.

So she'd beamed him with a Christmas gnome? Ugh. It sounded crazy.

But someone had. And she'd been there.

I'd wanted to talk to Grandpa about it before bed, but we had too many other people in the house and it seemed wrong to mess up everyone else's holiday vibe. So I went to bed and snuggled with JJ, but barely slept at all. Finally, after a night of thoughts and questions swirling around in my mind and barely any sleep, I went downstairs early on Christmas morning to clean the cats' quarters. The house was silent as I descended from the third floor. It reminded me of all those Christmas mornings when my sisters and I would sneak downstairs to see if Santa had brought us any presents. He always had—more than we'd ever asked for.

We'd lived here for a time, before my parents got their own house. This house was huge, and it had made sense when we were a young family and my dad was building his career and they were saving money. But then when Sam came along, my mother didn't want to completely take over her parents' house, so we moved.

I'd been devastated. I'd even asked if I could stay and live with Grandma and Grandpa. I loved following Grandpa around, playing with his badge and his official police hat, pretending to be on the force. We spent many nights snuggled up in the book nook right outside the room I was in now, reading together. When he was at work, I was baking with Grandma in the kitchen, or helping her with her garden. She and I would take long walks around the island. In the summer we'd go to the beach almost every day—she'd been a beach freak like me—and sit and read together. When we got too hot, we'd swim. She taught me how to boogie board, and we would ride waves side by side.

I brushed away a tear. I hated that she was gone. It felt wrong that we were still celebrating without her. But what else could we do? Life went on. And Grandma's house was now a cat café.

That part was kind of funny when I really thought about it.

Grandpa had left the Christmas tree lights on overnight for a little extra cheer. We had two trees this year, one for the main house and one for the cats in the café. Although we had a couple of younger babies, like Gimley, and they did like to climb it. As a result the lights were usually slightly off kilter and a couple of the decorations were always on the floor whenever I came down. I peeked into the room to find it was no different today. Apparently they'd had batting practice last night.

I straightened out the tree and cleaned all the boxes. As I was about to haul the trash out of the room, I caught sight of something on the little table next to the window. A shiny red bag that read LEE'S BOUTIQUE.

The present Lucas had brought last night. We'd been interrupted when he was trying to give it to me by the news that one of my best friends was under arrest.

I picked up the bag and peeked inside. There was a small, gift-wrapped box. I took it out and turned it around and around in my hand. The wrapping was gorgeous, shiny silver paper with a purple ribbon. It looked like he'd done it himself—it didn't have that perfect, polished store feel.

I held it for a long time, staring at it. Did I open it? Give it back to him? Ignore it? I had no idea. I felt tears prick my eyes and put the box back in the bag. Between him showing up last night and the murder, not to mention whatever was going on with Katrina, my emotions were going crazy right now. I'd been so happy to see Lucas— so glad he was okay—but so mad at the same time. And I couldn't let him know I was happy to see him. He'd think he could treat me however he wanted if I acted like I was okay with it.

But I'd really wanted to hug him and hear him out. He'd looked . . . sad. And like he'd lost a lot of weight.

I wondered what he was doing for Christmas.

"Hey." Val stuck her head into the room, startling me. "Merry Christmas. You need some help?"

"Hey," I said with a weak smile. "Merry Christmas. No, I'm good. Thanks."

"Ethan's not up yet. He was tired from all the defensive cooking last night. Grandpa had the truck packed up with the gifts before any of the rest of us were even up. Now he's out for his walk. Seriously, I have no idea where he gets his energy. I'm going to make coffee. You want some?"

"Are you kidding?"

"Thought so." She turned to go, then paused. "Are you okay?"

"Fine. Why?"

"Why?" She repeated. "Because last night was like an episode of some alternate-reality TV show?"

"It was kind of wild, wasn't it?" I sighed. "I can't believe this is happening to Katrina."

"Yeah. What's up with that? How could they think Katrina could hurt anyone? I mean, she didn't even hurt you when she babysat you—and you were tough."

She was trying to be funny, but I wasn't really in a laughing mood.

"Sorry. That was inappropriate." Val sighed. "I'm not as good at jokes as you. So what's going to happen to her?"

"She has to stay in jail until at least Monday when they arraign her. And that's only if they give her bail and she can make it."

Val stared at me. "Seriously?"

"Well, yeah. She got arrested. She's their prime suspect." I picked up a cat scoop, sighed, and put it down again. "Even though there are about five other people I can think of right off the bat who could've done it."

Her eyebrows shot up. "Really?"

I snorted. "For sure. That neighborhood where the guy lived is full of crazies. Including his own wife."

"Are you going to be able to help her?"

"Help her?" I asked. "How?"

Val shrugged. "I don't know. By figuring out who really did it. You're good at that. She could use your help, sounds like."

"I'm not really sure what I can do. I mean, they already arrested her."

"So? Innocent until proven guilty, right?"

I thought about that. Maybe she was right. Maybe I could help point the cops in the right direction. Especially since I was in the neighborhood a lot. Maybe there was a way to find out who the real killer was.

I kept my thoughts to myself, though, and finally she changed the subject. Alas, to an even worse one. "So what did Lucas say before I interrupted you? Sorry about that, by the way."

I turned away. "He said he was sorry. And he couldn't help it. Whatever that means."

"And you said . . . ?"

"Val." I turned, brandishing the litter scoop. "I don't want to talk about it. I have to feed everyone breakfast."

"I'll help," she offered, grabbing the stack of bowls. "So I take it you're still not going to give him a chance to explain?"

I considered what options I had to get rid of her. Aside from clobbering her with my litter scoop, I didn't see many. Val didn't take hints well. "I already told you how I felt about guys who vanish. And since when are you the big defender of men who behave badly? I know Ethan is perfect and all, but not all guys are."

"I'm not defending men who behave badly. I think Lucas is a nice guy," she said. "It seems really out of character for him. And I personally want to know what happened. Don't you?"

More than anything. But I was also terrified to know what happened. What if it had to do with some other woman? I didn't want to hear about that. I didn't think I could handle it.

"Not really," I said, wondering if Val knew I was lying. "I think what he did was really crappy, and I'm not ready to talk to him."

Val nodded. "That's fair."

"Good," I said. "I'm glad you think so."

She finished spooning wet food into bowls and distributing them. "I'll go make the coffee." Val headed out, then poked her head back in. "By the way, I don't think he's doing anything for Christmas."

"Val."

"Sorry. I just thought you would want to know. I know you don't like when people spend holidays alone."

"We're going to Mom and Dad's. I couldn't invite him if I wanted to—which I don't," I added, in case she was going to suggest I do just that. And of course I could if I wanted to. My parents would open their house up to the whole island if they could fit everyone. But did I really need to explain—again—why it wasn't a good idea to invite Lucas?

Val gave me her *Oh come on* look. "Mom and Dad always have plenty of room. And they welcome everyone. You know that. Anyway, I was just telling you." With one last, long look at me, she turned and headed into the kitchen.

Now I was cranky. I sulked while I filled up the bowls of dry food I kept out for a snack, changed the water bowls, vacuumed, and threw out the trash. I only started to feel better when JJ came in looking for me. He came over and rubbed his head against my leg, accepted my ear scratches, then plunked down on one of the beds to oversee the operations.

True to her word, Val returned shortly thereafter with a steaming mug of coffee. It was actually good, and sipping it made me feel better. But I was still sulking. I was the one who everyone should be feeling sorry for, not Lucas. Why did I get the feeling that everyone thought I was in the wrong here?

Chapter 18

All of us, including JJ in his brand-new Christmas harness, piled into Grandpa's truck—which wasn't exactly easy given the mound of presents, since we hadn't opened any last night per our usual tradition—around noon to head over to my parents. We would spend the majority of the day there, eating, watching Christmas movies, drinking, and napping. It was more relaxing than Christmas Eve, which had always been the more festive event for our family. On Christmas Day, you got the sense that it was already more over than not. The festive facades were slipping, the cheery music was dwindling and pretty soon everything was going to go back to the way it had been.

Or maybe it was just my mood. And last night had certainly not been festive. Between Lucas showing up and Katrina's arrest, they couldn't have made a Hallmark movie with more Christmas drama in it.

"Put on the Christmas music," Val demanded from the backseat.

Grandpa flipped the radio on. He'd actually gotten SiriusXM installed in his truck. He said it was partly for me, and partly so he could listen to the news. I didn't quite believe him but it still made me laugh. Especially

because I saw one of his presets was the Christmas chan-
nel Holly. George Michael from Wham! was currently
singing about giving his heart to someone last Christmas,
who gave it away the next day. I knew how he felt.

"So is Lucas joining us?" Grandpa asked, once we'd
turned off of our street and were driving through town.

"Et tu, Brutus?" I muttered.

"What's that, doll?"

"Nothing. No he isn't."

Grandpa frowned a little. "You two were interrupted
last night."

"Yup," I said. "The interruption was kind of important, no?"

"Of course. Just saying." He sighed and glanced in the
rearview mirror. I saw him catch Val's eye, which made
me think this was a whole conspiracy. Great. I sunk lower
in the seat, snuggling my face into JJ's fur, and stayed
quiet until we got to my parents' house.

My dad met us outside, and he, Grandpa, and Ethan
unloaded the gifts while Val and I brought the pies and JJ
inside. We'd been in charge of dessert and had made three
pies—apple, pumpkin, and my dad's favorite, blueberry.
When we got to the kitchen, my mother and Sam were at
the oven giggling.

"What's so funny?" Val asked, depositing her two pies
on the counter.

"Nothing. Your sister tried to make fudge." My mother
winked at me as I slid my pie next to Val's, deposited JJ
on the floor and shrugged off my coat.

"How do you mess up fudge?" Val demanded.

"You forget to stir it and leave the burner on too high."
Sam shrugged and hugged me. "Merry Christmas."

"Merry Christmas, sweetie." I'd barely gotten to spend
any time with my youngest sister since I'd been home.

She'd been away traveling, then she moved off-island for a short amount of time to pursue some kind of yoga training in Boston. "Did you finish your yoga training?"

Sam nodded. "But I'm not sure what I want to do still. I'm going to move back in here until I figure it out."

"You are?" I glanced at my mother over Sam's head, who shot me a look as if to say, *Don't ask.* It was kind of a running joke in our family. I was the typical oldest—responsible, ambitious, driven. Val was more serious, though. And really Type A. And Sam, well, she was the flighty but sweet youngest who had been babied by everyone. To my parents' credit, they just rolled with all of us. I'd never heard them say to Sam, for instance, *If you could just be more like Maddie.*

"Okay!" My dad came into the kitchen rubbing his hands together with glee. He was kind of like a little kid on Christmas too. "The presents are all under the tree. We should open them before dinner. Right, Soph?"

"Sure thing, honey," my mother said. "Let me just check on the stuffing. Sam, get rid of this mess." She handed her the pan with the burnt chocolate. "Maddie, want to get drinks? There's nondairy eggnog and pumpkin-pie soda."

"And rum," my dad said. "Who wants a mudslide?"

"Me," I said immediately, bending to pet Moonshine, the cat my parents had adopted at my grand opening earlier this year. He was a gorgeous black cat, who I could see was getting a little chunky. JJ was glad to see his old pal too. The two of them spent some time sniffing each other.

Once drinks were made and presents were opened, we all sat down to eat. I was grateful that the mood had been light so far, and I could be semi-quiet without a lot of attention. But eventually, as I knew it would, the conversation turned to Katrina.

"Have you heard any news?" My mother looked from me to Grandpa anxiously. "I'm so worried. I tried to call over to Lisa's but she's not answering."

Lisa was Katrina's mother. "I haven't," I said, glancing at Grandpa.

He shook his head too, scooping a bite of turkey and potatoes into his mouth. Once he'd finished chewing he said, "The arraignment won't be until Monday."

"Do you think she'll get out?" my mother asked.

"I don't know, Sophie."

"Mom. Dad. Do you know anything about the people on that street? Aside from Lilah, of course."

My dad frowned. "What do you mean, know anything?"

"Well, they all seem a little sketchy to me," I said. "And since we know Katrina didn't do this—"

"Maddie, you can't go accusing people randomly," Dad said. "If there's something not right about Katrina's arrest, the police will make that right."

"Yeah, but will they bother? Grandpa never thought they were that good," I said.

They both looked at Grandpa, who raised his knife and fork defensively. "Look. All I said was they work in a community that's . . . not that challenging. I can't remember the last Turtle Point murder. Can you?" he asked my parents.

They looked at each other, deep in thought. "Wasn't there that guy with the chainsaw?" my mother asked.

"Chainsaw?" Ethan repeated, looking at me.

"That was an accident," my dad said. "Manslaughter."

I debated the wisdom of asking for details and decided I didn't have the energy. I shook my head at Ethan. "We don't even want to know. But seriously, Dad. Some of those people seem a little nuts. Like June Proust." I circled my finger around my ear, a gesture I hadn't used since I was a kid.

"That's not nice, Maddie," my mother said, spooning some mashed potatoes onto her plate. "You shouldn't judge. No one knows what makes anyone else tick."

"Sorry, Mom, but it's true. She was so awful to us. You saw her in action. And the night he died . . ." I thought about her claw-like fingers gripping my wrist. "I feel like there's something off about her. Aside from her just being miserable. Ethan saw it too," I said, pointing my fork at him.

He nodded his assent, but kept eating.

My phone vibrated next to me on the table. I picked it up and glanced at the screen. A text from Lucas.

Merry Christmas, Maddie. Hope everything is OK. Wondered if we could finish our conversation?

I ignored it and put the phone facedown on the table again.

"I don't really know most of those neighbors," my dad was saying. "I do remember when that woman—Whitney, is it?—was in the hospital after that accident with her ex-husband. That was quite an event."

My ears perked up. "What happened to her? I know she's still recovering, but I never feel right asking."

"It was some sort of alcohol-related car wreck. It got to my desk because there were police and lawyers swarming the hospital for days." He shook his head. "And of course the newspaper was all over it."

I smiled. "Of course." I made a mental note to go look up the story. Or just ask Becky, since she had a photographic memory of everything the paper published. "But why lawyers?"

"Because they're both worth a lot of money, and she was clearly injured and unable to work for a while. They were in the process of an unfriendly divorce too. It was quite a mess."

"When did that happen?" I asked.

He thought back. "It was probably at the end of the summer."

"Wow. That's a long time," I said. "But she's so sweet and she still goes and gets food for the cats and tries to help as much as she can. Unlike the *others*." I wrinkled my nose.

My mother sighed. "Honey. We're trying to meet people where they are, remember?"

"That's fine, Mom. I just don't get why they need to be so mean about everything." My phone buzzed again. I ignored it.

Val looked at me pointedly. "You gonna get that? It sounds important."

"Nope," I said. "I don't think it's important at all."

Chapter 19

"Hopefully things will start getting back to normal today, JJ," I said to him the next morning, though I didn't really believe it. How could they, with Katrina still in jail? I couldn't help but think the arrest had been done strategically, so she would have to spend almost four days in a cell before she could be arraigned. I'm sure she was beside herself with worry about not only her situation, but the cats. Not to mention her own cats, who I was now taking care of as well. I was worried about all of it too.

JJ had curled himself into a ball on my pillow, inches away from my head. When I spoke, he opened one eye, regarded me, then closed it again, tucking his tail over his eyes like a blindfold. Guess he wasn't ready to face the day either.

I sighed and rolled over. The day after Christmas. Not the holiday I'd been expecting when I imagined my first holiday back home, like *really* home. I loved Christmas, and Christmas in New England, no matter how you felt about winter weather, was special. As much as I'd loved California, the season just didn't feel the same. So I'd romanticized this whole holiday season once I made the decision to stay here. It got even worse when Lucas and I seemed to be doing so well. I'd had visions of not only a cozy Christmas with my family, but with someone I loved by my side to help decorate the tree and watch corny Christmas movies.

Yeah, Maddie. Look how well that turned out. I pushed those images, as well as the one of the cheerfully wrapped little box, out of my mind. I still hadn't decided what to do with it yet. And I hadn't answered Lucas's texts. He tried a couple of more times to get me to respond last night. I'd ignored him, even though it hurt to do it. But I kept asking myself, is this the kind of guy you want to be with? Someone who can pull a disappearing act like that as if it's nothing?

And the answer was a resounding *No.* I'd been with enough bad boyfriends in my life and I was done with all that.

I threw off my covers, grabbed a sweatshirt and my slippers, and made my way down to the café. We were going to be open today—not that I was expecting a lot of traffic, but it still felt good to have a purpose. As I descended the stairs, the sounds and smells of normal things wrapped around me like a hug.

Ethan was in the kitchen, as usual, and Adele was in the café cleaning. I heard her classical music pouring out of the slightly open French doors. It always made me laugh. The fact that Adele, my gruff, two-pack-a-day crossing guard and cat-rescue warrior, loved classical music had never really computed with me, but she swore it helped the cats. I stopped by the kitchen for coffee and to say good morning to Ethan, then headed into the café. Adele had the cleaning under control so I went right out to the reception area, where I'd stashed a couple of boxes of deliveries that had showed up on Christmas Eve. In all the craziness, I hadn't even opened the boxes yet. I'd been buying more stuff for the café gift shop and couldn't wait to see what had arrived.

Having JJ as the mascot was a brilliant marketing strategy if I did say so, but if I could expand my line and start selling a range of items, all the better. So I'd started researching and strategically buying from vendors who I knew would be popular with the type of crowd I got. And one of my newest scores was stocking some of the artist Salvato's work.

Salvato was well known in animal circles for his rescue-animal line of paintings. I'd first learned about him when I was in California. His work was a big part of the famous Best Friends Animal Society in Utah, a rescue, adoption center, and sanctuary that was making a huge difference in the country. He'd done a project with them where he'd painted every dog that came in from a terrible dogfighting bust, showing the world their true personalities instead of the monsters portrayed by both the dogfighters and some members of the media. He'd been well known before then for an artist who never let himself be photographed and who stayed largely anonymous, but his fame shot to new heights after that line was released. Now you could not only buy his paintings, but prints, notecards, postcards, and even T-shirts with his designs. Best of all, he donated most of his profits to rescues around the country. He gave them to Best Friends for anything he did directly relating to them, and he also supported other organizations.

Chances were good one of these boxes was my Salvato order. I figured I'd get that unpacked and stocked today and start putting the pictures up on the website. I hauled the boxes out from where I'd stashed them behind the counter and sliced the first one open just as Grandpa walked in with a couple of plates. Apple cake, from the smell of it.

"Morning, doll," he said. "How are you feeling today?"

I shrugged. "Not great. I feel terrible that Katrina is stuck in that cell. They have to let her out at the arraignment, Grandpa."

"They don't *have to* do anything," he said gently, putting the plates down on the counter. "You know that."

I jabbed at the box with my box cutter. "I don't care. The whole thing is ridiculous. You have to tell those cops they have the wrong person."

"I talked to the chief," he said.

I looked up. "You did?"

He nodded. "Called him early this morning."

"And?"

Grandpa sighed. "He wasn't terribly receptive to me sticking my nose in, honestly. Especially now that I'm retired. Chief Dunn and I never . . . quite saw eye to eye."

"But that shouldn't matter if someone is innocent," I said.

"They have to figure that out for themselves, doll. And right now, they have a witness who saw Katrina's car there, and a bunch of people who saw her and the Prousts having a huge fight a few weeks ago."

That was news to me. "They did?"

He nodded. "That's what the chief said."

I thought about that. Something else she hadn't mentioned to me. I'd have to dig around and see what I could find out. But did it really matter? "So what? So did Avery Evans. They called the cops on her, for crying out loud." Not that I wanted to throw Avery under the bus, but I needed to make the point. "Grandpa. The reality is, they were super difficult and mean to anyone who tried to help the cats. So of course they had altercations. But this guy had to have other stuff going on in his life. Are they even looking? His wife is crazy as a loon. Have they looked at her?"

Grandpa shrugged. "While I'm not privy to the investigation, I'm sure they are looking at everything, Madalyn. Even if I disagree with the man sometimes, he runs a competent, albeit small and not terribly experienced, police force." He took a bite of his cake.

I watched, dumbfounded at his calm. "So you're really just going to go about your business and let them muck this up?"

"Of course not," he said around a mouthful. "I'm going to investigate on my own. He doesn't have to know about it. Well, at least until I have something to tell him."

That was more like it. "So what are you going to do first?" I smiled as I dug into the box, pleased to see it was indeed what I'd been hoping for, and pulled out a pack of notecards.

"Well, I'm going to see what I can find out about Virgil himself. Always start with the victim, as they say. What are those?" Grandpa stepped closer to inspect the notecards.

I pulled off the wrapper to see the various designs. As expected, they were gorgeous. I showed them to Grandpa. "This is the artist who does all the animal designs and donates most of his profits to animal rescue."

Grandpa took them and flipped through, pausing at the design of two dogs whose tails were twined together in a heart shape. I loved them because the illustrations were not cheesy at all—they depicted real-life shelter animals, even ones who didn't fit the traditional "cute dog" or "adorable cat" image. And he used colors really boldly in each too. I was hopeless at anything artsy, so I had no idea how to describe any of it, but his work filled me with peace and joy and occasionally brought me to tears. He had a whole Rainbow Bridge series that could literally tear your heart out.

"Lovely," Grandpa said, handing them back to me. He checked his watch. "I'm going to go for a walk."

"Okay. Be careful out there. It could be icy," I said. "And let me know what you find out!"

He waved me off as he left the room. He hadn't been gone for more than five minutes when I heard the doorbell. Ethan was closer so I let him get it, hoping it wasn't anyone for the café yet. It was only eight thirty and I wasn't planning on opening until ten, but sometimes people just showed up and I didn't have the heart to turn them away.

But it wasn't anyone here for the café.

Chapter 20

"Maddie?"

I turned, my heart thudding when I saw Lucas standing there. He looked exhausted, as if he hadn't slept at all, and even thinner if that was possible. "Hey," I said, trying to keep my voice neutral.

"Sorry to just drop by like this. . . . I tried texting you last night."

I averted my eyes. "Sorry. I was at my parents and my phone was in my bag. It was too late when I got home to get in touch." The lie rolled easily out of my mouth, but I figured it was better than completely stomping on his feelings. Like he'd done to me.

"I figured. Listen, do you think we could talk?"

"This really isn't a good time," I said. "I have to get some stuff done here and I'm opening soon."

"Oh. Sure. Of course. Well . . . is there another time that might work for you?"

I hated how formal he sounded, but of course I wasn't giving him any other option. "I'm afraid not." I reached into the top drawer of my desk and handed him the bag with the gift. "I appreciate the gesture but I really can't accept this." I wished I could erase the absolutely crushed look from his face.

He kept his hands in his pockets and didn't take the bag. "Maddie. Please. Can we just talk," he said, and the pleading note in his voice almost made me reconsider. I wanted to, so badly. I wanted to just forget about all of it and throw myself into his arms. Tell him how glad I was that he was home. But I knew how this worked. If he got away with it once, he'd feel like he could do whatever he wanted, and it would only get worse as the relationship went on. As much as I wanted to believe people change, my experience was that they didn't. And that meant more, bigger heartbreak in the future.

"I'm sorry," I said. "I really can't. Please take this." I put the bag on the desk and, avoiding his eyes, hurried upstairs where I locked myself in my bathroom and tried to convince myself it wasn't worth crying over.

I stayed upstairs until I was sure Lucas had left. I didn't want to chance going back downstairs if he was hanging around, hoping I'd give in. I wasn't sure if I knew what I was doing. All I knew is that the more I let people get away with stuff in my life, the more stuff they tried to get away with. It had always been that way with the guys I dated, and though I desperately wanted Lucas to be different, it seemed like he wasn't. So I needed to protect myself.

I waited twenty minutes then went back downstairs to pick up where I'd left off. JJ was in the café with Adele and the other cats. I went to my reception area and saw that the Lee's bag was still on the counter. I stuffed it on one of the shelves where I wouldn't have to look at it and flipped the sign on the door to OPEN. Then I returned to unpacking my box. My cell phone vibrated in my pocket. I pulled it out and peered at the screen. I didn't recognize the number, but it was local so I answered.

"Maddie? It's Dr. Kelly. Just wondering when someone is picking up this fluffy guy?"

I blinked, trying to reorient myself to the day. "Fluffy guy?"

"The black feral," he said patiently. "The one I fixed right before Christmas. He's fine to be returned now. I feel badly he's been in the trap for so long."

I was completely confused. Last I'd seen Toby, I'd transferred him to Katrina's care late Monday night. She hadn't mentioned when he'd be getting fixed but I figured she'd had it all lined up as she usually did. Although come to think of it, she usually let me know these things in case she needed a backup transporter. Then again, she'd been kind of busy getting arrested. And I was embarrassed to say it had totally slipped my mind with everything else going on.

"I'm so sorry," I said. "I didn't know he was still there. I'll be over in a little while."

"Great. Thank you."

I stuck my phone back in my pocket and checked the café e-mails. We didn't have any appointments today that had come in through our online scheduler, and I figured it was safe to say there wouldn't be a huge rush on the place. I asked Adele if she could stay for a bit and help any customers, then headed out. I was just sliding into my car when Cass drove up and parked behind me.

"What are you doing here?" I asked, getting back out of the car.

"You don't come to me, I come to you," he said. "Are we going somewhere?"

I smiled. I loved Cass. "I have to go pick up a cat and release him back to the woods."

"Let's go," he said, opening his passenger door for me. Cass drove a black Jeep Wrangler that wasn't really a great winter car, but he loved it.

I hoisted myself up into it and gave him directions to

Dr. Kelly's. Once we were on the road he glanced over at me. "How are you doing?"

"Not great," I admitted. "I need to help Katrina and I'm feeling a little overwhelmed about it."

Cas nodded. "And what about Lucas?"

I wrinkled my nose. "I don't want to talk about him."

"That's okay. But are you meditating?"

I suppressed an eye roll. I was an intermittent meditator at best, and while I knew it helped me, there was still a part of me resistant to it.

"I thought so. This is when you need it the most," he said. "That's where all your answers are."

"Yeah? Even Virgil's killer?" I knew I was being flip and hated myself for it, but I was feeling so terrible about everything I couldn't help it.

He glanced over at me with a small smile. "You never know what epiphanies you'll get when you meditate."

I slumped in my seat and kept my mouth shut until we pulled up at Dr. Kelly's door. He lived in Duck Cove not far from my parents, on the east border of Daybreak Harbor. He had always worked out of his home, which had a side entrance for his exam and surgery areas—kind of like our café now—and he had never gotten rid of all his equipment. After Dr. Drake went out of business and his partner left the island, we would've been vet-less if it wasn't for Dr. Kelly. Seemed like he knew his services would be needed once again on the island, so he'd been waiting in the wings.

"I'll be right back," I said to Cass and got out of the car.

His door was locked so I rang the bell. He opened it a moment later, smiling at me. Dr. Kelly was a pleasant, average-looking man. Average height, average weight, average glasses, average thinning hair. I didn't quite know how old he was but figured he had to be close to seventy if he'd been thinking of retirement. I remembered as a kid bringing our myriad of animal friends to see him, including my first cat Henry and the turtle Sam had saved when she was five years old. She had that turtle almost seventeen years before he died, and no one really knew how old he was when she found him.

"How are you, Maddie? It's nice to see you again," Dr. Kelly said now, stepping aside so I could come in.

"You too," I said, giving him a hug. "Thank you so much for helping the cats. And I'm so sorry. I didn't know Katrina's plan for him."

He waved me off. "Not a problem. It's certainly been a crazy week."

"It sure has. Can I give you some money for this?" I asked awkwardly. I had no idea what setup Katrina had in place for paying him. I know he did most of these surgeries at a giant discount, though.

But he shook his head. "It's all taken care of, not to worry. He's right in here. At least he was warm and dry for a few days." His voice sounded wistful. I know he cared very much about the cats outside also. He led me into one of the exam rooms, where my fluffy friend waited in his trap with a blanket over it.

"I was kind of hoping he wasn't feral," I said. "I'd love to find him a home."

"I know. Unfortunately, he is," Dr. Kelly said.

I sighed. "I especially hate bringing him back to that place," I said. "I worry about them over there. Those people . . ."

He watched me over the top of his glasses. "The situation out there has really turned tragic," he said. "How is Katrina?"

"I haven't talked to her," I said. "I imagine not good. She's arraigned on Monday." The words sounded surreal even with all the practice I'd had saying them over the past couple of days.

Dr. Kelly shook his head, pressing his lips together. "Katrina is a very good person. I have no idea what those police could be thinking. And just hearing about poor Virgil made me so sad."

"Did you know him well?" I asked. They didn't strike me as the type of guys who would run in the same circles, but the island was small and you never knew.

"Not well, but well enough. We've been on the Audubon Society board together for the past three years."

My mouth dropped open. "You . . . you're on the Audubon board? With him?" I'd heard rumblings that the island Audubon Society had been getting involved with the feral cat issue. It didn't surprise me that there were Sea Spray people on the board. I loved birds too, but I didn't agree with some Auduboners' philosophy that cats were evil creatures who needed to be removed from the streets to protect birds.

He smiled. "I am. Why?"

"I just . . . it seems . . . I didn't realize," I finished lamely.

Now he laughed out loud. "It is a very good organization, Maddie. With a noble mission. I know there are some who take things to the extreme with the cat-or-bird scenario, but most of us aren't like that."

I sniffed, but didn't say anything.

"It's actually the reason I joined the board," he added. "I wanted to be a voice for the cats as well."

That made me smile. An ulterior motive. I loved it. "Way to go, Dr. Kelly," I said, high-fiving him.

"Why thank you," he said, smiling modestly.

"So is it true that they wanted to get involved in the whole Sea Spray colony?" I asked.

He sighed. "There were a few people who expressed their support for the residents who were against the cats. But Virgil and I did a pretty decent job of swaying their attention to focus on other priorities."

I frowned. "Did you say you and Virgil?"

Dr. Kelly nodded. "I did. He didn't think it was appropriate for them to be involved either. He persuaded them to focus on broader issues."

I thanked Dr. Kelly for his help and promised him more cats soon. Then I grabbed Toby's cage and left.

I put the trap in the backseat and slid into the car. "Everything okay?" Cass asked.

I glanced at him. "This whole Virgil thing keeps getting more strange." I filled him in on the conversation with Dr. Kelly as we drove over to Sea Spray Lane to release my charge.

"Seems to me it would've behooved Virgil and all of his fellow cat haters to let Audubon step in and help get rid of the cats. I wonder why he didn't jump at the chance," I said. "His wife would've certainly wanted him to."

Cass pulled onto Sea Spray Lane and followed my pointing finger to Whitney's driveway. "Sometimes," he said in his Buddha-like way, "things aren't always what they seem, Maddie."

Chapter 21

Craig texted me first thing next morning. I was still in bed snuggled up with JJ, trying to do the new meditation Cass had given me yesterday for when I was feeling anxious. It was going okay but my mind, never a thing to be still, kept wandering. And of course when my phone buzzed I pounced on it, abandoning all hope of stillness and peace.

I frowned when I saw Craig's message.

I need to talk to you. Can I come by before work?

Sounds serious, I texted back. *What's up?*

Just need to talk to you. Is Leo home?

I sighed. JJ watched me with his big green eyes. "So much drama," I told him. "Craig is being very secretive. Maybe he's got some news about the real killer." That would be nice.

JJ squeaked.

I nodded. "I think we should hear him out too." I texted back.

Sure, I'm here. Grandpa is too.

Half an hour.

The eagle flies at midnight, I replied.

Apparently he didn't find that funny because he didn't reply.

I got up and JJ and I went downstairs. After I fed him breakfast I checked in on Grandpa, who was doing cat café cleaning duty that morning. I had told him a million times he didn't need to, but he insisted. Said he liked it. He sang to the cats and everything while he was cleaning. It was kind of adorable.

"Craig's apparently got some breaking news," I said. "Do you know what he's up to?"

He turned to me, adjusting his police-cat sweatshirt, a Christmas gift from Val. That was another one of his things—he wore silly cat clothes to the café whenever he was working in any capacity. "Not a clue. What'd he say?"

"He asked if he could come by. Said he needed to talk to me and asked if you were here." I shrugged. "He was being awfully cryptic. I guess that means he needs to talk to you too." I tried to make light of it but his text had sent my stomach churning again. I wasn't usually an expect-the-worst person, but this week had really thrown me off.

"Hmm." Grandpa frowned, but didn't comment. "Okay. Let me know when he's here."

"Okay. Did you find out anything interesting about Virgil yet?"

"Well, let's see. He was born in Boston and met June in college. He taught a justice course at Harvard for years. Really popular class. Popular teacher, in fact. Everyone loved him. Then he retired. About as far as I got."

It didn't seem that interesting to me. I went back upstairs to get dressed, squinting at myself in the mirror. This not-sleeping thing had been taking its toll. My eyes were puffy and I looked exhausted. I grabbed some under-eye

cream, moisturizer, and concealer and attempted to re-
pair the damage before Craig showed up.

That and some coffee made me feel more prepared to
answer the door when he knocked half an hour later. I
pulled it open.

He stood on the porch in his uniform, shading his eyes
from the sun. No snow today, and not-so-cold temps. Almost like spring. "Morning," he said.

"Hey. You didn't like my code line?"

He rolled his eyes and stepped inside. "Clever. I have
to get to work so . . ." He motioned me inside.

"Coffee?" I asked.

"Sure."

"Go sit. I'll grab it."

I poured coffee for him and topped off my own, then
carried them back out to the living room. Grandpa had
emerged from the café and he and Craig were talking
quietly.

I handed the mug to Craig with a questioning look
and sat across from him. "So did you find out something
about who really killed Virgil?"

Craig blinked. "What? No."

"No? Seriously? Then what's so super-secret urgent?"

He took a sip of his coffee, his eyes on the cup as he
returned it to the table. When he answered, it was with a
question to Grandpa. "Have you spoken to Katrina? Did
she tell you or the lawyer anything else?"

Grandpa shook his head. "I haven't spoken to her.
I don't believe Jack has either, but the arraignment is
tomorrow."

"Come on, Craig. What's going on? Did you find out
something that will help her?" I asked impatiently.

"If you mean have I been investigating with the Turtle
Point cops, no. You know I can't do anything relating to

official police work, right?" he said. "My chief wouldn't appreciate that. Especially if we're not asked to help."

"I know, but unofficially, you're helping, right? Can't you help Grandpa? I mean, she's your colleague. She does incredible things for the animals on this island. She works probably double the time she gets paid for. She's like a big sister to me. If there's anything you can do . . ."

"What do you mean, help Grandpa?" Craig asked, eyes narrowing as he glanced at Grandpa.

"She means help me eat what's left of this apple cake," Grandpa said, sliding a piece across the table while raising his bushy eyebrows at me over Craig's head.

Craig didn't look like he believed that. He glanced at the cake, then sighed. "Listen. I want her to be innocent like everyone else does."

His words chilled me. "What's up, Craig? What aren't you telling us?" I looked at Grandpa, who was silent, eyes on Craig.

Craig looked like he'd rather be anywhere else than here, but he took a deep breath and spoke. "There are some things you don't know about Katrina," he began.

I didn't like the sound of that. I leaned forward in my chair, my stomach a knot of anticipation. "Like what? I'm pretty sure I know most things about Katrina." I shoved my hands under my thighs to keep from playing with my nails. Did I, though? She was a few years older than me. She'd had a life while I was still a kid. She'd gone away to college for a while. I'd been off the island for a decade. Just because I liked to think of her as my old friend who rescued animals didn't mean there weren't other dimensions to her life.

"Like, when she went away to college, she was . . . involved in some things."

"Things," I repeated. "What kind of things?"

"Things," he said, but now there was a hard edge to his words, "like being in a radical animal activism group at her school."

"So she's always been an activist," I said, shrugging. "Most of us have, to some extent."

"Exactly. To some extent." He leveled me with his gaze. "I'm sure most of you weren't involved in an incident that left someone permanently injured."

I stared at him. What was he talking about? It certainly couldn't be my sweet friend, who cried over injured birds and once spent a night sleeping in the woods during the winter because she was worried about one of her ferals. I'd even seen her shed tears over a tree that someone wanted to cut down in her neighborhood.

What did he mean, "left someone permanently injured"?

I could feel my heart picking up speed. "Craig. I'm sure whatever you heard, it has to be a mistake. Katrina's hardly the type to be an extremist. She hates PETA, so that should tell you something about what she believes. She wouldn't have been involved in something like that."

Eyes still on me, Craig reached into his jacket, pulled out a medium-sized manila envelope and handed it to Grandpa, who hadn't said a word yet.

I resisted the urge to snatch it away. "What is that?"

"Reports from what happened."

Every fiber in my being screamed at me that I shouldn't take that folder. Whatever it was couldn't be good, if the look on Craig's face was any indication. I didn't doubt my friend, but at the same time . . .

"Can you be any more cryptic? Can't you just tell me whatever it is? I don't want to sit and read some old report from a hundred years ago." I waved the envelope away.

Grandpa, who hadn't said a word to this point, reached over and took the envelope. Leaving us to our debate, he opened it and began to flip through the pages.

"I'm still waiting," I said.

"Fine. Katrina went to college in Boston."

"Boston University. Yeah, I know."

"She hooked up with a group of animal people—who ended up being pretty serious about their cause. Extremists."

Oh, boy. This didn't sound good. And as much as I tried to brush it off, I couldn't tear myself away from whatever Craig was about to tell me.

"They did a lot of protests, a lot of sit-ins, they even released some animals from a lab at the school."

"Okay," I said. None of this sounded terrible to me. "So?"

"So then when that didn't get them the results they wanted, they apparently started to take it further. Threatening the researchers and the professors. Vandalism and damage to the labs. And ultimately, arson."

"Arson?" I stared at him. "What do you mean, arson?"

"I mean, they set someone's house on fire."

I could feel the blood drain from my face. "No. She would never—"

"They never found who actually set the fire. There was a whole group of them, and they all alibied each other."

"Was . . ." I swallowed. "Was anyone hurt?"

Craig nodded. "The house was supposed to be empty. It was the home of a prominent researcher, and he and his family were supposed to be away. But his teenaged daughter got sick and stayed behind at the last minute."

"Oh, Craig. No."

"I'm afraid so," he said.

"What happened to her?"

"She smelled the smoke but couldn't get out of her bedroom. She had to jump from a third-floor window. Broke her back and was paralyzed."

"Oh my God." I couldn't breathe. "This can't be true. Or it wasn't her, Craig. It couldn't have been her. Maybe she did get herself mixed up with a bad group of people, but she would've pulled out of some harebrained scheme like that. She would've known it couldn't turn out well. And Katrina isn't heartless." I got up from my chair and stalked around the room. "She's not one of those people who would sacrifice one life for another. She wants to save everything—that's her problem."

"I know you want to believe that, Maddie," he said. "But one of the eyewitnesses claimed they saw her at the house, a while before the fire broke out. They couldn't make any charges stick, but it didn't look good. She ended up leaving school not long after."

"Are these reports credible? Or was it just someone who wanted to point the finger at them? At her? Did they see others from this group, or was it just her?"

"There were a few of them. Allegedly."

"Okay. So maybe she was there, and maybe it was like, false pretenses or something. Maybe she thought they were going there to do something else, and they did this . . . awful thing instead." I paced the room again. "She didn't know, Craig. I'd bet my life on it."

"Maybe," Craig said, noncommittally. "I'm only telling you what the reports said."

Just the facts, ma'am. "Yeah, I know. The reports. So what does this mean, exactly?"

"It means that the prosecutor is most likely going to dig this up. And it's not going to look good for her."

"It doesn't mean she did anything wrong, Craig." I looked at Grandpa, who had set the papers down and was now watching us.

He sat back against the couch and rubbed his eyes. "It's not a positive thing, that's for sure."

I sank back down.

"It might mean something to the people on the jury, if it gets that far," Craig said. He looked to Grandpa for confirmation.

Grandpa gave a small nod.

"I don't want it to be true either. But if nothing else, it sets the stage for this crime. A woman who feels so strongly about animals that people who don't feel the same way are disposable. Sure, they can't prove it the first time. But if she saw something unjust happening again and couldn't make the person see reason, who's to say she didn't take matters into her own hands again?"

"You sound like you believe this," I said, incredulous.

"Just playing devil's advocate."

"You said she wasn't actually arrested for this."

"That's right. Not enough evidence."

"Then why are we prosecuting her? She's our friend!"

"I'm not prosecuting anyone. You can bet the actual prosecutor will have this information, though. And he won't hesitate to use it. Doesn't matter if it's true or not, Maddie. It's enough to plant reasonable doubt about what kind of a person she is when it comes to human versus animal."

We all let that sink in.

"Did you talk to her about this? Did you tell her you were digging up her past and ask her what she had to say?" I asked.

He shook his head. "I didn't. But Leo and I wanted to be prepared."

I looked at Grandpa. "You knew?"

He nodded. "I suggested it."

I didn't know what to think about that. "Do you suspect she did something, Grandpa?"

"No, honey. But I told Jack I'd help him. And Craig offered to help me."

I didn't have an answer for that. I looked at Craig.

"I was always curious," he admitted.

"Curious about what?"

"About why she came back early. She'd been so determined that she was going to leave the island, that she was going to go to veterinary school—I don't know. She had all these dreams and then all of a sudden she was back and there was nothing else." He lifted his shoulders in a shrug. "And I just wondered why."

This curiosity about everything around him was why Craig had become a cop. We're the same age, and Katrina was older—just enough that she could babysit me at my in-between ages, and just enough that it wasn't cool to hang out with me. But Craig was always so tuned in to what was going on around him, and if there was something that felt off, he wouldn't let it go. He'd clearly seen that Katrina had been struggling. I remembered her coming back. I remembered asking her about it a couple of times, because by then we were old enough—well, I was old enough—to be her friend. She said she'd just come back, that was all, and I'd let it go.

But Craig hadn't, and all these years later he'd still suspected something was off. Despite the fact that I hated his message right now, I felt respect and admiration bubbling up as well. It almost sent me off track.

Almost.

"So why didn't you ask her?"

"What?"

"Instead of sneaking around behind her back and gathering evidence—alleged evidence—against her. Why didn't you just ask her in the first place?"

I could tell he was startled by my question, but he recovered quickly. The only sign of a crack in his cop armor was the defensive crossing of his arms. "I doubt she would've told me this objectively."

"Of course it's not going to be objective. What happened to that girl was tragic—but if they never proved who did it, they shouldn't be assuming that it was Katrina or anyone else. You know I'm right. And I'm going to just ask her myself. Like you should have done in the first place."

Chapter 22

After Craig left, I turned to Grandpa.

"Don't you think you were a little hard on him, doll?" Grandpa asked.

"No! I can't believe you two went and violated her privacy that way."

"Maddie. This is police work. Look, Katrina was ordered by her boss to stay away from that neighborhood. She violated that order and went anyway. A man ended up dead. They are seriously looking at her, and if we want to help her, this is one of the ways we can do it."

Intellectually I knew he was right. That didn't mean I wanted to hear it. "I need to go out for a while. Clear my head," I said. "I'll be back in a bit."

I grabbed my coat and keys and drove to my parents'. I needed to get my mom's thoughts on all this. I let myself in through the side door. "Hello," I called, listening for my mother.

"In here, sweetie." Her voice floated out from the kitchen.

I followed the sound. "You won't believe—" I started, then paused when I realized she wasn't alone. Lilah Gilmore sat at the table with her.

As always, Lilah looked like she was dressed up for some fancy tea at the Plaza rather than an impromptu visit to my mother's house, with her pink suit and subtle string of pearls nestled around her neck. They had teacups and a plate of scones in front of them. From the fancy china plate and lacy doily they sat on, I gathered Lilah had brought them. My mother didn't bake that much, and when she did it was for a holiday or other special occasion. I didn't think Lilah visiting would warrant it.

"Why hello, Maddie," Lilah said, waving at me. I half expected to see lacy gloves, but her hands were bare. "Come have a scone!"

They did smell good. I went over and kissed my mother's cheek, then sat. She immediately got up and grabbed me a plate. "They're delightful," she said with a wink. "Blueberry lavender."

"Wow. Fancy." I plucked one off the plate and broke off a piece. It was still warm. "Sorry to interrupt," I said around a mouthful. "And this is delicious, by the way."

My mother passed the teapot. "I did teach them not to talk with their mouths full," she told Lilah dryly. "You're not interrupting, Maddie. Lilah just stopped by for a visit. So what won't I believe?"

"Hmm?" I was still engrossed in my scone. It felt like forever since I'd eaten that cinnamon bun this morning. Diet of champions lately, for sure.

"You came in and said 'You won't believe' . . . and then you stopped."

"Oh. Yeah. I forgot," I lied. "It wasn't important." I didn't want to get into the Katrina thing in front of Lilah. I didn't think Lilah believed Katrina did it, but I wasn't sure where her loyalties were.

Although I should've known that Lilah had come over to talk about just that. And now that I was here, the topic was even more ripe for discussion.

"Well, we were just talking about all the crazy excitement on our street," Lilah said. She waited for me to pour tea, then took the pot and topped off her own. "No one knows what to think. Between the thefts and the murder, you would think we were living in the projects in Boston!"

Thankfully I was chewing and couldn't respond to that one.

"It's shocking," my mother agreed. "Although no one—and no community—is immune to crime, Lilah."

"Isn't that the truth," Lilah said with a sigh. She turned to me. "And how is Katrina doing?"

"Not great," I said honestly, once I'd swallowed my scone. "She's in jail for a crime she didn't commit and we have no idea what's going to happen."

Lilah made a sympathetic noise. "I understand. It's very disturbing to think someone we know could have actually done this," she said.

"Well, it wasn't Katrina." I took another bite and washed it down with tea. "But I'm not sure if the cops are looking at other options."

"Hmmm." Lilah pretended to think about that. "Unfortunately so many people saw her having that terrible fight with the Prousts," she said, watching me closely.

My hand froze on its way to my mouth with another bite. So that had been true. "What fight?"

Lilah arched her eyebrows. "I thought for sure you would've heard."

I hadn't until Grandpa told me. "When was this?"

Lilah thought about that, taking a dainty bite of her scone. "Maybe a week ago?"

"What was the fight about?" I asked. "Did you hear them?"

"No." Lilah looked disappointed about this. "I heard about it from June. So I'm not sure if I heard the whole story. But she said that Katrina stormed up to their door and demanded a word with Virgil. They went outside to speak." Another arched eyebrow.

"But you don't know what about?"

"'I'm afraid not. There's just been so much tension," Lilah said. "It's so troubling. I wish everyone would be nicer to each other. I thought it was the usual winter blues coupled with holiday angst, but it seems to be so much deeper than that."

"Who has been fighting?" I asked. "Was Virgil having trouble with anyone else?"

She pretended to think about it. I was pretty sure she'd come over to my mother's to talk about this very subject and couldn't wait to gossip about Virgil's murder, and I'd just given her an opening. "Well, I don't know about trouble," she said. "He wasn't one for public displays of, well, anything. Now that Trey Barnes, he's another story. He doesn't care who sees him in a rage, or a drunken stupor, or any other foolish thing he's doing. Not that I'm surprised. He's not really . . . fit for the neighborhood."

"But Virgil?" my mother prompted.

"Virgil, yes. Like I said, he didn't really fight with anyone in the traditional way. But I do know he was having some . . . neighborly disagreements."

"Neighborly disagreements?" I leaned forward, eager for more information. "What kind of disagreements? Who with?"

"I really shouldn't say. I'm not sure it's appropriate, with what happened and all. It could look bad." Lilah worked at looking troubled by the dilemma.

"It already looks bad for Katrina," I pointed out. "And she didn't do it. Besides, we would never say anything."

"I knew I could trust you girls." Lilah abandoned her worried look and leaned forward. "For one thing, Virgil didn't like Trey Barnes. At all. I know a few times he threatened to throw his friends out of the neighborhood. It used to make Edie upset. Which made June upset. Those two are like this." Lilah held up crossed fingers. "Or at least they were. Lately they don't seem to be getting along well either."

"Really," I said, remembering their distance at the neighborhood meeting. "What happened?"

"I really don't know," Lilah mused, and I could tell it bugged her that she didn't know. "But I do wonder if it had something to do with their husbands. Then I saw Harvey Hackett arguing with Virgil about Virgil not showing up for the Audubon meetings. He was quite angry about it. Virgil was very stoic and not fighting back at the same level, but he surely said his piece." She sat back, a self-satisfied look on her face, waiting for our response.

I filed away the information about Trey Barnes, but something else seemed more important. "Wait," I said. "Harvey Hackett was part of the Audubon Society?"

Lilah nodded. "Virgil too."

Audubon meetings. The second time I'd heard about them. I hadn't been all that surprised about Virgil being part of that group, but Harvey?

"But they don't like cats," I said.

"That's not true of everyone," my mother said.

She was right. I thought of Dr. Kelly. Maybe Harvey had joined for the same reason. But my mind was racing back to the night of the murder. After the cops questioned me, when I'd heard Harvey and Monica arguing. Monica had said something about how it was going to "come out" that Harvey had been giving Virgil a hard time. This must be what they were talking about.

"He and Monica support the cats," I said. "Maybe it was an excuse to give Virgil Proust a hard time?"

Lilah looked at me with an expression I couldn't quite read. "He's a very nice man," she said carefully. "I do know that Harvey is very serious about the Audubon job. He was delighted to have Virgil on board. But Virgil never seemed as interested in it as June would've liked."

"June?" I was confused.

Lilah nodded. "June donates a lot to Audubon. She sat on the board for many years and offered up Virgil to take her spot. She had done the max term and she thought Virgil could help carry on her legacy."

I could hardly keep from making a face. Her *legacy*? Which included supporting the destruction of feral cats? I loved birds too, but I didn't think it had to be one or the other. Kind of like Dr. Kelly's philosophy.

"So why was Harvey upset?" my mother asked, shooting me a warning look. She recognized the signs of me about to go off on a rant.

"Because he also vouched for Virgil to be on the board, I guess. He feels it made him look bad that Virgil wasn't coming through." Lilah shrugged. "I'm not sure what prompted this . . . discussion, but he was shouting at Virgil in the street."

"Really? When?" I asked.

"A couple of weeks ago, now," Lilah said, after she'd taken a sip of tea.

"But don't you live at the other end of the street?" I asked.

Lilah nodded. "I do. But I was out for a walk and just happened to hear," she said with a wink. "It sounded quite contentious."

"So what did Harvey say?" I asked.

"He was reminding Virgil that this commitment needed to be taken seriously, and that they were doing important work that people needed to take seriously. I did hear him say that he could be removed from the board, no matter how much June donates. Virgil didn't seem to be phased by that. I think I heard him say, 'Let them remove me, then,' but he wasn't shouting so it was harder to hear him." Lilah looked annoyed by this.

"A one-sided fight, then." My mother smiled. "I have those with Brian all the time."

"Yes, but then Virgil did get mad," Lilah confided. "It was when Harvey threatened to talk to June about . . . well, whatever they were arguing about, I guess."

"Really? He was that scared of his own wife?" I asked in disbelief.

"Well, June can be difficult, as I'm sure you've noticed," Lilah said. "There's no doubt about that. So I think Virgil didn't want to deal with the fallout of all that. It was the only time he raised his voice back to Harvey."

"And he said . . ." I prompted.

"I'll tell you, when that man got angry you paid attention. He said something like, *'If you say a word about any of this to her I'll also be having a conversation with your wife.'*"

My mother and I exchanged a look at that one. What would he be telling Monica about? Was Harvey that afraid of *his* wife? But why?

It all seemed really murky but if anything, it gave more merit to my insistence that the cops had the wrong person on the hook for this murder. It seemed there'd been enough conflict in Virgil's life that the police had more work to do. Or was this just Lilah, exaggerating the conversation she'd heard to make it more interesting? "Did you tell the police this?" I asked.

Lilah nodded.

"When?"

"The night of the murder. They came around to all our houses to see if we had seen anything, or might be able to help them find the culprit."

But they'd still arrested Katrina. I thought about Harvey, arriving home at the exact time that I found the body.

Had that whole thing been staged? Had he only pretended to be out, and maybe parked his car around the corner and came back to do the deed? Part of me felt guilty for thinking this. Harvey seemed like a nice guy—he'd helped me out the night Virgil was murdered—and Monica was a sweetheart who loved cats. Could he really kill someone over a board position? I supposed anything was possible. People kill over much less.

Chapter 23

When I went down to the kitchen the next morning, Leopard Man and Grandpa were at the table having coffee and eating Ethan's famous—at least to us—cinnamon buns. Leopard Man wore a black suit with a leopard bow tie. It was the only obvious leopard-print item in his wardrobe today, which was a bit shocking. JJ was curled up in a ball on Leopard Man's lap, leaving orange fur clinging to the black material. I had no idea how they were eating anything. My stomach was full of butterflies. Today was the day we'd find out if Katrina could come home, at least until the rest of her fate was revealed.

Grandpa glanced up at me. "Morning, doll. How are you feeling today?"

"Fine," I muttered, trying to decide if I needed coffee or if it would upset my stomach even more.

Leopard Man, however, had a knack for both knowing when something was wrong and having a Shakespeare line ready for it.

"The course of true love never did run smooth," he said, motioning me to sit and handing me a cinnamon bun in a napkin. "Eat this. You'll feel better," he added.

Today's was a bit cliché for me. Or maybe it was just

my mood. Either way, it only spoke to part of my problem. But he was right about one thing. I hadn't eaten much yesterday, with everything going on. My appetite seemed to be mostly on the fritz these days. I sighed and slid into a chair, taking a small bite. It was, as expected, nothing short of remarkable. Ethan could be a gourmet chef. Or a gourmet baker. Why he chose to run juice bars and cat cafés with me was a mystery, but I was grateful.

"No true love here," I said once I'd swallowed. "But thanks for the reminder."

He smiled his best knowing smile at me, but let it drop.

I'd recently found out that Leopard Man had a name. I mean, I always knew he had to have a name, but I was fine not knowing it. I liked the whole mystique of having our own quirky island character. But his name was Carl, which had shocked me a little bit for the ordinariness of it. I'd told him I would never call him that, and he told me he'd be insulted if I did.

Leopard Man was one of the greatest cat advocates I knew. He adored the creatures. JJ hardly ever sat on anyone's lap, even mine, but as soon as Leopard Man showed up JJ was all about him. I thought it was adorable. And certainly a character reference. Plus, it totally didn't matter to him that his black suit was now rusty orange, which further enamored him to me.

"So why are you all dressed up?" I asked.

"Because you must dress appropriately for court," he said, as if that should've been obvious.

"You're coming to the arraignment? That's amazing," I said. "Thank you."

He nodded. "Of course. We cat people need to have each other's backs."

The courtroom was packed when we arrived. Aside from me, Grandpa, Leopard Man, and Jenna Randall—the

Chronicle reporter—most of the Sea Spray Neighborhood
Association had turned out for the big event. June Proust
sat front and center, eyes bugging out behind her glasses
as usual, if not more prominently given that they were
red-rimmed and puffy from crying. In between barely
concealed sobs, she took turns glaring at me, Grandpa,
and Katrina's lawyer. She also spent some time staring at
Leopard Man. I wondered if she knew him from around
the island. If she didn't, she had to be blind and/or living under a rock, but you never knew with some of these
people who thought they should only mix with their "own
kind."

He did have his fancy leopard coat with him, but he'd
removed it for the proceedings. I caught a glimpse of
leopard-print socks when he sat down on the other side
of me. Seeing them peeking out from under his pants leg
buoyed my spirits—it felt wrong for Leopard Man not to
be wearing multiple leopard-print items.

Other than this case, it didn't seem to be a big morning for arraignments. Aside from the murder, people had
actually behaved themselves over the holiday—hard to
believe. It wasn't always so. With the island empty of
tourists and more than half the businesses closed, cabin
fever ran rampant. The close quarters sometimes perpetuated domestic disputes, sadly. Grandpa had seen it many
times. People got bored, depressed, seasonal affective
disorder, whatever it was. Some people drank too much.
It was often a recipe for disaster. Or else the Turtle Point
community was just better behaved on principle.

Somehow, I doubted it. Someone had killed Virgil
Proust, and my gut told me it wasn't a random murderer
wandering the streets. Nor was it one of my best friends.

Finally, the bailiff brought Katrina in. I was glad to
see she wasn't in ankle shackles or anything like that,

although she was handcuffed. She looked so sad. It broke my heart. And simultaneously made me angry. Grandpa, sensing this, gave me a not-so-subtle elbow as a reminder to not do anything stupid like, say, start yelling at the judge.

He knew me so well.

Jack Gaffney waited behind the defense table, looking dapper yet appropriately somber in a pinstriped gray suit. When Katrina joined him, he bent his head and spoke softly in her ear. Whatever he said, she didn't look convinced.

June Proust turned her full-on glare to Katrina. I could see Katrina visibly trying to ignore her, but failing miserably.

Just before one o'clock, the doors opened and a man strode in, taking a seat in the back. Grandpa, who had turned to look, caught the man's eye and inclined his head in a nod. The other man returned the greeting with a curt nod of his own. He looked vaguely familiar to me, but I couldn't place him. I was dying to ask Grandpa, but at that moment the bailiff instructed all to rise while the judge took her seat. I was relieved. Sitting there felt like a pressure cooker was about to blow at any moment.

Once we had all settled back down, Judge Boyle, an affable-looking woman with killer highlights in her brown bob, surveyed the courtroom before flipping open a folder and skimming its contents. When she looked up, her laser focus went right to Katrina and when she opened her mouth, I could immediately tell that her affable demeanor didn't mean she was any kind of softie.

"Ms. Denning."

Katrina and Jack Gaffney stood in unison. "Yes, your honor," Katrina said. Her voice was hoarse, as if she hadn't used it much lately.

"I'm looking at a murder charge." Judge Boyle pointed a red fingernail at her folder. "I'm sure I don't have to tell you that this is very serious."

"Yes, your honor," Katrina repeated, a bit robotically, I thought.

"How do you plead?"

"Not guilty, your honor," Gaffney interjected.

The judge's eyes lingered on Gaffney for a moment, then shifted to the prosecuting attorney, a younger woman with a head full of curls who reminded me of Marcia Clark in the old days.

"Have you considered bail, Ms. Andrews?"

Andrews opened her mouth to answer, but Gaffney jumped in.

"If I may, your honor, I'd like to make note of Ms. Denning's reputation and standing in the community. She's a member of law enforcement as the animal control officer for Daybreak Harbor. In that role, she assists not only her town, but neighboring towns that don't have a similar role. She's responsible for saving hundreds of lives in this capacity." He spread his hands wide, his face earnest as he let the enormity of that sink in. "She has deep ties to the community and has lived here most of her life. She's not a flight risk. We're asking that Ms. Denning be released without bail until her trial."

The judge looked like none of that made a difference to her in any way. Andrews let out a snort of disbelief. "No bail? Your Honor. This woman is accused of *murder*, not stealing an ice cream cone. That's ridiculous. We'd like the court to deny bail."

"That's extreme, Your Honor," Gaffney said without missing a beat. "Ms. Denning stands by her innocence, and has never been arrested before."

The judge frowned as she turned back to her folder, then fixed her icy stare at Gaffney. "I'm afraid Ms. Andrews has a point. This isn't a shoplifting charge. This is murder. We take murder very seriously, at least in our town. While I don't believe Ms. Denning is a flight risk, I do think not setting bail would set a precedent that I can't live with. Bail is set at $200,000, and Ms. Denning may not go within five hundred feet of the Sea Spray community or any of its residents while awaiting her trial."

My mouth literally dropped. I looked at Gaffney, willing him to argue the point, but he stayed quiet. Andrews looked smug. I bet she figured Katrina couldn't make that kind of bail anyway, and she was probably right.

The judge slammed her gavel, making me jump, and glanced at the bailiff. "What's next?"

"That's our only arraignment, Your Honor."

"Dandy." She rose.

"All rise," the bailiff commanded.

Everyone rose hastily as the judge made her way back into her chambers. When she stepped off the platform, I could see how tiny she was.

The bailiff let Katrina back through the door she'd come in. I poked Grandpa furiously. "Two hundred thousand dollars? Seriously? She can't afford that!"

"Madalyn. Not here," he said, taking my arm and steering me toward the door. When we got there, though, he dropped it. "I need a minute."

I watched him head down the hall after the man who had come into the courtroom at the very end. Jack Gaffney and Leopard Man came out to wait with me. I looked at Leopard Man. "Who's that guy?"

"That is Chief McAuliffe," he said. "He took over when your grandfather retired."

"Oh wow. I didn't recognize him." I studied Grandpa's replacement, also Katrina's boss. I think I'd seen him once or twice at town meetings, but we hadn't ever met. He had a bit of a chip on his shoulder about Grandpa, since Grandpa did like to keep himself . . . engaged in the goings-on of the Daybreak Harbor police force. I didn't know if the new chief felt threatened by that, or by some of his force's loyalty to Grandpa, but he'd never been overly friendly to him.

They looked like they were having an earnest conversation now, though. I thought it was nice he'd come to support Katrina.

"I'll be back in a few moments," Leopard Man said, squeezing my shoulder, and then he left me with Gaffney.

I looked up at the lawyer. "Two hundred thousand dollars? That's the best you could do?"

Gaffney frowned at me. "I don't have any say over what bail amount the judge will set. This town is very cliquey. And they aren't used to murder charges." He shrugged and checked his watch.

"She doesn't have that kind of money!" I exclaimed.

Gaffney sighed. "Maddie. I'm sorry. I have no say in bail amounts. It's the judge's call." He glanced down the hall to where Grandpa was still deep in conversation with Chief McAuliffe. "I have to go. Tell Leo to call me later." And he strode off in the other direction, probably on to his next high-profile, high-paying case.

I wondered how much Grandpa was paying this guy. I stuffed my hands in my pocket, trying not to stew about it. I would have to figure out how to raise the money. Maybe I'd do a GoFundMe and tap into our rescue community. People who did rescue generally weren't rich, but they had big hearts—and if one of their own was in trouble, they had no qualms about stepping up to help. It might take us a while, but I was sure we could do it.

I pulled out my phone and texted Ethan to see if he could get it set up and then we could start to socialize it when I got home. So I didn't notice June Proust marching up to me until she was right in front of my face.

"You should be ashamed of yourself," she hissed, so close I could smell the coffee on her breath.

I took a startled step back. "Excuse me?"

"For coming here. And showing support to that awful woman after she . . . after she killed my Virgil!" She stared at me with those bugged-out eyes. This woman creeped me out.

"June. I'm sorry for your loss, but Katrina didn't kill anyone. Now please leave me alone." I turned to walk away, but she darted in front of me, quick as a beetle scurrying for a crack in the foundation. "You're all going to pay for this," she hissed at me, spittle flying from her mouth. She looked *insane*.

"Is there a problem?" Grandpa Leo had materialized behind her, and he didn't sound happy. Even June seemed to notice the shift in the air.

A younger, skinny man rushed over and grabbed June's arm. "I'm terribly sorry," he said, barely meeting my eyes. "Come on," he muttered to June.

She let the guy pull her away, but still shot daggers at me with her eyes. I wondered who the skinny guy was. I'd never seen him before on the street, but then again, some of the neighbors had stayed out of the whole thing.

Grandpa watched them until they were out of sight, then turned to me. "Where's Jack?"

"He said he had to go. And I'm guessing he didn't stop to offer up any money for Katrina's bail." I couldn't keep the disgust out of my voice.

Grandpa shook his head. "Maddie. You can't be like that. The man did his job."

"I don't care! There's no way she can afford that. I'm going to try to raise it for her, but it's not fair—"

"Maddie," Grandpa interrupted my tirade. "Don't worry. Please. I have a feeling it's all going to be taken care of. Come on, we need to go."

"What do you mean?" I asked, as we exited the court-house into the cold December day. Leopard Man stood near Grandpa's truck, hands in his fuzzy leopard coat pockets, whistling to himself. When we reached him, he winked at me.

"She'll be out by end of day."

Chapter 24

When we arrived home, Craig was there. He and Ethan were in the living room watching something on TV that looked violent. Grandpa didn't seem surprised to see him.

"Did you hear?" I asked.

"I did. He's a good guy," Craig said.

"What happened?" Ethan wanted to know.

"Katrina's bail got set at two hundred thousand dollars," I said.

Ethan's eyes widened. "Whoa. How is that good?"

"That's not the good part," I said impatiently. "Leopard Man came to the rescue and put up her bail. It's like he's this guardian angel just waiting to swoop in and make life better. He's so incredible." I nearly swooned.

When Leopard Man's true identity had come to light recently, he hadn't loved the attention or the fact that people now knew the truth about who he was. But he was making the most of the situation by remaining his quirky, elusive self most days—except when he was courting Ellen the librarian around town or making sizable donations to things that mattered on the island.

Like Katrina's bail. If she had to wait around for her trial in jail, it would have killed her. I was certain of it. I'd still offered to try and raise the money, but he'd basically told me not to waste my time and to go save more cats.

We needed more people like Leopard Man in this world.

"That's great," Craig said, but his lack of enthusiasm was kind of obvious.

"What?" I asked. "Is there some problem with that?"

"Not at all."

"Then why so subdued?" I looked around for my hat. I had promised to pick up Katrina once all the paperwork was done and didn't want to be late.

"I'm not subdued."

"You so are." I plucked the hat off the top of a cat tree and pulled it over my hair. "Hurry up and tell me why. I have to go pick her up shortly."

Craig sighed. "This is the problem with knowing everyone on this island for your whole life."

I arched my eyebrows at him.

Ethan, taking the cue, rose. "I'm going to go to the general store. I want to make us some veggie burgers tonight."

"You might want to get Grandpa a real burger," I called after him. He waved his acknowledgment as he headed into the kitchen. I turned back to Craig. "So?"

"I'm just worried about how this is going to go down."

"How what is going to go down?"

"This trial."

"How do you know she's going to have to go on trial?"

He gave me a look. "Because that's what happens after you've been arrested for a crime."

"So you don't think they're competent enough to find the real killer?" I asked.

He pressed his lips together so they almost disappeared. "I didn't say that."

"You don't have to. They aren't looking for anyone

else, so that says it all. Which is why we need to do something about it. Hey, your chief was there. At the arraignment." I'd wanted to ask Grandpa what they'd been talking about, but after all the excitement with Leopard Man posting bail, I'd forgotten. "You think he'll help Grandpa figure out who really killed Virgil?"

Craig was silent.

I rolled my eyes. "I know, I know. It's official police business."

"It's not that, Mads. It's . . ." He sighed. "Forget it. Go pick up Katrina. We'll talk later."

"Okay." I shrugged into my coat and zipped it. "Hey, how's Jade?" I asked.

His gaze shifted away. "She's fine."

I waited, but that was it. Guess he didn't want to talk to me about his love life. "Great," I said. "Next time you come over, don't be so chatty, okay? I couldn't hear myself think." I grabbed my bag and headed out the door, leaving him standing there.

The county correctional facility that served the entire island was in Fisherman's Cove, the smallest town on the island. It was on the other side of Turtle Point. This town was less of a tourist draw. There was no quaint downtown, just small, no-nonsense homes for the fishermen who still made their living out on the sea. Most people who came to visit never came out this way, if they even realized there was another town at all. However, there were great beaches and state parks out here. When I wanted to go to either in the height of summer, I usually went to Fisherman's Cove to avoid the crowds.

However, it was a male prison, so Katrina couldn't stay there. Instead she'd been relegated to the lockup at the Turtle Point PD, which really wasn't a long-term solution. I wondered what they would've done had she not made bail. She probably would've been sent to a women's facility on the mainland. Which also would've been unbearable for her.

When I pulled up at the police station, Katrina stood outside shivering in the freezing cold air. She had on a pair of sweats, her hiking boots, and a cargo jacket over a T-shirt. I realized it must've been what she was wearing when they'd picked her up the other night.

"Why are you standing outside?" I asked when I'd pulled the car over and she opened the door. "You're going to freeze. How come they didn't let you get warmer clothes?"

Katrina slid into the car and slouched down in the seat. "Just drive," she said. "I want to get as far away from here as possible."

I cranked up the heat and obliged. "Are you okay?" I asked when we were a safe distance from the jail. I knew it was kind of a stupid question, but I didn't know what else to ask her. *Why were you there that night? What were you doing at Virgil Proust's house?*

None of those would be good, so I went with the obvious.

She shot me a look and didn't say anything.

"Okay. Well, I know that was a dumb question, but I had to ask. I bet you're hungry. I'm taking you to my place. Ethan's making veggie burgers. And I'm guessing fries, since you can't have veggie burgers without fries." I was kind of babbling.

But now she looked panicked. "I can't visit anyone. I need to go home."

"Katrina. You're not visiting. We're family. You're coming for dinner. And staying with us is totally an option. It might be better than going home alone."

"I need to see my babies," she said. "They've been all

alone." Katrina's two cats, Fred and Ethel, were her whole world. Somehow, despite what she did for a living, she'd managed to keep her permanent crew at two. Most rescuers had a houseful.

"Adele and I have been taking care of them. Did you really think we wouldn't?" I asked. "They're fine! They can't wait to see you. And if you want, we can bring them to our house. There's plenty of room. So think about it over dinner and then we'll go pick them up." I wasn't leaving her any wiggle room. I didn't want her to go home alone. Grandpa and I had already discussed it.

Plus, I wanted to know if she'd talk to us at all. About why she'd been there in the first place, and what had happened. And what the fight with Virgil that she'd forgotten to mention had been about. But mostly, I just wanted her with me where I could keep an eye on her.

"Who posted my bail?" Katrina asked suddenly.

My hands tightened on the steering wheel. I wasn't sure if I was supposed to tell her, but it probably wouldn't be a secret for long anyway. "Leopard Man," I said.

"Really?" She sniffled. "He's such a good man. How can I ever repay him?"

"Show up at court," I said. "So we can get this nonsense over with and get you cleared of this. Katrina. Seriously. What happened that night? Why were you at the Prousts' house?" I couldn't resist. It was one of my biggest problems—when there was an elephant in the room, I had to try to move it.

Silence. Then my phone began to ring.

Cursing it, I reached for it and answered.

"Are you on your way back?" Grandpa asked.

"Yes, we're almost there," I said.

"Good. Your sister got one of the guest rooms ready."

"Awesome," I said. "We'll see you soon." I hung up

and turned back to her. "So? You were about to say something."

She hadn't been, but I really needed her to.

"Maddie. I don't want to talk about it right now," she said.

"But you were there," I pressed. "You told Grandpa and the lawyer that you were there. Why would you go over there? You said you were staying out of the neighborhood for a while."

I could feel her glare even without turning to look at her. "This is what you used to do when you were the pain in the butt kid I had to babysit," she said.

I half smiled. "Leopards never change their spots. So?"

"I needed to check on one of the cats," she said. "I heard it was hurt."

I frowned. "Which cat?" I hadn't seen or heard about one of the ferals needing medical attention. Not to mention, the cat probably wasn't at Virgil Proust's house.

She waved me off. "Doesn't matter. I couldn't find him."

"So you weren't technically at Virgil's house, then. You were just in the neighborhood. Is that what you meant?"

"Yes. Of course that's what I meant." She didn't look at me. "The lawyer probably misunderstood."

Something about her story was off to me, but she clearly wasn't saying anything else. I kept my mouth shut for the rest of the drive until we pulled into the driveway. "Did you actually see Virgil? Before . . ." I couldn't finish the sentence.

Katrina stared out her window so I couldn't see her face when she responded, but her voice was flat. Like scary flat. "Yeah," she said. "Yeah, I did."

Grandpa materialized next to the car, opening Katrina's door for her and offering a hand to help her out. "Hey there, beautiful," he said, wrapping her in a hug. "Hey, Leo," she said, her voice muffled against his shoulder.

With a sigh, I turned off the engine and got out. I really wanted the full story about that night, but it was like pulling teeth.

And I wasn't sure why.

Chapter 25

We convinced Katrina to stay over. It didn't take much. She was exhausted and I could tell she really needed some good food, a warm bed, and comfy clothes. Grandpa and Ethan took care of the food (Grandpa's famous chicken noodle soup and Ethan's veggie burgers and fries), and Val took care of the guest room, complete with candles, a brand-new pair of jammies she'd picked up for her, flannel sheets, and the fuzziest blanket we had. Which left me in charge of going to get Katrina's cats and some clothes for her.

She protested briefly, saying that she should come with me, but we all talked her out of it. When I left, she was wrapped in the blanket on the couch with Grandpa's soup, a bourbon, and some comedy that Ethan insisted would fix everything.

I wished it was that simple.

I got into Grandpa's truck and started the engine. While it was warming up, I called Becky and put her on speaker. "Katrina's out," I said when she answered.

"That's good," she said. "How is she?"

That was the million-dollar question, wasn't it? "Not great, but she was glad to have real food and a blanket that didn't smell like felons."

"I'm sure. So what do you think?"

"She didn't do it, Beck."

"I know she didn't do it," Becky said impatiently. "Jeez, she's my friend too. I'm not that ruthless. I just mean, what do you think is going to happen?"

"I don't know. Lilah Gilmore said Virgil wasn't getting along with a bunch of his neighbors. And that she told the cops that. But they still arrested Katrina."

"Not surprising. The Turtle Point cops aren't the best to work with."

"What do you mean?" I asked, my antennae rising.

She paused for a moment. "Nothing bad," she said finally. "I don't mean they're corrupt or anything. It's just that nothing ever happens out there unless it's something stupid like some stolen bikes—"

"Or stolen decos," I added.

"Exactly. So they kind of Keystone Kop–it when something big happens. I don't want to say they don't know what they're doing, but . . ." She let the sentence hang unfinished. "I couldn't even get an official statement for two days on the arrest, and that's an easy one. I also think they're not used to talking to reporters about a case like this. Anyway, keep me posted."

I promised her I would as I turned into Katrina's driveway. I pulled my wad of keys out of my pocket, found hers, and headed up to the door. I scooped up the mail from that day that had been pushed under the door and brought it into the kitchen, adding it to the pile I'd already created on the counter, then I looked around for Fred and Ethel.

They were snuggled up together on their cat tree, watching me impassively. They were bonded siblings whom Katrina had rescued when they were kittens. They were almost twelve now.

I got them into their crate without a problem, then

headed into the bedroom to get clothes. I picked out some
sweats, leggings, and flannel shirts and packed them into
her backpack, along with an extra set of pajamas and
some socks, then paused to think what else she might
want. She'd been so tired she hadn't even given me any
instructions before I left, which also wasn't like her. I
saw her phone charger on her nightstand and stuck that
in the bag along with the book she seemed to have been
reading. I glanced at the title. The newest Liane Moriarty
book. That surprised me a little. Katrina was more of a
thriller gal.

But then again, I guess I didn't know everything about
my friend.

I picked up the backpack and looked around one more
time. "We ready?" I asked the cats.

They blinked at me.

"Okay, then." I stooped to pick up their carrier and as
I did, I noticed one more envelope that must have been
stuck under the door. It was halfway under the mat, which
was why I hadn't noticed it the first time. I pulled it out.

It was blank. Which meant it hadn't come in the mail.
And the envelope hadn't been closed all the way. It was
basically open, so I peeked inside.

Cash. Wrapped in a piece of paper. I pulled it out and
unfolded the paper. It didn't say anything. I counted the
money. Three hundred dollars. I placed it back into the
envelope and put it with the rest of the mail, tucking it
underneath.

Who had left her that money? The anonymous cat donor? She'd mentioned that someone had been giving her
money. Leopard Man, I guessed.

Now I was curious, though. I flipped through the mail
to see if there was anything else there that would shed
some light, but nothing caught my attention. I poked
around a little bit, feeling guilty, not even knowing what

I was looking for. Well, that wasn't true. I was looking for something that would tell me what Katrina and Virgil fought about, and why she was at his place the night he died.

Which was kind of a long shot.

Unless . . . I hesitated. I wondered if she kept a journal. As soon as the thought entered my mind I shoved it out. That would be the ultimate betrayal. Worse than Craig poking around in her past. How could I even think of doing that?

"Get it together, Maddie," I ordered myself. "You are not going through your friend's journal. If she even has one. Get out of here and go be supportive."

I went back to the kitchen and picked up the backpack and the cat carrier. I was just about to leave when my phone buzzed. Val. I stopped to answer it.

"Hey. You still at Katrina's?"

"Just walking out the door. What's up?"

"She forgot to tell you Fred is on medicine. It's in the cabinet right next to the stove."

"Roger that." I stuffed my phone back in my pocket and went back to the kitchen. I flipped open the cabinet, found the pills easily enough—it appeared to be for some kind of stomach ailment—and shut the cabinet. As I did, my eyes fell on the calendar Katrina had tacked to the cabinet door.

I glanced at the block for December 23, the day Virgil died. Nothing on there but *pick up mom's meds*.

But now I was curious. And it was better than going through her journal. I pulled the calendar off the door and flipped back, checking dates over the past three weeks. Nothing made any reference to Sea Spray Lane, Virgil Proust, or anything else suspicious. I figured as much, but had to check.

I was just about to hang it back up when I noticed an

address scrawled at the bottom of the November page. It
had no appointment or even a day associated with it. Just
525 Bluff Point Drive.

Curious. It didn't sound familiar to me. Maybe she'd
gotten an animal call while she'd been home and scrawled
the address on the nearest available piece of paper.

I hesitated, then copied it into the Notes on my phone.
At the very least, I could Google it later.

I felt better knowing Katrina was safe at home with us.
She was happy to have her cats, and she went straight to
bed with them when I returned to the house. All in all, I
was feeling pretty good before I went to bed myself. The
only downer was getting a text from Lucas, telling me
he missed me more than anything and could we please
speak.

I didn't answer.

I also felt like it was time to talk to Katrina. Now that
she was home and she knew we were trying to help her,
she would see that she needed to tell Grandpa and me
everything, so we could figure out the best approach with
her lawyer. Unfortunately that included needing to know
about this terrible event from her past too. As much as
I hated to admit it, Craig was right. Whether or not she
had been responsible for what happened, if her name was
attached to it in any way, it wouldn't look good and we'd
need to take a proactive approach.

I had no idea if she would talk to me about it. Sometimes I think Katrina still saw me as the younger kid she
used to babysit, even though we were both adults now. A
part of her would always want to protect me, and I loved
that about her. But she would talk to Grandpa. Of that, I
was positive.

Before I went upstairs, I headed down to Grandpa's
office. He'd disappeared down there earlier. I assumed he

was doing some sort of work relating to Katrina. When I poked my head in, he was engrossed in something on his computer, but when he saw me he clicked away from it and sat back in his chair. "Hi, doll. What's up?"

"What are you doing? Did you find out anything yet?" I knew I was being a pain asking him every five seconds. Especially when I knew how Grandpa worked. When he first started investigating something, he need space to gather data and organize his thoughts. In my (admittedly very limited experience) working with him on cases, he didn't like to talk about it a lot at that point, until he'd coalesced the thoughts in his brain.

"Working on it," he said simply, which confirmed my assessment. "You need something, Maddie?"

"I think we should talk to Katrina," I said. "About everything. Get her to tell us what she was doing out there. And . . . we should ask her about the college thing. Even though she's going to be angry about that. We probably shouldn't tell her Craig found out."

"He was trying to help her."

"Do you believe it?"

"Do I believe that Katrina had anything to do with what happened to that young woman?" Grandpa sighed. "I never spoke to her about it, Maddie. I know what I read in the report, which didn't have overwhelming evidence against her. I will say if she was caught up with the wrong people and found herself in a situation, she may have been an active participant, however unwilling."

I hated to hear that, although I completely understood it. "We have to ask her, Grandpa."

"Her lawyer will figure it out. That's why we have Jack. He's a pro at this stuff."

I realized that Grandpa might be a little bit afraid of the answer too. Because otherwise he would've already had the conversation with her. "Right. But Jack doesn't care if she really did it or not," I said slowly. "Jack will only care about what he can redirect the jury to believe. Isn't that what you always told me?"

Grandpa nodded slowly. "That's right."

"So he's not going to really ask her if she did this. Just like he doesn't want to know if she killed Virgil Proust. Which I know she didn't, but still. He just wants to know enough that he can convince the jury there's reasonable doubt."

Grandpa remained silent, but his slight nod was enough.

"Well, great. But I still need to know." I pushed my chair back. "And you're her private investigator, aren't you? Wouldn't you want to know too?"

Chapter 26

When Grandpa and I went looking for Katrina the next morning, we found her in the living room with a cup of coffee. JJ, Fred, and Ethel were all cuddled up next to her on the couch. So that's where JJ had gone. I'd wondered why he wasn't snuggled up on my head when I woke up. He was so sweet. He always knew who needed him most.

"Hey," I said. "How'd you sleep?"

"So good," she said gratefully. "Thank you for having me here. And for the coffee. It's delicious." She smiled, but it faded as she looked from me to Grandpa. "What's wrong?"

"Nothing's wrong. We wanted to talk to you, if you have a few minutes." Then I realized it was the middle of the week. "Unless you have to get ready for work. Or are you taking some time off? You should take some time off."

She smiled, but there was no mirth in it. "You could say I have some time off." Her gaze lingered on Grandpa for a moment.

Grandpa sat down next to her and took her hand. "It's going to be alright, Katrina. I promise."

She looked like she didn't quite believe him, but no one challenged Grandpa. She squeezed his hand.

"What happened?" I asked. "I feel like I'm missing something."

Katrina sighed. "Leo, did you tell her about my suspension?"

I stared at Grandpa. "No, he didn't."

"It really wasn't my place," Grandpa said.

"Well, our fabulous chief suspended me," she said bitterly. "Doesn't want to give the public the wrong idea that he's letting a murderer run loose on their tax dollars."

I looked at Grandpa. He gave me a curt nod of assent. So that's why the chief had been at the arraignment, and why he and Grandpa were so engrossed in conversation. I'd thought he'd come to support her. Guess I'd been wrong again. My judgment about people was really lousy these days.

And it was probably why Craig had acted so weird yesterday too.

"So who is running the shelter?" I asked.

"No one," she said.

"No one?" Grandpa and I repeated in unison. We looked at each other.

"How can that be?" I asked.

She shrugged. "Because it's not important to him. He's got dispatch monitoring calls and apparently has volunteers feeding and walking the dogs. Mick is on call for when real calls come in, but he's doing it off the side of his desk. He's actually good," she said when I wrinkled my nose. "He cares. But the chief won't let him spend any real time on this. They're not going to do . . . anything like what I do. Unless he does it on his own time. Which he totally will, but that's not realistic."

I knew exactly what she meant. The animal control officer was, by charter, required to respond to any complaint or request that came into the department. An animal had to be held for a minimum of five days. What happened after that largely depended on the animal control officer. Some of them, the ones who I felt didn't actually *like* animals, euthanized the animal pretty quickly, citing space and financial restrictions. It was even worse for wild animals, especially one that was sick or injured. They had no voice, so what happened to them was often not pleasant. Katrina was a horse of a different color. She worked pretty much around the clock, outside of her regular duties, to take in animals that there wasn't space for in the facility so they got a fair shot. If the veterinary budget was over, she paid out of her own pocket.

And this business about Mick Ellory caring enough about animals that he'd work on his own time? I'd believe that when I saw it.

"So they're basically not going to go out of their way to help any animals until this gets sorted out?" I felt my blood pressure rise and looked at Grandpa. "You have to do something."

Grandpa sighed. "Madalyn. You act like I'm still in charge."

"Grandpa, come on! You can do something about this. I know you can." I gave him my best pleading look. Katrina watched him hopefully too.

His gaze went from me to her then back to me. "We need to make sure you're back at your post very soon," he said to Katrina. "So we have to clear your name. And speaking of that. We wanted to talk to you about some information that came to our attention."

Katrina froze for the slightest of seconds. "Information?" she asked casually, but I saw her hand shake as she lifted her mug. "For what, my lawyer?"

Grandpa nodded. He still held her hand. "We wanted to make sure Jack had everything he needed and in enough time. I'm sure the prosecution is going to come across this information while preparing for the trial, if they haven't already. But it's about what happened while you were at college."

Katrina's entire body deflated, right in front of us. She set her mug on the coffee table next to her, looking like a punctured balloon. Even her cheeks seemed to have sunk into her face.

"I figured," she said in a voice that sounded like shards of broken glass. "Something like that will always come back to haunt you, right?"

Neither of us said anything, just waited for her to continue.

"I was young and fired up, and animals were always my thing," she said. "I felt like I was actually out in the world, in a place where I could help make a difference instead of stuck out here on the island. I got involved in some animal rights groups in college. One of them wasn't just college kids creating petitions. It was a group that included college kids, but was run by other people. Adults with agendas."

"PETA?" I asked.

"No, but similar," she said.

"But you hate PETA," I said. "Because they do bad things to animals just to prove a point."

She nodded vigorously. "I do. But I didn't know that then. This group took a lot of pages out of PETA's book, but they hid it nicely. And they sucked me in." She stroked Fred. "I was overly enthusiastic and raring to save the world. You know how it is. They smelled me coming a mile away. The cute leader was so charismatic. He laid it on thick. Told me how much they needed me. Needed people like me in their group, fresh blood, yada yada. And I fell for it. I fell for him too, as cliché as that is. Brandon," she said, tasting the name on her tongue and making a face. "He was a lot older than me, and I was the perfect target."

"When did you realize they were . . . not what they made themselves out to be?" I asked.

Katrina kept petting Fred, her eyes focused somewhere on the carpet in front of her. "There was a lab in the science building. They tested on mice. Which a lot of people protested anyway, but it never did any good. So they staged a break-in and took all the mice out. This wasn't terrible because they didn't do anything bad—aside from the break-in. They saved all the mice," she added. "Brought them to a rescue. But I was worried about getting in trouble. I didn't, though."

We both glanced at Grandpa. His face remained impassive, but he inclined his head, encouraging her to continue.

"The next time they got us together for an *important mission,* it involved a person. There was some guy who was pushing to test on beagles. Can you imagine?" Even all these years later, I could see how much it bothered her. It bothered me too, and I could see how a young girl could've been swept up in the injustice of it and the desire to make a difference. "They wanted to get him to back off, to stop petitioning the school to do it. I told them I was in. They wouldn't tell us the plan ahead of time. We met late at night—of course—and went to this guy's house. Where they proceeded to give us all rocks and instruct us to break as many of the guy's windows as possible."

"And did you?" Grandpa asked.

Katrina kept her gaze steady on her mug. "I took a couple of rocks and went around back. As soon as I was out of sight I took off. I didn't want to be part of that. It seemed . . . serious."

"Vandalizing someone's house *is* serious," Grandpa said. "That was a good choice. So what happened next time you saw them?"

"Brandon came to my door the next day. He was angry. Accused me of not being dedicated to the animals.

To him. Manipulated me hard. When I was properly begging for forgiveness and a way to make it up to him, he
told me about the next plan."

"Which involved the fire."

Katrina nodded. "Of course he left that part out, but
yes."

"So tell us what happened," Grandpa said. "Was it
against the same person?"

"Yes. He got permission to bring in the dogs. Which of
course made me feel even worse, like if I had stepped up
that night . . . maybe he would've backed off. He told me
the plan was to destroy their house. I told him that was
crazy, that there had to be a better way. He insisted that it
was the only way to make a statement."

"Did he tell you how?" Grandpa asked.

I didn't realize I was holding my breath, waiting for
what came next.

"He wouldn't, until we were on the way there. There
were five of us. We stopped at the gas station to fill up a
bunch of gas cans. That's when I realized. I went to get
out of the car and take off, but one of the other guys . . .
pulled a knife on me." She still wouldn't look at us, so
completely lost in her story. Her face was white and she
wasn't even speaking to us. It was like she'd been waiting
to tell this story for so long and finally had her chance.

"We got to the house. I was crying. Asking them not to
do it. They all took turns making fun of me, then threatening me. They made me touch all the gas cans."

For fingerprints, I realized. If they were going down,
she was going with them. I felt tears prick my eyes. I
couldn't even imagine being put in that situation.

"And then . . . Brandon was trying to make me light
the match. I wouldn't do it. His friend actually cut me."
She lifted her sleeve and rubbed at a scar on her arm. I'd

noticed it before—it stretched the length of her forearm—but I'd always assumed it had to do with an animal. And I'd never asked.

"Then I gave in and tried, but I couldn't. My hands were shaking and I'd never been good at matches." She laughed a little. "It's why I never got into smoking. But finally they figured we were going to be spotted, so they stopped trying to make me do it. Brandon's little mini-me actually lit the match and tossed the rags. Then they took off and left me there. I took off into the woods and hid for hours until I felt safe enough to walk home. I didn't even hear . . . the rest of it until the next day."

I couldn't take anymore. I went over and wrapped my arms around her, not even caring that I was displacing the cats. "I'm so sorry," I said, hugging her tight. "I wish you had told me."

She pulled away and looked from me to Grandpa, her eyes fierce. "I never wanted to tell you this. Either of you. I knew you would've been so disappointed in me. Like you are now."

"No." Grandpa shook his head. "You needed help. You didn't do anything wrong, Katrina."

She squeezed his hand gratefully, grabbing mine with her other hand. "You guys . . . you're like my family. You have to believe me. I didn't set that fire. Just like I didn't kill Virgil Proust. And I need help figuring out who did."

Chapter 27

Grandpa and I, in unspoken agreement, waited a few hours, then left the house to debrief on Katrina's story. She'd told us a lot today, and I felt sorry for her. And definitely sorry for the girl she'd been back then, charged up to do good and bring justice to animals and ending up a scapegoat for a bunch of people with a larger agenda.

"So what do you think?" I asked Grandpa finally, when we were in his truck and had turned the corner heading to town.

He glanced at me. "I think that she was a young kid who got put in a bad position, and that she's regretted it every day since. I feel sorry for what she went through."

I blew out a breath of relief. "Me too."

"I wish she would've pressed charges on those boys," he said.

I shrugged. "She was probably scared."

"I'm sure she was. It doesn't mean they should've gotten away with it. And the fact that she knows who did it . . ." He let the sentence trail off.

I felt my body go cold. "Could she still get in trouble?"

"There was no murder involved, only personal injury.

Statute of limitations on arson in Massachusetts is six years. Same for kidnapping."

"Kidnapping?"

He pulled into a parking space in front of Bean, my favorite coffee place. "Those boys kidnapped her when they made her stay in the car by knifepoint."

I sat back, the full realization of what she'd gone through dawning on me.

"The family could go to civil court, but none of them would do jail time at this point. It was, what . . ." he did some quick calculations. "Nineteen, twenty years ago?"

I nodded. "Roughly."

He shook his head, lips pressed together, no doubt thinking about how the injured person probably felt like it was yesterday. I sure was.

"Katrina didn't kill Virgil," I said.

"I know. Did you find out what was she doing there that night?"

"She says she had to check on a cat."

"Jack told me she specifically said she was at the Proust house."

"She told me he must have misunderstood."

We got out of the car and went into the café. I ordered for us while Grandpa got a table—a vanilla latte for me and a black coffee for Grandpa. I got us a raspberry muffin to share and headed over to sit.

The truth was, I didn't buy Katrina's reason myself. And it didn't line up with the other things I was hearing. Being in the neighborhood was one thing. Being at Virgil Proust's house was another. The only reason I could think of for her to go there specifically would be to confront them with something. Which would look really, really bad.

But I didn't say any of that. "I'm sure she had a good reason," I said when I slid into my seat. "To be there.

Especially if she had been told by her boss not to go. What's up with him, by the way? Why did he suspend her?"

"It's political, Maddie. You know that."

"Well, it's wrong." I took a bite of my muffin. Good, but not nearly as good as Ethan's.

"He felt that he didn't have a choice." He didn't opine on his feelings about that. Grandpa sighed. "Look. I love Katrina like she was one of you girls. I would do anything for any of you. And that means she's innocent in my mind unless or until the evidence overwhelmingly points otherwise. I think there's something she's not telling us, but I don't think it's that she murdered that man. I also think the case they have against her is flimsy at best. They're a good police department, but inexperienced with murders. And they want a fast solve, so of course they're going to take the easy path. And don't you repeat that to Craig," he added.

"Of course not." But it didn't make me feel great to hear it. "We need to strategize. There are a lot of crazy characters who live in that neighborhood. Did you find out anything juicy about any of them yet? Or maybe the matching Christmas gnome in someone's trash that could give us a clue?" I was being facetious of course, but deep down I hoped it just might be that easy.

Instead, Grandpa reached into his jacket pocket and pulled out a small black notebook. I recognized it immediately. It was the same kind of notebook he'd used throughout his police career. He'd always had one on him, and when I was a kid and used to go visit him at the police station there was usually a stack of them on his desk. He never used anything but those notebooks for work. I think he had kind of a superstition that if he used anything else he wouldn't successfully close the case.

Grandpa flipped open the notebook to the first clean

page, and clicked his pen. He didn't answer my question, but I kind of expected that. He was clearly still in the information-gathering stage. "Tell me your observations about this neighborhood and its people."

I launched into a description of the neighbors I knew, which houses they lived in and how they were placed on the cul-de-sac, and what I knew about each, including Virgil. Then I told him about Lilah's insights from the other day when I'd stopped by my parents' house. The Audubon board, Harvey, Trey Barnes. Edie and June having some kind of falling out. He said nothing while I talked, just took extensive notes. When I finished giving him the brain dump, I paused for breath.

He finished scribbling then looked up at me. "Given the people you know—who, by the way, aren't the only potential suspects—who are you most concerned about?"

"June," I said immediately. "Honestly, she seems off, Grandpa. I'm not just saying that because she's mean about the cats. She really seems unstable."

"I can see why, given what you told me about her smashing his phone. And I saw her approach you at the courthouse. She looked disturbed." He flipped back a couple of pages and underlined something. "Who else?"

I thought about that. I wanted to give him my best answer. I kind of felt like a cop in training right now. "I wouldn't have said it before, but . . . Lilah mentioned the whole argument with Harvey. I would've chalked it up to nothing much, but I heard Harvey's wife saying something about how people were going to find out about them being at odds. It seemed weird to me. And like Harvey was trying to keep up this really positive facade about him and Virgil."

"Did the cops hear this?"

I shook my head. "They didn't even want to talk to Harvey after they talked to me. I mean, I guess they talked to him when they arrived, but they were definitely more worried about me."

"Well, you found him. That doesn't surprise me." Grandpa consulted his notes again. Every now and then he would pause and circle something, or make some kind of symbol. I watched with interest. I loved watching other people's work processes. I found it fascinating.

"What else?" he asked again, looking up at me.

I had to tell him the rest of it. "There's one more thing . . . involving Katrina. It sounds like it was right around the time she got banned from the neighborhood." I told him what Lilah said about her alleged fight with Virgil. "She never mentioned it to me, though."

He wrote that down too.

"So what do you think?" I asked. "Is there any way you can find out anything about June?"

He didn't answer right away. Then he said, "The fight with Hackett was about the board meetings?"

I nodded. "That's what Lilah said."

"That Virgil wasn't showing up for."

"I guess not."

"First thing we should do. Check if there's a pattern. Was it every meeting? Some meetings? How often? Maybe we can track his activity to something else. Something he didn't want anyone knowing about."

"Okay," I said. "We need the minutes. Are those public?"

"Hmm." Grandpa thought about that, tapping his pen on the table.

Suddenly I sat straight up. "Never mind! It doesn't matter if they're public. Dr. Kelly is the Audubon secretary."

"The vet?"

I nodded. "He mentioned it in passing when I was there

the other day. I'm sure he'd be happy to help. He loves Katrina."

"Then," Grandpa said, "we should talk to Dr. Kelly."

I nodded. "Tomorrow," I said. "We don't have a lot of time to waste."

"Sounds good to me. By the way, you may want to check with your parents. They scored an invite to the funeral."

"Virgil's funeral?" I asked, surprised.

"Yes. Apparently it's a private affair, but the CEO of the hospital is always welcome."

I smiled. "Well, it wouldn't be right if their daughter didn't go pay her respects too, then. Especially given my . . . proximity to the situation."

"Exactly what I was thinking," Grandpa said.

Chapter 28

We finished our coffee in record time and left Bean. I wanted to get to Dr. Kelly as quickly as possible, and I wanted Grandpa as my secret weapon. Although I planned on charming the good doctor for his minutes, I figured it wouldn't hurt to have Grandpa's silent backing in this endeavor. Although I knew Dr. Kelly adored Katrina and had a feeling he wouldn't resist the opportunity to help her out of this mess if he could.

Grandpa insisted on driving, so we hopped into his truck and drove to Duck Cove. I hoped Dr. Kelly was home. I didn't want to call first. Catching people off guard for stuff like this generally worked better, in my amateur opinion. I was relieved to see his old Dodge minivan parked in the driveway when we pulled up.

I tried the side door leading to the vet office first. I wasn't sure if he worked today. I wasn't even sure if he had regular hours anymore or just took people when they called for appointments. Either way he had to be back pretty close to full time. For a small island, there were a lot of pet owners. But the door was unlocked, and when I stepped inside Dr. Kelly's wife, Janet, glanced up from the little desk. She brightened when she saw me.

"Hi, Maddie! How are you, sweetheart?" She came around to give me a giant hug, and when she saw Grandpa she gave him one too. "And Leo. It must be my lucky day to see two of my favorites." She grasped each of our hands and squeezed. "How are *you*, Leo?"

"I'm good, Janet," Grandpa said, looking a little embarrassed by all the attention.

"Well, I should say so. You have yourself a whole new career, not to mention your beautiful first-born granddaughter back in the fold. It must be so comforting."

"It's great to be back," I said, saving Grandpa from having to be all effusively sentimental. Especially since he was in police mode. "We're having a lot of fun."

"Wonderful! Now what can I do for you? Did you bring a cat?" She looked around to see if we had a carrier with us.

"No, not today," I said. "Actually we were wondering if we could talk to Dr. Kelly, if he has a moment?"

"Oh, of course," she said. "He's just finishing with someone now but they're almost done. Have a seat." She waved at the little seating area with the same little orange chairs that I remembered from when I was a kid.

Janet, not one for silence, kept up the small talk while we waited, asking about Val and Sam, and of course my parents. I did most of the talking. Grandpa was funny when he was in work mode—he had a one-track mind.

True to her word, five minutes later her husband came out, followed by a man with a beagle. It made me think of Katrina's story, and I felt awful again. "He should be feeling better in no time," the doctor was saying. "Call me with an update in a few days."

While Janet took care of the man's bill, Dr. Kelly turned to us. "Well, hello again Maddie. And Leo. Good to see you, sir, as always."

"You too, Doc." Grandpa stood and shook his hand. "Can we have a moment of your time?"

"Of course. Come on in." He led us to his little office, which was no bigger than my mom's walk-in closet. "What's going on?"

"Dr. Kelly," I began. "you told me you're on the Audubon board with Virgil Proust. And that you're secretary."

Dr. Kelly nodded a bit warily. "Yes."

"I understand that the meeting minutes are public record and I wondered how I might be able to get a look at a few of the more recent ones?" I blinked innocently at him. "I'm not quite sure where to look online. When I did a search, I couldn't find them."

Dr. Kelly's face relaxed. "Sure. I can do that. And I'm afraid that's my fault that you can't find them online. I haven't posted them to our site. I do need to get myself back on track." He looked properly chastised for putting off this job. "How far back would you like to go?"

I wondered why he had looked so freaked out when I first mentioned the board, but I guess when someone asks you about a murdered guy, most people would probably get a little freaked.

"The past year?" I asked, glancing at Grandpa. He nodded.

Dr. Kelly flipped open his laptop and clicked around a bit. A minute later his little printer stirred to life and pages began slipping out.

"Thanks, Doc. We really appreciate this," Grandpa said.

"Not a problem."

"Okay if we take them?" I asked.

He nodded. "Absolutely."

Well. That was easy. I sat back, satisfied, and waited for the pages to finish printing. Once they were done,

Dr. Kelly gathered them, clipped them together with a purple paper clip, and handed them to me.

"Let me know if you need anything else," he said, glancing at Grandpa. "And good luck with whatever it is you're looking for."

When we got in Grandpa's truck, we both turned and looked at each other. "That was easy," I said.

Grandpa shrugged. "The minutes are public record. And it's the Audubon Society, not the U.S. Department of Defense."

We continued to look at each other.

I said, "He knows something. And he was awfully glad that I didn't ask him about anything that would specifically lead to it."

Grandpa nodded approvingly. "See, I told you. You should've been a cop. Although your parents wouldn't have forgiven me if you had." He lifted his chin when I looked at him questioningly. "They told me early on. I think they could see it themselves. Short-sighted of them. You are a natural. Anyway. I think you're absolutely right. So whaddaya say we get an early dinner, go over these minutes, and see what we can decipher on our own? I'm starving."

I brightened. Food sounded like a fabulous idea. The muffin just hadn't done the trick. And a drink sounded even better. "Me too. That sounds great. Where do you want to go?"

"I know just the place," Grandpa said.

Chapter 29

"Has this always been here?" I asked as we walked into the Blue Heaven Café. I didn't remember ever seeing it before. Granted, I'd been away from home for a decade, but I felt like I would've totally remembered a place as adorable as this. It was on the water—let's face it, most places were out here on the island—but it didn't have all the trappings of a regular, waterfront place. Meaning, it wasn't full of lobsters or boat paraphernalia. Rather, it had an eclectic, Mediterranean/Spanish vibe that reminded me of a place Ethan and I used to hang out in San Francisco, making me miss my "other" home for a minute.

Grandpa nodded. "It was always a place for the older folks," he said with a wink.

I took in the different-colored walls, the jazz posters hung around the dining room, and the live band setting up in the adjacent bar space, and shot him a disbelieving look. "Really?"

We followed the hostess to a table in the back near the fireplace. A waiter immediately arrived with two waters and a scotch for Grandpa. I eyed it. "Guess you've been coming here for a while," I said with a chuckle.

"Chief Leo is our favorite," the waiter said proudly. "And for you, miss?"

I ordered a martini and we got a Mediterranean sampler to start, with all kinds of goodies from hummus to olives to grape leaves. I pulled out the pages of minutes and divided them up, taking the first half of the year and giving Grandpa the most recent ones, and dove in.

The first thing I noticed was that Virgil had attended only one meeting out of the six that I had. The very first one of the year, where new members were sworn in. I didn't recognize any of those names, so I skimmed that part. The meeting was short, without a lot of business aside from new members. I paused to pop an olive in my mouth and glance at Grandpa, who was intently reading. The room was filling up now. In the bar area, the band started playing reggae music. I hid a smile.

He saw me grinning and frowned. "What?"

"Nothing. Just didn't know you were a reggae guy."

He seemed indifferent to my observation. "The music is different all the time," he said. "Besides, reggae is great music. Very uplifting. Your friend Cass comes here often," he added.

"Cass does? Really?" I guessed it didn't surprise me, even if reggae was on the menu. Cass loved anything feel-good. Something else I didn't know about a good friend. It seemed I needed to start paying more attention to the people in my life.

The waiter reappeared to take our orders. We decided to split the seafood paella. "This place is awesome," I said happily, scooping some hummus onto a grape leaf and popping it into my mouth. "Maybe we should bring Katrina some takeout to cheer her up?"

Grandpa pointed to the papers. "Yes. Or we could find the real killer. That would cheer her up more."

He was right. I was getting distracted. I went back to

the next month—no Virgil—and skimmed the rest of the topics. A discussion about whether to charge for admission to the sanctuary, which I thought was a little much and was glad to see they voted it down. The most recent "State of the Birds" research report took up the rest of that meeting.

I flipped the pages and started on the next one. No Virgil, again. We were in March now. I glanced at Grandpa. "So far he's been to one meeting. The first one."

Grandpa nodded. "He hasn't been to any that I've reviewed yet. But I've only done two."

"These meetings are boring," I said.

He half smiled. "I have a feeling they're about to pick up." He tapped the paper in front of him. "Mr. Harvey Hackett just introduced the problem with the Sea Spray feral colony."

My eyes widened. "You're kidding." I grabbed the paper and skimmed, my eyes sliding back up to Grandpa's. "Harvey? Why would he do that? He and his wife are cool with the cats. I thought he was on the board to help them."

"I didn't get to see it all, since someone snatched the paper away," Grandpa said pointedly.

Sheepishly I handed it back. "What month is that?"

"September."

"What did he say about it?"

"I'll tell you once I finish reading," Grandpa said.

I sighed. "Fine. But hurry."

He gave me one of his looks and went back to the papers.

Now I was impatient to get to October, but Grandpa didn't do well with being rushed. I went back to April and May. No Virgil at either, and no topic that had anything to do with Sea Spray or its people.

Finally Grandpa finished with September and picked

up October. I tried to concentrate on my stuff but wasn't succeeding. I resorted to eating more of the appetizer platter to keep occupied.

"Well," he said finally, just as the waiter arrived with the paella. "Harvey brought up the cats and said it was becoming a problem in the neighborhood. That he's been noticing a lot more bird carcasses than usual, and the neighbors were getting very upset about it."

My spoon stilled halfway to my plate, paella sauce dripping onto the tablecloth. "Why would Harvey say that if he and his wife are advocates for the cats?"

"I have no idea," Grandpa said. "But Virgil showed up to the next meeting in October."

"He did?"

Grandpa nodded. "And when the Sea Spray colony came up, he admonished the group for diverting their attention from the bigger picture and advised them to stay out of it."

My mind was in overdrive trying to process this. I'd already known that Virgil—for some odd reason—had tried to divert the attention from the cats. But Harvey was the one who'd brought the issue up in the first place? That seemed . . . out of character. Especially since Monica was such a cat person. "So Harvey stirred this pot?"

"Seems so. And Virgil Proust told them to stand down, basically."

"Even though in public, Harvey is a friend of the cats and Virgil and his wife are calling the cops on a volunteer?"

Grandpa lifted his hands, palms up, in a *Don't ask me to explain it, I'm just telling you what I read* gesture.

"Huh." I sat back in my seat, my paella forgotten. Why would Harvey do that when he claimed to want to help the cats? And why would he lie about it?

Grandpa, however, dug in. "Still got November and

December to go," he said with a mouthful. "Who knows what kind of turn this'll take?"

I wasn't sure I wanted to know, at this point. I excused myself to go to the ladies room. Not quite sure where it was, I headed into the bar area where the band was in full swing and the crowd was getting happy. I had to walk by a small group of people dancing up a storm in the middle of the room and I paused for a second to watch. I love music and I love to sing, but dancing had never been my forte. I'd rather watch people dance—they always looked like they were having so much fun.

Especially one woman in particular. She wore an outfit that would make a belly dancer envious, and she was really getting into it. She had moves too. I watched as her partner, a handsome dark-haired man, spun her around until she landed right smack in front of me.

And my jaw dropped.

It was Whitney Piasecki. Of Sea Spray Lane. Whitney with the "bad" leg who used a cane to walk everywhere. Unless, of course, I was crazy. Or she had a twin. But if she didn't, her cane was nowhere in sight and she looked like she would have no need for it anyway.

The way her eyes widened when she saw me, I knew I wasn't wrong.

"Maddie!" she exclaimed, her eyes darting around in that panicked way people had when they were cornered. "What are you doing here?"

"Having dinner with my grandpa," I shouted over the loud music. "What about you?"

The guy she'd been dancing with was still trying to dance, but eventually realized she'd stopped and stepped over to us as the song ended.

"Hello," he said, giving me a big smile. "I'm—"

"This is Dominic," Whitney broke in. "My physical therapist."

I saw his eyes flick to her, but to his credit, he said nothing and shook my hand.

"Maddie," I said. I resisted the urge to comment on how much physical therapy seemed to have changed since Ethan broke his leg a couple of years ago and I took him to therapy until he could drive again. At a facility. With machines and other therapists and patients. We'd never once been to a dance club in that capacity.

Whitney took my arm and pulled me away from the dance floor, exaggerating her walk again to a limp, as if I hadn't just seen her shaking her tail feathers with some handsome guy. "So crazy to bump into you! But lovely to see you. How are you?"

"I'm fine," I said. "It is crazy, isn't it? I didn't mean to interrupt your . . . session." I waved at the dance floor.

"You're not interrupting at all! Dominic is such a dear, he's agreed to use alternative therapies to get my leg back into shape again. Dancing is just such a wonderful way to feel better! So much different than walking or those strength exercises they're always making me do. I'm so tired of this injury," she said, reaching down to rub the offending limb for effect. "And it's so lovely the hospital lets him use the training he feels is right instead of forcing him into some *protocol*." She laughed nervously, waiting for my response.

Honestly, I didn't know what to say. I wasn't about to call her out in the middle of a dance party. Whitney's leg injury—or seeming lack thereof—was really none of my business. "That's great," I said. "I hope it continues to improve. Listen, I was actually on my way to the bathroom so I'll see you later, okay?"

"Okay, honey. Have a good time with Grandpa." She gave me a hug. "I'll have more cat food waiting when you come tomorrow. How's Katrina? Poor thing!"

I assured her Katrina was much better since getting

out of jail, then extracted myself and went to the ladies'
room. As I washed my hands, though, I wondered why
Whitney would pretend to have a bad leg. I remembered
seeing her at June Proust's door the day I was out with my
mom, and how angry she'd been at them before storming
off with her cane.

Whitney hated the Prousts. And she loved the cats. At
least, all her actions pointed toward that conclusion. So
what if she was faking a leg injury so people wouldn't give
her a second look? Could she have killed Virgil in a fit of
rage and then pretended to be the weak, injured neighbor
who couldn't even put up her own Christmas lights?

I hated the way I was thinking, but I couldn't help it.
Between her and Harvey, I felt like nothing was what it
seemed. Kind of like what Cass has said the other day.
Shaken, I finished up and headed back out to Grandpa,
avoiding eye contact with anyone in the bar. When I sat
down, he glanced up from his reading.

"What happened?"

I smiled, trying to keep everything I was thinking off
my face in case Whitney was watching. "Why do you think
something happened?"

"Because I know you," Grandpa responded patiently.
"So what is it?"

I sighed. It was never any use trying to hide anything
from Grandpa. "One of the Sea Spray neighbors is here.
The one with the leg injury. She's dancing." I filled him
in on what I'd seen, and my potentially crazy thought
process.

He listened, then made a note. "Okay, now we're getting somewhere. In the meantime," he tapped the paper in
front of him, "something else interesting in here from the
December meeting."

The last meeting before the murder. I leaned forward
eagerly. "What?"

"The poison petition," he said. "Harvey suggested it."

I stared at him, stunned. "You're sure? It's not a typo?"

"Unless someone is doctoring the minutes, it says it in plain English."

I sank back in my chair. This whole exercise just reinforced that idea that you never really know anyone. "You think Monica knows?"

"I don't know, doll," Grandpa said. "But at least we have some options for Katrina."

Chapter 30

Wednesday morning. The day of Virgil Proust's funeral. I woke up to Katrina shaking me. When I opened my eyes, she loomed over me, looking very serious. Startled, I jumped up. "What's wrong?"

"Nothing. Well, everything." She covered her face with her hands. "I just got a call from Mick. He's got a dog that needs help and he's tied up with something at the station. He can't leave. Can you call Craig for me and see if he can help?"

I rubbed my eyes, trying to focus, pressing my hand against my chest. "You scared the crap out of me. What can Craig do?"

"He can get me the address and I can go get the dog?"

I gave her a look. "Because you never want your job back?"

She sighed. "Fine. Can he at least go get the dog? Maybe you can go with him? I'll take care of the café. He'll just need to get the keys from Mick."

I couldn't say no to a dog in trouble. I reached over, grabbed my cell phone off the nightstand, and texted Craig.

Help.

He responded back nearly immediately.

What happened? Are you okay?

Come over and I'll explain, I replied.

So you're okay?

I'm fine but I need your help.

This better be good.

I tossed the phone on the bed. "He's coming. Now can I please go to the bathroom?"

I barely had time to wash my face, brush my teeth, and throw some clothes on before Craig was at the door. When he saw Katrina and me standing there, he frowned.

"What's the emergency?"

"Come on in and we'll tell you." I tugged his sleeve until he came inside, then handed him some coffee. He wasn't wearing his uniform. "Are you off today?"

He nodded. "I did a double yesterday."

"And we woke you. Sorry," I said, wincing.

"It's fine." He regarded Katrina. "How are you doing?"

"Crappy," she answered. "But you can help me feel a little better."

We gave him a quick rundown. I could tell he wasn't thrilled about this, but he agreed to help.

"Thank you so much," Katrina said, giving him a hug. "Maddie will go with you and get the dog settled."

I nodded. "You don't have to stay. I just need to be able to get into the center."

"Okay, let's go." He finished his coffee and handed me the mug. "And then you can buy me breakfast."

He was true to his word. We picked up the keys from Sergeant Ellory—well, Craig did, I waited in the car— then picked up the dog, a poor stray black lab who was extremely friendly. After we got the dog set up in an empty kennel and gave him food and water, I left a note for the volunteers to scan him for a microchip and then we headed to the diner on Bicycle Street, where I bought Craig the breakfast he'd very much earned.

I was happy to do it and thankful he'd helped us with the dog. While we waited for our food, I told him so.

He waved me off. "No problem. How is Katrina?"

"You heard her. She's crappy." I sipped my orange juice. "But she told us the story about that thing in college."

"She did?"

I nodded and gave him the abridged version, pausing only when the waitress came by with our food.

He listened to the whole thing without a word. When I was done, he ate a few more bites then said, "It sounds like an awful experience. I hope that it doesn't come up in front of a jury."

"Me too. God, Craig. The cops have to find out who really did this. Isn't there someone there who you can talk to?" I stabbed my omelet in frustration.

Craig polished off his pumpkin pancake. "What is it you think I can do, Maddie? I can't tell them how to run their investigation." He took a sip of his coffee.

"No, but you can tell them about the other suspicious people who could've done this."

"I think they know enough to check out the spouse. It's usually the first place cops look."

I rolled my eyes. "I watch *Law and Order*. I know that. But how *seriously* would they look at her? She's a lifer there, she's got money, I'm sure she's got something on someone on the force. They probably did the bare minimum questioning and that's it. In fact, I know that's it. Lilah Gilmore told them about seeing Virgil having an argument with someone and they still arrested Katrina."

Craig didn't look impressed.

"Craig." I leaned forward, pushing my plate aside. "His wife is nuts. She smashed his phone into pieces during a public meeting."

Craig took the last bite of pancake and tossed his napkin over his empty plate. "But so what? Husbands and wives fight all the time. It doesn't mean they kill each other in most cases."

"No, but in some cases they do."

He sighed. "Okay. You're right. In some cases they do."

"June is strong. She grabbed me the other day and man, she could hold on." I rubbed my wrist just thinking about it.

His eyes narrowed at that. "Why was she grabbing you?"

"When she was accusing me and my friends of killing Virgil. The night it happened. The cops saw the whole thing."

"You're kidding. What did they do?"

"Finally they took her out of sight—once Ethan jumped in." I smiled thinking about it, but he didn't look amused.

"That's not cool," he said. "They should've done something."

"Grieving widow and all that." I made a face. "But seriously." I ticked names off on my fingers. "There's June. There's Trey Barnes, the young guy who's married to the old lady. Lilah said Virgil threatened to throw his friends out of the neighborhood or something. There's Harvey Hackett, who threatened to tell June about Virgil not showing up at these meetings. Which apparently made Virgil really mad. And there's something weird going on there—he and his wife have been really cool about the cats to our faces, but I found out he's the one

who started the whole poison petition thing. I didn't tell
Katrina," I added hastily. "We don't need her knowing
who it was. Virgil, of all people, shot it down. And then
there's Whitney, who is really good to us and the cats, but
she's faking this leg injury. And she hates the Prousts." I
filled him in on that story too.

"Jeez." He rubbed his temples. "All this on that fancy-
pants street, huh?"

"Yep. You see what I mean? Someone needs to investigate them and all their secrets."

"I get the feeling someone already is," Craig said dryly.

I crossed my arms over my chest. "Grandpa and I are,
yes. But we could use more help. Like someone who actually has an in with the police."

"And you think I do?"

"You're a cop!"

"On another force. With a boss who doesn't want to
get involved."

We had a stare-off for a few seconds, then he sighed.
"Come on. I have to bring you home. I have some stuff
to do."

"Oooh, like what? Big date with Jade today?" I teased
as we walked out the door.

But he looked really uncomfortable. "No. We aren't
seeing each other much anymore." He strode ahead of me
so I couldn't see his face.

I rushed to catch up. "Oh no! Why not?" I was genuinely surprised to hear that. They'd looked so tight at
Christmas. And although it was a little weird that they
were dating, I really did want it to work out for them.

Craig shrugged. "Just wasn't working out. Look, I
have to go."

"Craig." I reached for his arm. "I'm sorry."

He returned my gaze. "Thanks."

At that exact moment, Lucas walked around the corner.

He had a dog with him. That was a special service he offered—pick up and drop off for his grooming clients. This one was adorable. A squat little black-and-white pit bull that looked like he or she was smiling. I did love dogs—I just hadn't thought about having one right now because, well, I had a house full of cats.

My instinct was to drop down and say hello to the dog, who had seen us and was already wagging his or her tail. But I didn't want to look like I was encouraging conversation. Especially in front of Craig, who watched with narrowed eyes.

Then Lucas glanced up and realized we were there, and his entire face fell. For a split second. Then he replaced it with a carefully blank expression. I realized what it must look like, especially since I had been holding on to Craig's arm when he came around the corner, and opened my mouth to explain.

Then realized I didn't need to explain. After all, this was the guy who had vanished on me for a month without a word.

"Hey," Lucas said, lifting his hand in a slight wave before awkwardly shoving it back in his pocket.

"Hey," I returned, because Craig said nothing and I didn't want to be completely rude.

Lucas tugged on the dog's leash, but he (she?) had planted him or herself on the sidewalk, waiting for some love.

I gave in and reached down to pet the dog. The animal sniffed me, tentatively at first, then began kissing my fingers in earnest. "Cutie pie. What's his"—I glanced up for confirmation from Lucas—"name?"

"Oliver."

"Hi, Oliver," I said, scratching his ears. "You're a doll."

I could feel Lucas watching me. I avoided his eyes as I stood up and turned to walk away.

"Maddie," he said, but I cut him off.

"I have to go." I followed Craig down the sidewalk. When I got a few feet I turned back. "Cute dog though."

He didn't reply. I could feel his eyes on me as we hurried down the street to Craig's car.

Chapter 31

Wednesday, December 30: eight days after the murder
Virgil's funeral
4:00 p.m.

I pushed my parents' doorbell and practiced my most innocent look. My dad opened the door a few minutes later, suit jacket in hand. When he saw me, he raised his eyebrows. "What are you doing here, hon?"

"Hi, Dad." I reached up and gave him a kiss, then stepped past him into the hallway. "I'm coming to the funeral."

"Madalyn. You know it's not open to the public."

"I'm not the public," I said. "I'm the girl who found his body. I kind of think I've earned it, no? Besides, who's going to turn Brian James's daughter away?"

He gave me that look that said he desperately wanted to argue with me but knew he wasn't going to win.

"Brian, who was at the door?" My mother's voice floated down from upstairs.

"It's Maddie," he called up.

"Maddie?" I heard her heels on the floor upstairs, then she appeared on the stairs, leaning over so she could see me. She'd been in the middle of putting her long curls in an up-do. One side still hung down, brushing her shoulder. "What are you doing here?"

I was getting kind of sick of that greeting. "I'm coming to the funeral."

"Oh, Maddie." My mother sighed. "Are you sure that's the best idea? How did you know about it anyway?"

"You told me," I lied. "Plus you're going, and you were right there with me sticking up for the cats."

"I know, but—"

"And you've known Katrina forever. You totally vouched for her. So I'm not seeing a big difference here between you and me." I crossed my arms and thrust my chin up defiantly. "I'm coming."

"I'll get the car," my dad said, and slipped outside.

"He's always hated conflict," my mother mused. "Crazy, given his job." She refocused on me. "Okay, well. You're here, so you might as well come. Just behave, okay?"

"Behave? What do you think I'm going to do?" I asked. "Accuse someone of murder? Oh, wait. That's their MO."

She was already on her way back upstairs to finish pinning her hair up. I think she ignored me on purpose.

When we arrived at the church, there were only a handful of cars there. "Low turnout?" I said.

"It is a private event," my mother said.

"Right, but I thought that just meant they wouldn't let any gawkers in. I figured that meant that all the rich Turtle Point people could go."

I saw my dad and mom exchange a glance, but neither of them replied. My dad parked and went around to open my mother's door. I thought it was so cute he still did that. We all went inside together and took a seat on the left side, a few pews back and across from the Prousts—the perfect angle for me to watch them.

I surveyed the room. Most people were gathered up front. I could see June holding court, wearing a black dress that had as much style as a Hefty trash bag. I recognized a couple of people from the neighborhood. Lilah was right up front, as expected. I didn't see Edie, though. I spotted Dr. Kelly and his wife.

A young man with a ponytail that reminded a bit of Virgil's sat in the front pew but didn't speak to anyone. I recognized him as the scrawny guy who'd pulled June off of me at the courthouse. I poked my mother. "Who's that?"

"He must be their son," she whispered. "I'd heard they had a child, but he doesn't live around here."

That didn't surprise me at all. Poor kid. I couldn't imagine growing up with June as a mother. The church door opened again. I felt the rush of cold air and turned to look. The man who strode down the aisle looked familiar, but it took me a minute to place him.

When I did, I frowned. It was the guy I'd seen dancing with Whitney Piasecki at Blue Heaven. The guy she'd tried to tell me was her physical therapist. Dominic. I remembered because anytime I met someone with that name I immediately thought of that stupid Christmas song "Dominick the Donkey," and then I always associated that person with that song for the rest of their lives.

But that aside, this made no sense. Whitney hated the Prousts because of their feral-hating ways. So why was her boyfriend—at least I assumed it was her boyfriend and for some reason she didn't want anyone to know—here at Virgil's private funeral?

I leaned over to my mother and poked her. "Hey. Do you know that guy?"

She followed my finger to where the guy had gone up to June and was speaking in a low voice. "No. Never seen him before. And don't point, Maddie. It's rude."

I watched the conversation unfold. Whatever he was saying to June, she looked like she had no interest in it. Or him. She finally said something and he gave up, going to sit next to the guy my parents thought was the Prousts' son. I watched as they shook hands.

I leaned over my mother to get my father's attention and asked him the same question. "I can't really see his face, but he doesn't look familiar," my father said. "I'll look again when he gets up. Why?"

I shrugged. "I've seen him before but I'm curious about why he's here."

I could tell my father wanted to ask me about that, but whoever was playing the music for the funeral started, and a bunch of melancholy notes floated out of the eaves above us. It had been a long time since I'd been in a church. As a little girl, I always wanted to sit in the balcony where the music came from during mass. But since we usually only went for holidays, it was so full by the time we arrived that we never had a shot. I turned to look up there, and my eyes fell on an unexpected mourner in the back. Leopard Man.

He didn't see me watching him. He was engrossed in the music, singing along. Why on earth was he here? Especially given the scenario with Katrina? He didn't seem like the type of company Virgil Proust would keep enough to secure an invite to a private event, although clearly there were a lot of secrets in this little community.

I kept myself busy people watching during the service, which thankfully wasn't terribly long. Near the end, the young man from the front row—who was, in fact, Virgil and June's son, Virgil Junior—got up to do the eulogy. Everyone leaned forward a bit in their seats to hear what he was going to say.

He stood there for a moment, surveying the crowd with a dour look on his face. His eyes were small like June's, and he was tall and lanky like her. But when he spoke, I could hear the elder Virgil in his voice—that deep baritone and quiet confidence.

"Thank you all for coming to remember my father," he said. "I know there were a lot more people who wanted to come say goodbye, whose lives he touched in some way, but at his core my dad was a private person. He was never happier than when he was in his study reading, or painting, or doing his charity work."

Painting? Charity work? I was curious now. Did he mean the Audubon board? If so, he'd apparently kept his lack of enthusiasm to himself.

Young Virgil went on for a few more moments, talking about memories from his childhood, holidays, and one particular memory where his dad had helped him rescue a squirrel who'd gotten his foot stuck in a crack in a wall behind their house. He didn't mention any of the recent neighborhood unpleasantness, or the fact that someone had murdered his father. Which I suppose would've been inappropriate for a eulogy, but seemed odd just the same to ignore this giant elephant in the room. The whole time, June stared at her son like she'd never seen him before.

When he sat back down, the priest went through the rest of the service. Finally, it was over. As people started to rise, the priest said, "Mrs. Proust wishes to invite everyone back to her home for a small celebration of Virgil's life. Thank you all for coming."

I turned to my parents. "We going?"

"Going where?" Dad asked.

"To the Prousts'."

He looked at my mother, then back at me. I could see what he was thinking: *If we don't go, it's one less way my daughter will be involved in this mess.* "I don't think so, Maddie—"

"Oh, come on. It would be rude not to," I said, looking at my mother for confirmation. "Right?"

My mother chewed on her lip. "It might be a little rude, but I'm not sure if we—"

"Sophie! Brian!" A woman walking past our pew bent over and clasped my father's hand. "So lovely to see you. You're coming to June's, right?" She looked eagerly at my mother.

"Um. Of course," my mother said, pasting a smile on, avoiding my father's eyes on her. "We can't stay long—"

The woman dismissed that with a wave of her hand. "Not to worry. I just think it's important to be there to support our friends." She squeezed my father's hand again, then dropped it and headed to the front of the church.

My dad looked at my mom. She shrugged. "Really, Brian. What was I supposed to say? These people want us there because of you, after all."

I hid a smile. My mother always knew the best way to rationalize things so my dad had to see it her way.

He had nothing to say to that. With a sigh, he ushered us out of the pew. "Come on. We're not staying long. And Maddie, you're staying with me," he instructed.

"Jeez, Dad. What do you think I'm going to do?"

"I have no idea. And that's what worries me."

Victorious, I stepped out of the pew, scanning the back of the church for Leopard Man. I didn't see him. He must've taken off right when it ended.

Chapter 32

Truth be told, I was glad that woman had cornered my mother. I really wanted to go to this thing, as crazy as it sounded. I wanted a chance to talk to the people in Virgil's life when they would, theoretically, have their guard down. And if they saw me at a function like this as a member of the prominent James-Mancini family rather than one of the wackadoodle cat ladies traipsing around the woods during a snowstorm, I'd probably have a better chance at finding something out. Like why Whitney's "physical therapist" was here.

I got in Grandma's car and followed my parents the short distance from the church to the Prousts' home. I looked at the houses as we drove by, observing them in this different light. I wasn't here today to feed cats (although I would be later) so I tried to see if it felt any different as a "normal" visitor. Anyone driving by would probably think nothing except what a fancy neighborhood it was, with big, stately, sort-of pretty homes. A regular person might try to make up stories about the kinds of families who lived in these houses. They wouldn't know that someone's head had been bashed in with a Christmas gnome, and that there seemed to be more secrets along this street than in most teenaged-girls' diaries. I did wonder about this gnome. Had it belonged to the Prousts? It seemed . . . less than classy by their standards. So had the killer brought it, or found it along the way?

I was also dying to talk to Virgil Junior. I wondered if he'd talk to me, or if his mother would forbid it. Or if I should focus my attention on Whitney's boyfriend.

As if my father had read my mind, he materialized at my side when I was getting out of the car. "Listen, Maddie, I know you want to help Katrina. But please don't go in here asking these people a ton of questions and playing detective, okay?"

"Brian, leave her be," my mother said automatically. She'd walked over to us, no doubt to play peacekeeper if needed. "If Maddie talks to anyone I'm sure she'll be discreet."

"Not the point, Sophie," Dad said. "This is someone's funeral and that kind of thing doesn't have a place here."

"Then you should tell the police officer that." My mother pointed.

I followed her finger and sure enough, there was one of Turtle Point's finest, a man I didn't recognize. I wondered why they'd bothered to show up at all. I knew that as far as they were concerned they had their killer. They'd made that clear enough. Had June invited him?

Impulsively, I hugged my dad. "Don't worry. I promise I won't embarrass you."

"That's not what I was saying," he began, but I silenced him with a wink.

"Kidding. Let's go." I led the way to the Prousts' front door, offering June a sympathetic smile when she let us in.

I saw the initial flash of anger in her eyes before she dismissed me, turning her attention to my father. "Brian. How kind of you to come." She sniffed and dabbed at her eyes with a tissue. "We lost a great man."

My mother and I exchanged an eye roll behind her back. Apparently June had forgotten how she'd hurled his phone at a wall in a fit of anger before he died. And the way she was so polite and deferential to my dad made me want to gag.

"I'm so sorry for your loss," my father said. He was the one truly polite person in the family.

"Please, come in." June pointed to the living room, where people were gathering. Someone had put out a food spread. There was even a little bar with a man standing behind it, ready to serve drinks.

Even death was fancy in these parts.

Someone approached my mother and began talking, so I used the opportunity to slip into the room and survey the small crowd. Still no sign of Edie or Trey Barnes, which was odd given that Edie and June were allegedly so close. Even if they'd had a falling out, wouldn't such a tragic death have overridden that? I would think Edie would have wanted to be here for her friend.

I did see Whitney's "physical therapist," though. He stood alone over by a painting, drink in hand, back to the crowd, either lost in thought or lost in the piece of art. It was too perfect. I went up behind him and stared at the picture too. It was one of those modern pieces that didn't really seem to have an actual point of focus—rather it was a swirl of colors and designs that kind of exploded together in an unexplainably soothing way. There were bright reds, oranges, and yellows and the whole thing reminded me of a sun rising on a blazing hot summer day full of the promise of memories made.

"Gorgeous, right?" Whitney's guy commented.

I'd almost forgotten he was standing there, I'd been so mesmerized by the painting.

"It really is," I said.

"He was quite the artist."

I turned toward him. "Who?"

The guy looked at me like I was dense. "Virgil."

I frowned. "Virgil Proust? He painted this?"

"Sure did." The guy nodded proudly, like he'd just told me his kid had painted it. "And many more."

I remembered Virgil's son during the eulogy, mentioning how Virgil loved to paint. "I didn't know."

Now he turned to face me, giving me his full attention. "Yeah, you didn't seem like you were part of this crowd. I'm Paul Durant." Then he squinted at me and his face reddened. "Didn't I meet you—"

"At Blue Heaven. Maddie James."

"Yeah." He blew out a breath. "Sorry about that. Whitney panicked. My name really is Paul," he added, "not Dominic. Thank God because I hate that stupid Christmas song about the donkey."

I couldn't help it. I started to laugh, and once I did I couldn't stop. Even when I realized people were staring at me. Including my dad, which was what sobered me enough to get it together. Paul Durant watched me with an amused look.

"You okay?"

"Yes." I cleared my throat. "Sorry."

"No problem. I get the sense laughter isn't easy to come by in this house. How did you come to be acquainted with Virgil?"

"Oh. Um. Well, my dad." I waved vaguely in the direction of where I'd left my parents. "He knows everyone in town. He runs the hospital. And I'm actually helping out with the neighborhood feral cat problem."

"That's right!" Paul snapped his fingers, then he glanced around and lowered his voice. "Whitney mentioned that the night we, ah, saw you." He looked sufficiently embarrassed about that. "Listen, she's a wonderful woman. She didn't want to lie about her leg. But her ex is a truly terrible human and was going to cut her insurance once she recovered . . ."

"It's fine," I said, holding up a hand. "You certainly don't owe me an explanation." Not to mention, I didn't want to be party to insurance fraud along with everything else. "So, what about you?" I asked. "How do you know Virgil? And, is Whitney here? I didn't think she was that . . . friendly with the Prousts." I made a show of looking around, although I wouldn't have been able to miss her if she had been.

He seemed very interested in the painting again. "Ah, no. She isn't." He sighed. "You're right. She had a huge issue with June Proust. That's why she didn't come."

I waited, but he didn't say anything else. I pondered my choices here. I could be polite and let it go, which to me wasn't much of an option. I had a limited window of time to help Katrina, and getting the opportunity to talk to this guy seemed like the Universe trying to help me out. Also he had kind of opened the door by acknowledging he did not, in fact, share a name with an Italian Christmas donkey.

I decided the heck with it and pressed on. "So then you knew Virgil outside of Whitney's neighborhood? Are you from the island?" I was pretty sure he wasn't. I'd never seen him before the night at Blue Heaven.

He shook his head again. "No, I'm not. And yes, I know Virgil outside of Whitney. Through work."

He lapsed into silence again, but now we were getting somewhere.

"Through teaching? Wasn't Virgil a professor?"

Something crossed his face, but it was so quick I couldn't be sure. "He was, but that's not how I know him." He gestured toward the painting. "I'm Virgil's agent."

My mouth dropped. It took a minute for me to make

the connection between what he was saying and the paint-ing. "Agent? Like, art agent?"

He nodded.

"He actually sold paintings?"

Paul smiled. "A few."

"Wow." I turned back to the painting and studied it again. This piece of art was quite good. I'd put it in my house. "So are any of these other paintings his too?" I waved around at the various art pieces in the room.

"A couple of them, yeah," Paul said. He pointed at a painting of the sea in some kind of tumultuous storm. "He was a tremendous talent. The art world has suffered a loss for sure." He sounded sad.

I stepped up to the picture and studied it. It was a common-enough concept, but the way Virgil had used grays and blues and greens together and even the depic-tion of the waves was different. Stunning. And somehow slightly familiar. Had I seen some of his pieces before and simply not known it?

"So did Whitney introduce you as Dominic because it's a secret that you represented Virgil? Or because she was hiding the leg thing?"

"I don't think that had anything to do with Virgil," Paul said dryly.

"I'm guessing you aren't a physical therapist, then," I said. "But I can imagine that it must be difficult repre-senting him when your . . . girlfriend?" I looked to him for confirmation. When he nodded, I went on. "When your girlfriend feels the way she does."

He clearly didn't want to talk about this, and as luck would have it for him, June Proust saved him. She barreled toward us and grabbed his arm with that claw-like hand, pulling him away from me into a corner where she started talking a mile a minute. Probably about how he shouldn't speak to me.

Ugh. I didn't want to be anywhere near that woman. I turned to find my parents but they were engrossed in conversation with another couple I didn't recognize. For a small, private affair, there were a lot of people in this room. It hadn't seemed like that many at church. It was starting to get hot in here, even though the house was ginormous and there was probably a ton of other places in which to congregate. I grabbed a sparkling water from the bar and went to go find one.

Weaving through the people, I stepped into the next room, which was another living-room type space. This one had a deck, so I made my way over there, opened the door, and stepped outside. I didn't notice Virgil Junior was out there until I'd turned to shut the door behind me and he'd scared the crap out of me.

"Oh! I'm so sorry. I didn't know anyone was out here."

"No problem." He barely met my eyes.

"Hot in there," I said.

He muttered something I didn't quite catch. Up close, I saw how much he looked like his mother. That same slight build, the small eyes, the dour face with the lips pulling down in a permanent disapproving look. I felt sorry for him. I couldn't imagine growing up with her as my mom.

That sympathy made me try a little harder. Plus he'd just lost his dad. "I'm very sorry for your loss," I said.

Now he looked at me. I saw that his eyes weren't as beady and dull as June's, now that we'd actually made eye contact. They were curious, and a tiny bit sad. "Who are you again?"

"My name is Maddie James. My dad is the CEO of the hospital." I left out the bit about the cats, as I figured June would've already told him my friend had killed his father.

"I see," Virgil Jr. said. "So you knew my dad?"

"A little," I said. It was only a tiny white lie. I did know him a little. "It's really tragic what happened. It seems so crazy. I mean, this is such a beautiful neighborhood . . ." I trailed off, realizing I was babbling now.

Virgil Junior acknowledged all of this with a slight incline of his chin. "Beautiful neighborhoods can be ugly too," he said, his gaze going out to the backyard.

It missed the mark a little bit as far as poetic sentiment, but I knew where he was going. I followed his gaze. I could see into the woods from here, and even caught a glimpse of one of the cat shelters. I wondered if June would wait out here, trying to see if we were straying too close to her property line.

I turned my attention back to Virgil Junior, who was lost in thought. "I didn't know your dad was an artist," I said. "He did beautiful work."

"He did," Virgil Junior said, then lapsed back into silence.

Talkative, this one. I tried again. "So was it more of a side hustle? I didn't know you could get an agent to sell a few paintings if you did it as a hobby. But then again, I don't know anything about the art world, so that's not surprising, right?" I laughed at my own joke, but Virgil Junior was now watching me with a look I couldn't quite read.

"Side hustle," he said, with a wry smile. "Yeah, my dad was pretty good at those. Excuse me, would you?"

He got up and walked back into the house, leaving his drink on the table.

Chapter 33

Since no one but Paul Durant seemed interested in speaking to me, and even he didn't want to talk about his client or his girlfriend, I busied myself looking at paintings and trying to figure out which ones were Virgil's until my mother came over to tell me we were leaving and handed me my coat. I guess that meant I was going too, even though I had my own car. My dad was probably afraid what I would do without a chaperone. I didn't fight it though. I didn't think there was anyone else in here who would talk to me, and being this close to June creeped me out.

Out on the porch, when I stopped to pull my scarf around my neck, I spotted Harvey Hackett. He'd just gotten out of his car and was heading toward his front door.

"You guys go ahead," I said to my parents. "I need to chat with Harvey for a minute. Thanks for bringing me. I'll call you guys later!" I turned away before they could protest and hurried next door.

"Hi, Harvey!" I waved, catching his attention just as he slid his key into the lock.

"Hi, Maddie. How are you?"

"Fine," I said. "I went with my parents to pay my respects to the Prousts."

He looked puzzled by that, but nodded. "I understand. I would've gone, but . . ." he trailed off.

"Yeah, I imagine it's not fun having neighbors you don't really get along with," I said. "I'm sorry about that. It must be hard to look at people who can be so mean to animals. Especially the way you and your wife feel about cats." I watched him closely.

He reddened a little and glanced down at the driveway before he shrugged. "We got along fine." His tone wasn't convincing, and he must have realized it.

My mind was racing frantically on how to get him to talk about Virgil and the board without sounding like I was fishing. I should've been more prepared, but I'd seen an opportunity and grabbed it without really knowing my next move. "I just met his art agent, actually. I had no idea Virgil was an artist."

Harvey squinted at me in a way that made me think he had no use for artists. "Yes, I heard that too. Anyway, it was nice to see you—"

"Harvey. I know you and Virgil were on the Audubon board together," I burst out, then cringed as soon as the words came out of my mouth. So much for smooth.

He gave me an odd look, his hand dropping from his doorknob. "We were," he said. "Sort of."

"Sort of?"

He shrugged. "Virgil was really not that involved. I think he only did it for his résumé. He wasn't very reliable."

"I had no idea you were part of that organization," I said. "Don't they hate cats?" I blinked innocently at him.

Harvey's face turned even more red. "No! I mean, birds are the priority of course, but the group has nothing against cats. Why are you asking about the board anyway?"

"I'm really curious about it," I said. "I get that Virgil and his wife didn't want the cats here. But I heard there was a lot of controversy about whether the board should get involved with the situation here. Since you and Virgil were the two residents on the board . . ." I let my sentence trail off.

"Where on earth did you hear that?" Harvey's laugh was forced. "Listen, the only controversy was me telling Virgil a few times that if he wanted to be on the board he should probably show up more, but that's it. The topic of feral cats always comes up in one way or another at Audubon meetings all over the country. It's because there are definitely some people who blame the cats for bird populations declining. But here, we did our best to turn people's attention elsewhere. We have a new report on how many birds we've lost in this part of the country in the past fifty years under review, for instance, and I wanted to make sure we didn't lose focus on that."

I nodded, pretending to understand. "So Virgil wasn't really into this whole thing. You think it was June making him do it?"

He nodded. "I do." He glanced behind him as if he thought June might be listening. "In Virgil's defense, June . . . she's bats, you know. Well, I don't have to tell you. You've seen it."

"I have," I said sympathetically. "She gave you a hard time too, I heard."

Harvey nodded again, emphatically, seemingly happy to point out June's shortcomings. "She's at my door all the time, telling me how awful my children are and how they're in her yard doing hideous things. I can only imagine what it was like to live with her. Almost felt sorry for him." He looked like he wanted to go on, but caught himself and shut his mouth. "Why so many questions about Virgil, though?"

"I'm sure you know my friend is their number-one suspect in his murder," I said.

He nodded. Opened his mouth as if to say something, then closed it again.

"She didn't do it," I said.

"And you're trying to find out if someone else did? That's a big job, Maddie. And possibly a dangerous one."

Was it me, or was there something threatening to his tone? I shrugged. "I'm helping my grandfather. He's doing some private investigating."

Harvey frowned. "Into Virgil's murder?"

I hesitated for dramatic effect, then nodded. "Yes. And honestly, I'm really worried about June." I leaned closer, conspiratorially. "I saw her take his phone and smash it. I can't help but wonder if she was disturbed enough to . . . well."

"Oh, she's got some problems, alright," Harvey said. "I wouldn't doubt that she'd be capable of something like that. I said as much to Monica."

I raised my eyebrows. "You're serious?"

He nodded. "She had a temper."

I didn't disagree, but he'd thrown her under the bus pretty quickly. "Thanks, Harvey. Hey, one more question," I said, as if I'd just remembered. "Was Virgil the one who brought up the feral cat issue to the Audubon board? And the poison petition?"

He frowned, then glanced around again as if he thought someone was eavesdropping. "I shouldn't be talking about this, but yes, he was."

I made a sympathetic noise. "I know you and Monica care so much about the cats. It must've really bothered you."

"Oh, it certainly did," he said, nodding vigorously. "I just remember being so shocked about him introducing the petition to poison them. I was the first to vote against it."

He was a liar. A bald-faced liar. What else was he capable of?

"Daddy!"

Harvey whipped around at the sound of his son's voice. One of the kids stood inside the front door, waving madly.

"Daddy, I need to talk to you!"

Harvey glanced back at me, clearly relieved. "I have to run, Maddie. I'm sure I'll see you soon." He pulled the door open and stepped inside. He turned to look at me one last time before he ushered his son through the door, pausing, then closing it firmly behind him.

I walked to my car, trying to put this information together in my mind. Harvey had argued with Virgil in the middle of the street because neither of them wanted their wives to know what they were really up to. He'd lied about his stance regarding the cats and tried to make it look like Virgil was the bad guy at the Audubon board. And now he was flat-out lying to me about all of it.

Could he have also lied about where he was that night? Could he have left his house, parked out of sight, then snuck back to the neighborhood to bash Virgil over the head with a Christmas gnome?

Chapter 34

I couldn't wait to debrief Grandpa on what I'd learned at the funeral. He'd been asleep when I got home the previous night, but I figured we'd connect first thing this morning. While I waited for him to come downstairs, I poured myself coffee and used the time to google *Virgil Proust, artist*.

No hits.

I frowned. "Guess he wasn't that famous after all," I said to myself.

"Who?"

I turned to see Katrina standing in the kitchen doorway. She had her cat carrier with Fred and Ethel in one hand and her duffel bag in the other. I frowned. "Where are you going?"

"Back to my place. It's so sweet of you guys to have me here but I need to get back into my routine." She smiled a half smile. "For as long as I have it."

"Katrina, no. I don't want you to be alone." I put my mug down and crossed the room to her. "Is there something else we can do for you here? Do you want more privacy?"

"No, Mads, please. You guys have been amazing. I

just need to spend some time alone. Honest, I'll be fine. Now"—she smiled, a little too brightly—"who's not famous?"

"Uh." I frantically tried to think of an answer that didn't involve the guy she was accused of murdering, but in the end I couldn't come up with one. "I was looking up Virgil," I said. "They were talking about his art yesterday. And I met his agent."

She went white.

"Katrina? I'm sorry, I didn't want to mention him but I didn't want to lie."

"No, no, it's fine." She stepped away from me, shaking her head. "I have to go."

"How are you getting home? I'll drive you," I offered.

"I already called an Uber. It should be here any moment. Thanks for everything, Mads. I'll call you tomorrow."

I watched her go, trying to ignore the sinking feeling her departure was giving me. I felt like a terrible friend, but I couldn't force her to stay. I did wonder, though. She'd asked for our help but still seemed standoffish and unengaged about the whole thing, even going out of her way to change the subject or, like just now, removing herself from any related conversation. It could be because she was trying to deal with the whole arrest/bail/awaiting-trial thing—everyone had their own ways of dealing—but it felt weird to me.

My cell phone vibrated in my pocket, jolting me out of my thoughts, and I pulled it out and glanced at it. Craig.

"Hey," I said. "What's going on?"

"You home?" He sounded serious.

"Yeah."

"Good. I'm outside. I need to talk to you." Before I could say anything, he'd disconnected.

Now what? I headed to the door. He was already at it.

"What in the world is going on?" I asked as he strode

past me into the house like he was on a mission. "If this is more stuff about Katrina I'm really not in the mood—"

He cut me off with a raised hand. "Not Katrina. Maddie, I need to tell you something. About Lucas."

That, I wasn't expecting. And hearing Lucas's name made my stomach drop, as if I'd just begun the plunge down the particularly steep descent of a roller coaster. I steeled myself, at the same time reminding myself that Craig had never been a Lucas fan, mostly because I was. If there was more to it than that, he'd never let on. "What?" I asked.

"It's about . . . while he was away."

My heart sped up even more, leaving me feeling shaky and untethered. I had to work to get my feet figuratively under me again. I moved to the couch and sank down. "Sit. You're making me nervous. How would you know about while he was away?" I asked.

Craig reluctantly perched on the edge of a chair. "I did some checking in . . . the system."

"What system?"

He waved me away. "It's not important what system. It was bothering me, though, especially since he's been sniffing around you again."

"Sniffing around me?" I laughed, but the sound was forced. "Really, Craig?"

"Look, do you want to hear this or not?"

Not really. "Fine, go ahead," I said in a bored tone to let him know I was only entertaining this because we had a history.

"He was in jail."

My jaw literally dropped. I'd seen the phenomenon in cartoons but didn't really think it was a thing in real life. However, it happened. I stared at him. "What . . . what do you mean 'in jail'? For what?"

"In Virginia. I couldn't get details. I wasn't really

supposed to be doing this because it's not related to anything I'm working on, but I was able to get the basics. Assault and battery was the charge."

This was making no sense to me. I wasn't that bad of a character judge . . . was I? My sweet, considerate Lucas, who had never even raised his voice in my presence, had been arrested and charged with hurting someone? I didn't want Craig to know how shaken I was by this news, so I tried to cover it under a sarcastic tone. "Who was he assaulting and battering?" I asked finally, when I was sure my voice would work without shaking. His family lived in Virginia—I did know that. But who would he have assaulted?

"I didn't get that information," Craig said.

"So what happened? He was in jail, and then . . . what? Is he going to trial? How did he get out?"

"Like I said, I didn't have access to the whole file."

"Well, you're just a fount of information these days, aren't you?" I said. I couldn't help the bitterness I heard oozing out of my tone.

He looked taken aback. "What do you mean?"

I shrugged. "Katrina's secrets, Lucas's secrets. You seem to know it all."

"Hey. I just wanted to help Katrina. And you," he added. "Since I know you're still hung up on the guy."

"I am not *hung up*," I snapped. "And I don't know how helpful it is to dig up people's secrets that clearly they're ashamed of and not wanting the whole world to know about!"

"I hardly think I'm the whole world," Craig responded dryly. "It's not like I called Becky and asked her to feature the news on the front page."

"Not funny." I glanced down when JJ jumped into my lap—seriously, this cat had a sixth sense for when I needed him—and kept my eyes averted. I didn't want

Craig to see how hurt—and shell-shocked—I was at this news. I knew it would be all over my face. I wanted to know more, but I didn't think he actually knew any more. I'm sure he would've been happy to tell me if he did. Seemed like he would always carry this grudge against Lucas. He would always think we would've gotten back together if Lucas hadn't been in the picture.

"Are you going to tell everyone? Did you already tell Grandpa?"

He gave me a look through slanted eyes. "I wouldn't do that. You don't have to worry about it. Anyway, I just thought you should know." He turned and headed for the door.

"Where are you going?" I demanded.

"To work," he said through gritted teeth, his hand on the doorknob.

"Now?"

Craig sighed and let go, turning around to look at me. "Yes, now. Why do you care? You didn't exactly want to hear the news I shared. You made that perfectly clear."

I clenched and unclenched my fists, not sure what I wanted—what a surprise. Finally I sagged onto the couch and dropped my head into my hands. "I'm sorry. I know I'm a jerk and you were just looking out for me. And I know you always do," I said, glancing up at him. "I just . . . don't know what to think about all this. And I'm hurt. And angry. I'm hurt and angry and I don't know what to do about it."

It felt good to say that out loud. Even with Becky, it had been hard to verbalize that. Anger was easier. It made me look less weak. But I knew anger came from hurt, and I had that in spades.

He came and sat next to me, slipping an arm around my shoulder. "I know. I'm sorry, Maddie. I really am. And I wish I could've gotten more details for you."

I smiled a little sadly and leaned into him. "I do too, but I also don't."

"I know that too. But I wouldn't want him trying to hide it from you either."

"He's been trying to explain," I said. "I just haven't let him. I guess my gut knew I wouldn't like it."

We were silent for a moment, then he glanced at his watch. "I really have to go. I'm here if you need anything."

I put on a brave smile. "Thanks. I appreciate it."

He gave me another squeeze, then rose and headed out the door, leaving me with my thoughts and questions. I hadn't realized I could feel any worse about this situation, but apparently it was possible.

Chapter 35

"Jail," I said miserably, swirling my drink around in my glass. "He was in jail. In Virginia. For assault and battery. He went to Boston, ended up in Virginia, and went to jail. Can you believe it?"

Val, Ethan, Becky, and I had gone out to celebrate the new year, even though I didn't feel like I had much to celebrate. I still hadn't found Virgil's real killer, Katrina was still facing a murder charge and had gone home to be alone, and now I find out that my kind-of boyfriend had been in jail. This wasn't the way I wanted to ring in the new year, although I was happy to put this year in the rearview mirror. Aside from moving home and opening the cat café, things had been mostly crappy to say the least.

We were at Jade Moon, where basically the only good party on the island was happening. Since, you know, most of the island was deserted at this time of year. Which was awkward, since I knew Craig and Jade were having problems. And I couldn't help but feel like she blamed me. I'd caught her sneaking glances at our table, but she hadn't come over to say hi yet. Although she could just be busy and I was crazy. Which was becoming more and more possible given the circumstances.

"It doesn't make sense," Val said. "There has to be a reason. Maybe he caught some guy abusing a woman and stepped in, and the cops got called and he was hauled away. It was a misunderstanding! Had to be." She looked at me, waiting for me to perk up at this possibility. "Craig couldn't find out anything else?"

Ethan nodded. "It's not a crazy idea. We'd need the details to really get a good picture of this."

Becky and I just stared at them.

"What?" Val asked indignantly.

"Nothing," I said. "I would just love to know when you became such a romantic."

"Or a fiction writer," Becky added.

"Oh come on! Lucas isn't a criminal. I'm not buying that." Val sat back and crossed her arms. "And by the way, you'd know the story if you gave the guy five minutes to explain it. Then you wouldn't bc over here making up your own fiction about how he's suddenly become a"—she cast around for a fitting crime—"rapist or drug dealer or something."

She kind of had a point, but I didn't want to have this conversation again.

"So get this," I said, desperate to change the subject. "Jade and Craig aren't seeing each other anymore, apparently."

Val's eyes widened. "Really? Why?"

"I have no idea. I asked him about her and he just said they weren't seeing each other at the moment. Or something like that."

"That's too bad," Ethan said. "I wondered why he wasn't here tonight. Unless he's working, of course."

"*At the moment.* What does that mean?" Becky asked.

I shrugged. "But he was telling me about it when Lucas came around the corner. I could tell he thought he'd interrupted something." I smiled. "Good."

Val pressed her lips together but didn't say anything about that. Instead she said, "That's too bad. I kind of thought they were good together."

I gave her a funny look. "You've been thinking about Craig's love life?"

Val shrugged and kissed Ethan's cheek. "My own is going so well, and you don't want to talk about yours, so . . ." She winked.

"Not funny. And I have no love life." I crossed my arms over my chest in defense.

Val just looked at me.

"What?"

"You could," she said.

And suddenly, we were talking about this again. I looked at Becky for help, but she had none to offer. She lifted her shoulders in a shrug. "She's kind of right, much as I hate to say it."

I looked at Ethan. He held his hands up in a gesture of surrender. "I'm not saying anything."

I glared at all of them and tipped my glass back, swallowing the rest of my special New Year's Eve martini, the name of which I couldn't remember at the moment. I put my glass down and held up my finger. "No more talking if that's all you can talk about. I'm getting another drink. Who wants another drink?"

"Me," Becky said, amused.

"Me too," Val said, looking less amused.

"Here." Ethan handed me some bills. "Me too but I'm buying."

I plucked the bills out of his hand. I never turn down a free drink. "I'll be right back." I was feeling just tipsy enough that going up to talk to Jade seemed like a good idea. I scoped out the bar and found one lone seat near the end, so I hopped on the chair and waited for her to notice me.

It took her a long time. Although in fairness, it was pretty busy. One of the other bartenders came over, but I said I was waiting for Jade. He shrugged and walked away, tapping her on the shoulder and pointing at me.

Jade took her time coming over. When she did, she nodded, but didn't smile. "Hey."

"Hey," I said.

"What can I get you?"

I rattled off the drinks, then leaned over to grab her arm when she nodded and prepared to walk away. "Wait."

She paused, glancing down at my arm, then back at me.

"I actually wanted to talk to you."

"I'm a little busy," she said dryly, waving her hand at the crowd. "Talk to me about what?"

"Craig."

Jade's jaw set. "What about him?"

"I heard you guys weren't really seeing each other anymore."

"And?" Jade pulled the cloth from her back pocket and flicked it at a nonexistent spot on the bar.

"And I . . . was sad to hear that," I said. I was starting to feel a little stupid. Also, she wasn't totally receptive to this conversation. I wasn't sure why I'd thought she would be—maybe I'd assumed it would be like two friends dishing about guy troubles—but clearly she didn't see me that way. And why should she? We were acquaintances at best. I liked Jade, but that didn't mean we'd gotten tight.

Maybe making this decision based on two drinks hadn't been the best idea.

"Really," she said, sounding unimpressed.

"Yeah. Really."

"I figured you'd be delighted," she said. "Now you get another chance."

I stared at her. "Why would I be delighted? And what do you mean, 'another chance'?"

"Oh, come on, Maddie," Jade said. "Look, I have work to do. And I'm sure you want your drinks." She turned to walk away.

"Jade. What happened with you two?" I blurted out. "Because I hope it's not that you think he has a thing for me or something. Or that I was trying to get him back. Look, it was a long time ago. When we dated. We've stayed friends, that's all. My parents have known him all his life, and he worked for my grandfather, so he's like family. That's it. Honestly." I was babbling, but I couldn't help myself. I don't know what it was about Jade, but I always felt a little awkward when I talked to her.

She watched my impassioned speech without a word, making me feel like I needed to keep filling the space with my voice. Which kept getting louder to try to rise above the noise level in the bar, which was also getting louder as the night went on.

Jade worked pretty hard to keep the *I couldn't care less* look on her face, but I could see her eyes were sad. "I don't really think it's any of your business," she said. "And if there's nothing between you two, why do you care? I'm not in the market for a relationship coach."

"Of course I care. Because he's my friend, and I hope you are too," I said. "And I want him to be happy. He's done nothing but help my family, and I'm just trying to help him. If you don't want to hear what I have to say, fine. But I had to say it."

Her face softened a bit and she looked like she might be about to drop the attitude and say something genuine, but at that moment a group of four rowdy guys sauntered up to the bar, laughing and talking loudly. Jade's eyes narrowed. "Great," she muttered. "Like I need this kind of trouble."

I glanced over at the guys and then did a double take.

One of them was Trey Barnes.

Chapter 36

I sucked in a breath. "Do you know them?" I asked Jade.

"Unfortunately," she said. "They come in here a lot." She looked like this was not a good thing.

I was dying to ask her why, but she had turned away to go make my drinks and take more orders, since the bar was getting fuller and fuller as the night went on. I stayed where I was and watched Trey and his friends. They reminded me of a group of frat boys. One of them in particular rubbed me the wrong way, the way he catcalled any woman who entered his field of vision—especially Jade. Trey was the quietest of the bunch, but that wasn't saying much.

I wondered again how old this guy was. He couldn't be more than forty. Maybe forty-five, if he took really good care of himself. His wife seriously had to be around seventy. Ugh. Just the thought of it grossed me out.

I considered my options. I would probably never get another chance to talk to Trey without his wife's hawk eyes on us. And I was clearly failing in my attempts to narrow down my suspect pool. Maybe he knew something about what was going on in the neighborhood. He always seemed to be home, so maybe he was privy to some of the goings-on that happened out of sight of the others.

Decision made, I slid off my seat and went over to them, bracing myself for the inevitable. It came immediately when the most-vile member of the group saw me first and leaned forward with a salacious leer.

"Well, well," he said, and I realized he was clearly on something aside from booze. "Hello, gorgeous. Looking to start the new year off right?"

I recoiled and, trying to ignore him, focused on Trey. "Hey. Do you remember me?"

He squinted at me through a haze of God knows what, but a glimmer of recognition did appear in his eyes. "Yeah. Aren't you the cat girl?"

I smiled a little. "That's me. Can I talk to you for a second?"

He looked uncertain, but his friends all started poking him and laughing. Seriously, were these guys twclvc? I saw Jade watching us and hoped she didn't think I was trying to pick up one of these buffoons.

"Go for it, Barnes," one of the others said, shoving him in my direction. "And then bring her back for us when you're done."

I stared, openmouthed, and then snapped my jaw shut and stabbed my index finger at the guy. "Watch it, you piece of crap, or I'll—"

"I got this," Trey muttered. "Leave her alone," he admonished his friend. "She's got police contacts. Relatives or something. Right?" He stared hard at me, obviously trying to remember.

"Yeah," I snapped. "I do. A lot of them."

The other guys frowned and made a couple of more comments that I couldn't quite make out, but they backed off.

Trey looked at me. "Whaddaya want to talk to me about?"

I motioned for him to follow me and led him out into the hallway where the restrooms were. It was a little quieter out here, at least. I positioned myself near the back exit so we weren't blocking the bathrooms, then turned to him. "I need to talk to you about Virgil Proust."

Some kind of emotion I couldn't quite pinpoint skittered across his impaired brain and manifested on his face. He narrowed his eyes and folded his giant arms across his broad chest. "My dead neighbor? What about him?"

"I'm trying to figure out how he got that way," I said. "Because my friend didn't kill him."

"How you know that?" he wanted to know. "The police think she did."

"They're wrong," I said bluntly. "Someone else did. And I feel like it was close to home. Since you . . . live there, I wondered if you knew how Virgil and his wife got along."

That made him laugh. "Got along? You mean hated each other?"

I knew it. "They did?"

"Well, she ain't exactly the nicest lady ever walked the earth. I should know. She's buddies with my wife." He grimaced a little at that. "June was always whining to Edie about everything Virgil was and wasn't doing."

My ears perked up at that. Of course Trey must've heard some of their conversations. "Did she complain about anything in particular?" I asked, trying to keep my tone casual.

"What *didn't* she complain about? He wasn't around enough, he didn't respect her, he didn't do as she asked—the usual nagging crap. Whining about how he probably had a girlfriend. Which, who could blame the guy?"

I tried to keep my distaste for this guy off my face. What a charmer. Was Edie Barnes so desperate for a guy—or for some arm candy—that she had to resort to this? Although she didn't seem that nice either, so maybe they deserved each other.

"Were you and Virgil close?" I asked.

He gave me an *Are you serious* look. "Nope."

I guessed he wasn't going to elaborate on that.

"Did you guys get along? Not get along?"

Now his eyes narrowed into slits—and they weren't entirely friendly. "We got along fine . . . when he minded his own business," he said.

From this vantage point I could see how big this guy really was. He had to be six one or six two, and clearly must spend most of his day in the gym. His biceps were like boulders. I was trying to figure out how to get him to elaborate when a giant ruckus from the bar grabbed both our attentions.

His head snapped around. "What the . . . ?"

I pushed past him and headed back to the bar in time to see cops descending on Trey's buddies. Like, a swarm of them. They had moved everyone away and were hand-cuffing them, while another cop stood guard, hand on his gun.

Holy crap. What was this about? I looked behind me, but Trey was gone. I watched the rear exit door at the end of the hall thunk shut. I made my way back out to where Jade stood at the bar, watching the police lead the guys out. Conversation started to buzz again, drowning out the loud silence that had descended while everyone had watched that play out.

"What happened?" I asked.

"I called the cops to see if they could come just be a presence. Those guys are trouble," she said. "They've caused issues in here before. But when the cops got here, they realized they have warrants out for two of them. Drug dealing. The other one tried to slug one of the cops." She tossed her hair and turned back to the bar. "Good riddance."

Chapter 37

New Year's Day. It was officially next year. Funny, it didn't feel any different. It felt exactly the same, and that was a distressing thought.

After all the excitement at the bar last night, we'd left and come home to ring in the new year in a less-fraught atmosphere. Which meant watching the ball drop with Anderson Cooper and then me slinking off to bed, where I laid awake for hours thinking about Trey and his creepy friends. Drug dealers? Seriously? And why had he run out the back door? Would he have been arrested with the lot of them, or was he just being cautious?

And then he'd made that comment about how he got along with Virgil when Virgil "minded his own business." He'd clearly been under the influence of something, but wasn't that usually when people were the most honest? I had to call Craig and tell him. Maybe it was nothing, but maybe it wasn't. And he was in the strongest position to get the Turtle Point police to pay attention. I also had to talk it over with Grandpa and see what info he'd uncovered the past couple of days. Between Katrina leaving and Craig's shocking news about Lucas, not to mention getting through another holiday, I hadn't been in the frame of mind to focus on the murder. And Grandpa had been mysteriously absent most of yesterday, out "checking on a few things," as the cryptic note he'd left put it.

In the meantime, JJ and I had a big day. I'd gotten up way too early to go feed the ferals, and later this morning we were hosting senior citizens from the senior centers around the island on a special café tour. Grandpa, who had always supported the senior centers in his official capacity, had suggested it and had secured a volunteer bus driver—along with a bus—to pick them up in shifts and bring them over to the café. We had seniors coming from every town.

I was really looking forward to this. First of all, JJ was a common visitor on the senior-center circuit. He loved to meet people, and everyone adored him. We made it a point to visit one of the centers every few weeks, although lately I'd been so busy with the colony and my own personal drama that I hadn't gotten there.

Also, I loved showing off the café, and I loved the seniors. It was a bright light in a string of bad days and I was desperately latching on to it and trying not to worry. And it was still nagging at me that I hadn't been able to reach Katrina since she'd gone home—I was worried about her being all alone. She had to be in a bad space.

But I couldn't do anything about it now. I turned to JJ, who was curled up into his usual ball on my pillow.

"You ready, bud?" I asked. "You've got some people to charm. I have a feeling we're gonna sell a lot of JJ's House of Purrs tote bags today."

When we got downstairs, I popped in to say good morning to Ethan, who was heading out to "work" with the crew on his garage-turned-café. He had enthusiastically named himself part of the construction crew, and while I didn't think he was adding a lot of value to the work itself, the guys enjoyed him and it gave him something to do during our slow season. I filled a mug with coffee and went into the café. Grandpa was already in there.

"I was about to come looking for you," I said. "We have to talk."

"Here I am. We have a lot to do for today." He rubbed his hands together. "And while we do that we can debrief. You first. How was the funeral?"

"In a minute." I wasn't even sure if he knew Katrina wasn't here, and I needed to tell him.

His face turned grim when I described her speedy exit from the house yesterday. "She was already leaving, but when I mentioned Virgil . . ." I shook my head. "I understand the whole thing has traumatized her, but still." I took a deep breath. "And it kind of worries me for another reason."

I walked Grandpa through what I'd learned—Virgil's art career, Whitney's boyfriend as his agent, his son's disdain for his father's "side hustles"—whatever that meant—Harvey's lies, and my chance New Year's Eve meeting with Trey Barnes and his band of merry men at Jade's bar, as well as his cryptic comments. Especially the one about June "whining about Virgil having a girlfriend." I wasn't loving where my head was going.

"Well," Grandpa said. "Seems I did some nosing around at the hospital for nothing. You were way ahead of me."

"Hospital?"

He nodded. "I went to find out about this alleged physical therapist of Whitney's. Pretended I was an old guy with an appointment who must've gotten it wrong when they told me there was no Dominic on staff."

I had to giggle at that. "That's a lot of effort. Couldn't you have called?"

He shrugged. "It was kind of fun to play a shuffling old man. But in all seriousness, do we like this Trey guy as a suspect?"

I threw up my hands. "That's just it. I don't know who to like anymore. And since when do we use that word? I thought that was for TV."

"Give me a break," Grandpa said. "I'm in character as a PI."

Oh, boy. I ignored that one. "I'm worried," I said. "I'm worried that Katrina was seeing Virgil Proust." The words tasted terrible on my tongue, but I'd drawn the conclusion in the dark of this early morning as I lay in bed going over and over everything in my head.

Grandpa sat down heavily on one of the café chairs. "Well. It seems our investigations have collided."

"What do you mean?"

"I got my hands on Virgil Proust's cell-phone logs from the month before he died."

My eyes widened. "You did? How?"

He smiled. "I still have friends in high places."

"And?"

The smile faded. "That's the interesting news." He paused.

I tried to control my impatience. Grandpa hated being rushed. But I couldn't last that long. "And?"

"Katrina and Virgil exchanged a lot of calls. And texts."

And there it was. Looks like I was right. Which didn't bode well for Katrina. But it also didn't bode well for June, in my mind, if she knew. Or even suspected. "Like how many is a lot?"

"A few a week, at least. Calls and texts from her personal cell and some calls from her office."

I stroked Simon, the tiger cat who'd just crawled onto my lap. He'd been really coming out of his shell recently. When I first met him I wasn't sure how adoptable he would be—he was scared of everything and hid all the time. But Katrina told me to give it time, that he'd come around. She'd been right.

"That looks bad," I said. "But, if she was seeing him and she liked him, she wouldn't kill him."

Grandpa nodded. "Unless he broke it off." He left the rest of it unsaid—that it happens all the time.

He was right, but that didn't sit well with me. Katrina had never been the type who got all angsty about guys. Not that I knew about, admittedly. She much preferred her animals. I didn't even know the last time she'd been on a date.

Unless she just wasn't telling me about them.

"It could also be bad for June," I pointed out.

Grandpa nodded thoughtfully. "True. But I'm not getting the gut feeling about her. It is interesting, though, that you mentioned that Trey Barnes character." He pulled out his notebook and flipped pages. "That's the fella I also read about in the call logs. Seems there were a few complaints about him and some of his associates. Minor things like disturbing the peace and drunk and disorderly. No arrests, though."

I thought back to the bunch of idiots who'd been dragged away by the cops last night. "Jade mentioned drugs. Who called on him?"

"I thought you'd never ask. It was Virgil."

Chapter 38

As the bus full of senior citizens pulled up outside I waited in the doorway, mulling over what Grandpa had discovered. Virgil had called the cops on Trey. He'd had fast and loose fingers when it came to calling the cops, for sure. Not only had he tried to get our volunteer arrested, but he'd also tried to get his own neighbor arrested. Not that Trey and his friends seemed to have any trouble doing that on their own, but still. That couldn't have gone over well on the street, even if nothing had come of it. Or between June and Edie, who were allegedly best friends. Would that have caused the recent rift Lilah had mentioned? Was that why she hadn't been at Virgil's funeral?

Unless Virgil had done it with the promise of anonymity, but even anonymous callers weren't all that anonymous. Especially considering Edie Barnes's money and reputation as a squeaky wheel. And while she struck me as the type who kept Trey on a short leash, she also seemed like she wouldn't want anything—or anyone—sullying her reputation.

The doorbell rang. I pushed it all out of my mind and welcomed my visitors to the café with a smile, delighting in their *ooh*s and *aah*s when they saw what we'd done with the place—and especially when the cats started to come out of the spots to be adored.

Grandpa was getting some adoring too. Clearly he was a catch in the senior community. I watched, amused, as some of the more determined ladies competed for his attention, asking him all kinds of questions about the house, the cats, how he was doing since the loss of his beloved wife. He was the star here. I happily took a backseat and let him show everyone around and be the center of attention.

We had buses coming every ninety minutes, staggering trips from each of the four senior centers on the island. Ethan had created a special menu for the day and kept the coffee, tea, and Italian cookies and pastries flowing. The cats were happy aside from poor Simon, who'd had a minor incident with Mr. Callaghan's cane and was hiding in his cubby. And our visitors seemed to be genuinely enjoying themselves. I grabbed a couple of cookies and some tea and busied myself behind the counter, organizing some of the T-shirts that had arrived this week. As I pulled a stack out to fold, my eyes fell on the gift bag Lucas had brought. It was still here. I still wasn't sure what to do with it. It mocked me now, all glittery and inviting. I reached out to touch it.

"You've really done a great job with the place."

I snatched my fingers away, not sure why I felt guilty, and looked up to find Stewart Payne, one of the senior center volunteers, smiling at me from behind his bushy white beard. At sixty-five, Stewart could have easily been using the senior center instead of volunteering at it, but he was like Grandpa—never aged and certainly never slowed down. Probably one of the reasons he and Grandpa had been friends for years.

I came around the counter to hug him. "I didn't know you were here!"

He grinned and planted a loud kiss on my cheek. "I

snuck in the back. You look like you're doing good, Maddie. I'm pleased to see that."

"Thanks, Stewart. How are you?"

He shrugged, patting his big belly. "Still eating too much pizza. Just living the dream. Leo loves this place, you know."

"I do know." I watched Grandpa show one of the senior ladies how Simon liked his belly rubbed. She swooned a little, and not just over the cat.

"I'm glad you could give him a new chapter." Stewart nodded. "Of course, I'm sure he's still policing in his spare time."

"You know it. Grandpa couldn't stop that if he tried."

"He looking into this Proust matter?" Stewart asked. "I hope so. 'Cause we all know Katrina wouldn't hurt a fly."

I nodded. "He is." I didn't want to say too much if Grandpa hadn't mentioned it to him.

Stewart scratched his beard again, his face solemn. "Poor guy. Put up with so much but had a heart of gold."

"Virgil?" I couldn't hide the skeptical look on my face. "You knew him?"

"Yeah. He was a good guy, Maddie. Why don't you think so?"

"I don't know. I didn't really know him. But he and his crazy wife made our lives miserable for trying to help the feral cats in the neighborhood. His wife is just mean. And did I mention crazy?"

Stewart made a noncommittal sound.

"I'm serious! When she wasn't accusing Katrina of murder, she was accusing the rest of us of stealing things. And honestly, I wouldn't be surprised if *she* did it." I wasn't going to go there, but I couldn't help it. I got so mad when I thought about it, and even more so when people tried to defend June.

But Stewart's eyes widened and he shook his head earnestly. "Oh, Maddie. That's not the whole story."

"What do you mean?"

"I mean, yes, June could be very challenging. But that was the illness. It manifests differently in everyone, and she, well, she had some anger and aggression issues."

"Wait." I was having a hard time keeping up. "Illness?"

He nodded. "June has dementia."

I stared at him. "She does?" It certainly explained a lot. And maybe I felt kind of terrible right now, but I hadn't known. I'd never had personal experience with dementia, but Ethan's grandmother had suffered from it. He'd told me some stories, but not in great detail. But I wondered why no one had ever mentioned this. Especially Lilah Gilmore.

"She does," Steward said. "Virgil kept it very quiet. She didn't want anyone to know. And really, neither did he. It had gotten worse over the past year. Especially recently with all the activity out in their neighborhood. . . . And of course the stress of that potential lawsuit."

That caught my attention. "Lawsuit?"

He nodded. "Someone was threatening to sue them. There was an incident where June thought a young woman was trespassing and made Virgil call the police. They threatened to arrest her but didn't and then the family came back and said the woman had been emotionally distressed or something like that. Millennials." He shook his head. "But you probably know all this."

I nodded carefully. The Avery Evans suit that had apparently never come to fruition. "I heard some of it. That was our volunteer. She was just trying to feed the cats. But you said June made Virgil call?"

Stewart nodded. "Yes. He tried to talk her out of it but when she got like that . . ." He shook his head. "Virgil was a good soul and took very good care of her, despite her treatment of him. She wasn't the easiest woman even before her illness. But he always tried to placate her while not causing too much damage to anyone else. I know he was truly sorry that girl was so upset. That's why he quietly paid off her parents so they wouldn't go through with it. He knew June couldn't take the stress." He glanced around, then held up a finger. "But you didn't hear that from me. At least not the part where he paid them off."

"That's terrible." Maybe I had misjudged Virgil. And Grandpa's gut wasn't gunning for June. But I wasn't entirely ready to let it go yet. What if she hadn't been aware of her actions and really had done something to hurt Virgil, maybe without meaning to?

I said as much to Stewart. He considered it. "It's possible someone could go to that extreme, Maddie, but I've never seen it and I've worked with a lot of dementia cases at the center over the years. Besides, June couldn't have done it. She was at her support group at the center the night Virgil was killed. I can personally vouch for her because I was working, and I called her friend to pick her up when the police called over."

And Grandpa's gut struck again. That was a rock-solid alibi, I realized with a sinking feeling. The list of suspects was dwindling. "Which friend?" I asked.

"Edie Barnes. Far as I knew, she was the only one who knew the real deal about June. Aside from Virgil and their son, of course. Edie was June's secondary emergency contact."

I leaned against the counter, feeling some of the wind leave my sails. If anything, June's illness was just another reason why Virgil might have been looking for some comfort outside of his real life. Which brought me full circle back to Katrina. I still didn't believe she'd killed him, but if she'd been seeing him, she needed to come clean now.

"Hey, Stewart," I said as he prepared to usher his charges back to the bus. "How do you know all this? About Virgil?"

He grinned at me. "We've been playing poker together for years. You learn a lot about a guy during an all-night card game." But then his smile faded. "Sure am gonna miss those card games."

Chapter 39

I didn't want to alert her that I was coming, so I showed up at Katrina's house with no advance notice. I figured she'd be home. She hadn't been out much lately. Not that I blamed her. She'd basically had her job taken away and has a murder charge hanging over her head.

I was right. Her car was in the driveway, and her lights were on. She answered the door right away. I knew she wasn't feeling great, but I was shocked at how terrible she looked. She'd lost weight, and she had been thin to begin with. Her sweatpants hung off her, and her hair was pulled back in a messy ponytail. Her bangs were too long, and dark circles under her eyes aged her by at least five years. She didn't look thrilled to see me, which made me sad. At the same time, I felt a surge of anger. If she'd just confided in me in the first place, maybe we could've avoided a lot of this mess.

"Hey," she said listlessly. "What's up?"

"I need to talk to you," I said, moving past her.

"Well then come on in," she said sarcastically to my back.

Fred jumped down from his window perch and raced over to me, rubbing against my leg. I bent to pet him, giving me a moment to get myself together. Finally I rose and turned to face her. She stood against the door, arms crossed over her chest, watching me as one would an animal they were wary of. She didn't ask me to sit.

"So what's going on?" she asked finally.

I took a deep breath. "I need to ask you something, and I need you to be honest with me. Because I'm really trying to help you."

She winced a little at that, probably remembering the last time we had something to ask her. "Go on."

"Katrina. You know I love you like a sister. And I know you didn't hurt anyone. But you have to tell me. Were you having an affair with Virgil?"

By the range of emotions that raced across her face, I could tell that whatever she'd been expecting from me, it wasn't that. Her reaction was so shocked, I realized it couldn't be true. I'd known her a long time and she wasn't that good of an actor.

"Was I . . . having an affair . . . with Virgil?" she repeated, as if tasting the words, finding them disgusting, and trying to spit them out. She looked like she didn't know whether to laugh or come after me. "Maddie. Did you seriously just ask me that question?"

I stood my ground. "What am I supposed to think? You guys were calling each other all the time. You admitted you were at his house that night, although you never actually said why, aside from some story about checking on a cat that makes no sense. June had serious problems, and they clearly weren't acting like a married couple. So"—I lifted my arms, palms up—"what would *you* think?"

"What would *I* think?" Katrina walked slowly around her kitchen. "I'm not sure. But I certainly wouldn't jump to conclusions, especially ones like that, and run around accusing someone—my friend—without gathering the right information. But I guess you and I are different."

The way she was looking at me made me want to crawl into a hole, but I kept my gaze on her. "Then why were you at Virgil's house that night, if you weren't seeing him? Because I know you weren't murdering him."

"Well," she said, "thanks for the vote of confidence." She yanked her door open, eyes flashing with anger. "I think you should leave."

"Katrina, come on. Talk to me."

"You don't want to talk, Maddie. You just want to point fingers. Listen, I would appreciate it if you just stayed out of it. I know I asked for help, but I changed my mind. I don't want your help. I'll take my chances with the lawyer. And I'll pay your grandfather back every cent for that as soon as I can, believe me. But in the meantime, just forget about all of it. Now please leave."

That wasn't what I was expecting. "You can't—you need our help. I know you didn't kill Virgil. The police aren't interested in looking at anyone else. Just tell me what was going on, Katrina. Whatever it was, we can figure it out."

"I asked you to leave." Her eyes were so cold. "Now."

I walked slowly to the door and turned around to try one more time, but she slammed it in my face. I had to take a step back so it wouldn't hit me. I could hear her throw the deadbolt in place on the other side.

I waited a moment, my face burning despite the cold, then walked slowly toward my car. I'd been so sure I'd found at least one of the answers, but now I mostly just felt like a jerk. And like I'd lost one of my best and oldest friends.

Chapter 40

I couldn't sleep. Which was nothing new lately, but last night it was particularly bad. I kept replaying the scene with Katrina over and over in my mind. I still felt like there was no other obvious conclusion I could've come to given the information I had, but either she was a really good actress or my conclusion was flat-out wrong.

This thing was getting crazier and crazier. I'd excluded June as a suspect given her situation and alibi, but aside from that development, I hadn't narrowed my list down any further. And whether Katrina and Virgil were having an affair or not, I know she didn't kill him. There had to be something I was missing. Finally around five a.m. I gave up, grabbed a notebook, and sat down on my bed, opening to a fresh page. I felt like Grandpa, but I needed to see all of this in one place.

I made a numbered list and added Katrina next to number 1. I hated to do it, but I needed to sort through the facts and, like it or not, she was a big part of the story. I jotted down a few notes—"seen in the area the night he died"; "lied about it"; her number in his call logs."

Next I wrote down Whitney's name. Whitney loved the cats and hated the Prousts, and she'd been lying about her injury. Which meant it was a lot easier to get around then she wanted people to think. And I'd heard her sort of threatening the Prousts. Well, June, but since Virgil was protecting June, he wouldn't have taken too kindly to that. Plus, her boyfriend—whom she'd also lied about— was Virgil's art agent. I wrote Paul Durant as number 2A. Had something happened there? Some kind of professional dispute that had driven him to murder? He'd seemed like a nice enough guy, but if enough money was involved, people could flip on a dime. Money was always a great motivator. I made a note to see what I could find out there and circled it.

Number 3 was Harvey Hackett. Harvey, who I'd thought was an ally for the cats, had actually tried to convince people to poison them. And he'd been seen fighting with Virgil in the street, and Virgil had actually threatened *him*. Maybe Harvey had gotten really angry about that and decided to pay Virgil back? It seemed extreme, but it was still a possibility. And there was the conversation between Harvey and Monica about him "giving Virgil a hard time." Whatever that was, they hadn't wanted the police to know about it.

Then there was Trey Barnes. I underlined and circled his name. Virgil had called the cops on him. He didn't seem like the type who would've taken kindly to that. And if he was hanging out with sketchy characters like the ones at the bar the other night, who seemed to have a not-so-great relationship with law enforcement. . . . I thought of Jade's harsh words about him and his friends. Nothing much fazed Jade, so the fact that she'd reacted so negatively to these guys was a red flag.

For the heck of it, I googled Trey's name. I didn't find much. A guy who worked at CrossFit in Colorado; a financial advisor in Connecticut. Nothing on any social profiles for a Trey Barnes who fit his description and location. He appeared to be tagged in a couple of images from other social accounts with shoddy privacy settings, one at a gym and another at what looked like a party on a beach. On the third page of the search, I found a small marriage announcement. Edie Wright married Trey Barnes on February 19, 2016. So they hadn't been married very long. But there was nothing else on the Trey I was interested in.

I skimmed through the rest of the pages, then sat back, thinking. I wondered if Trey had any kind of an arrest record. Grandpa hadn't found one in Turtle Point—the only mention he'd found was the time Virgil had called the cops on Trey.

But maybe he was doing his partying and subsequent bad behavior in other places. Like the old adage about not going to the bathroom where you ate.

I wrote June's name down too, then crossed it out. She had an alibi and I needed to accept it and let it go no matter how much I didn't like the woman, illness aside.

I waited until six—a much more civilized hour—then picked up my phone. I hadn't talked to Craig since he'd broken the news about Lucas. Or since I'd spoken to Jade. I wondered if he had heard about that yet . . . and if he was still talking to me.

But after a moment, he answered.

"Hey," I said.

"Hey."

He sounded fine, so I jumped right in. "You ever heard of a Trey Barnes being arrested in Daybreak Harbor?" I asked.

"Barnes? I'd have to look. Common name. Why?"

I gave him a quick overview of the situation in Jade's bar the other night, and what I knew about Trey. He didn't say anything when I mentioned Jade, so I didn't either.

"I'll look into it," he said.

"Really? You promise?"

"Yes, of course. I'll check when I get into work today."

I thanked him and hung up, pondering my next move. I'd been thinking about Leopard Man at Virgil's funeral. While I knew Leopard Man probably knew everyone on the island and then some, he wasn't friendly with everyone. And he certainly wouldn't be friends with a cat hater.

So why had he been there?

Well, wondering wasn't going to get me anywhere. I needed to ask him, and luckily I had an idea of where I could find him. I just had to wait until an even more civilized hour.

In the meantime, I had cats to feed. I threw on some clothes, brought JJ downstairs to feed him, then hopped in Grandma's car. Instead of heading straight to Sea Spray, I drove to Cass's shop first. He owned the building and lived in the apartment above it, so I figured chances were good he would be there.

He was already in the shop—the lights were on. I got out and went to the door. When he unlocked it, I handed him one of Ethan's muffins. "Time to take a quick drive?"

Cass looked completely unfazed at the fact that I'd shown up at barely six thirty in the morning. He blew out his incense, picked up his coat, and put his arm around me. "For you, anything."

Once we were in the car, he glanced over. "Where are we going?"

"I have to feed the ferals," I said. "You don't have to get out of the car."

"I am always happy to help." He unwrapped his muffin and took a bite. "Delicious."

"I'll tell Ethan you said so." I pulled up at a red light and glanced over at him. "Craig found out Lucas was in jail while he was away."

Cass's face didn't change. He was so good at the Zen thing. "What happened?"

"I'm not sure. Craig couldn't get the full file."

"And you haven't asked Lucas to explain?"

I hit the gas a little too hard when the light turned green. "No."

"Do you think you might?"

"I don't know," I muttered.

Cass continued to eat his muffin. At least when he judged me, he didn't show it. "That's probably the only way you're ever going to know," he said.

"What if he lies?" I asked. "How will I ever know if he's telling me the truth?"

Now he did look at me. "Because I taught you how to know. And because you didn't really need me to teach you in the first place. You always know, Maddie."

Chapter 41

With Cass in the woods with me, feeding the cats went quickly. It was actually nice to have him there. No one would mess with Cass, so I wasn't worried about running into anyone with bad intentions. I finished up by filling the water bowls in Whitney's shed. Cass had gone back to warm up the car. As I came out of her backyard and slid into the driver's seat, I saw Edie Barnes up at the end of her driveway in a robe and slippers despite the snow still on the ground. For someone usually so put together, she looked like she'd gotten no sleep last night. Her usually perfect shoulder-length hair was flat on one side. She was peering into her trash can. I wondered if she'd lost something, and if so why she hadn't sent Trey out to find it.

"Mind if I stop?" I asked Cass.

"Of course not."

I rolled up to Edie's driveway. Cass rolled down the window and leaned over to smile at her. "Morning, Edie. Everything okay?"

She, in turn, glared at me and then turned a suspicious look on Cass. "Everything's fine. Why?"

"I didn't see you at Virgil's funeral," I said.

The fact that I was at Virgil's funeral seemed to surprise her, but she recovered quickly. "I wasn't feeling well."

"Well, I hope you're feeling better. Is Trey ill too? He left the bar so quickly the other night."

Now her face went a sickly gray. "The bar?" she asked in a deadly quiet voice.

I nodded. "Jade Moon. New Year's Eve. I guess because you weren't feeling well he was out with some friends."

Her mouth was working but no sound came out. I felt a little bad now. She clearly had no idea what her husband had been up to, or that he'd been out at Jade's.

"He's fine. Thanks for asking." She turned to head back to her house, sliding a little on the slushy snow as she hurried away.

Cass and I looked at each other. "She certainly didn't seem very happy to speak to you," Cass said.

"No," I murmured. "She certainly didn't."

I dropped Cass off and arrived at the library around ten. I was relieved to see that Ellen St. Pierre was working. She was not only one of the librarians, but more importantly, Leopard Man's girlfriend—a recent development. She stood in the lobby speaking to a harried-looking woman with two young children. She pointed upstairs, and once the woman walked away dragging the kids—one of whom was throwing an impressive fit—she shook her head and came over to give me a hug.

"Poor thing has devil children," she whispered into my ear. "But don't tell her I said so." Stepping back, she held me at arm's length and looked me over. "How are you, Maddie? You look skinny. Are you eating?"

At least one good thing had come of this whole Lucas

ordeal. "I am, Ellen. I just needed to lose a few pounds." I smiled reassuringly. "I'm looking for our favorite leopard. Is he here?"

"In his favorite chair," she said, pointing to a small reading room off the main room. "Waiting for me to get done. We have a hot date tonight," she said with a wink.

I wasn't sure I wanted to know about that. "Didn't you just open?" I asked, glancing at my watch.

She nodded. "He just likes to be around me." She clasped her hands together and brought them to her lips. "It's so sweet."

That it was. "Thanks, Ellen." I hurried into the other room.

Leopard Man was in a chair next to the window. He had an open book on his lap, but he wasn't reading it. Instead, he was gazing out the window. He turned when I came in and smiled.

"Ah, Maddie. I bear a charmed life." He closed his book and rose to kiss my cheek. "To what do I owe the honor?"

"I'm sorry to bother you," I said. "But I had two questions for you."

"Delightful!" He clapped his hands. "What's the first? I hope I know the answer."

"Are you the one giving Katrina anonymous donations for the ferals out on Sea Spray? And paying the vet costs?" Something else I'd been wondering, although I wasn't sure it was related.

"Alas, that is not me. Although it's a lovely idea," he mused. "I should do in the future. And the second question?" He waited expectantly.

"This one's a bit more pointed," I warned him.

He inclined his head in a *go ahead* motion.

"I was wondering why you were at Virgil Proust's funeral?"

Leopard Man regarded me seriously, those piercing eyes on mine, his whimsy falling away. "Because he was a friend," he said finally. "And I count myself in nothing else so happy as in a soul remembering my good friends."

"*Richard the Second*," I said, snapping my fingers.

He smiled. "Very good."

My Shakespeare skills aside, this seemed weird. "But no, seriously. You were friends?"

"Yes. For many years." He motioned for me to come sit. I dropped into the comfy chair across from him.

"Why?" I asked finally. "He didn't like the cats. And they tried to stop us from helping them."

Leopard Man shook his head firmly. "No, Madalyn. That was not Virgil."

"Then it was his wife. And I know she was sick, but still. He went along with it." I crossed my arms stubbornly. "I thought that would be a deal breaker for you."

"It surely would've been. But that wasn't him. He did not go along with anything that would have endangered a cat."

"You were really that good of friends? Does Grandpa know?"

Leopard Man nodded. "Yes, we were friendly. Not best friends, but friendly. Your grandfather knew."

But had never mentioned it to me. Not that it really mattered, but still. "How did you know him?"

"He had an office near where I parked my trailer years ago. One day, we started talking. He liked my tail," Leopard Man remembered with a wistful smile. Leopard Man's tail was famous around the island. He wore it on days when he was in an especially good mood. "After a while, we began meeting at least once a week for coffee and conversation."

That caught my attention. "An office? For what?"

Leopard Man looked at me strangely. "For his work."

"Yes, but what kind of work?" I asked impatiently.

"I believe it was multipurpose," he said.

"Like a studio? I learned he was an artist."

"Why, yes he was." Leopard Man looked pleased that I knew that.

"Did he still have it? Like recently?"

He nodded. "Virgil owned it."

"And he went there a lot, even recently?"

"I imagine so. It's where he did most of his work."

"Did he really do that much painting? I googled him and didn't find anything about him. Do you know if he used it for . . . anything else?"

Leopard Man studied me again. He did that a lot during serious conversations and I always felt he was looking right into my brain.

"Maybe you should see for yourself," he said finally, then offered me his arm. "Care to take a drive?"

Chapter 42

Since Leopard Man didn't drive his ancient truck around unless he was moving his horse trailer/house, we got into my car and headed west. He didn't tell me where we were going, just offered step-by-step directions. Finally we ended up on Ocean Boulevard, the winding road that ran parallel to the ocean and spanned each town. It appeared we were heading to Fisherman's Cove, the town at the westernmost tip of the island.

Finally Leopard Man pointed to a turn. I glanced at the street sign as I took the sharp left: Bluff Point Drive.

Why did that sound familiar? I mulled it over as I cruised down the street and ultimately found myself in a little village of cottages. Beyond them, the ocean sparkled in the winter sunlight. I followed his pointing finger to the end of the little street and parked, then looked questioningly at him. "You used to live out here?"

He smiled. "As much as I've lived anywhere on the island, yes." He pointed to an area of beach a little ways away from the small houses. "I parked over there. It's probably the longest I stayed anywhere. It's lovely here. Quiet."

I surveyed the cottages. They looked empty. Which

made sense, given that it was winter. People probably didn't stay out here year-round.

Leopard Man got out of the car. I followed him to the last cottage, nearest his old parking spot. The door was turquoise blue with swirls of color splashed through it.

Leopard Man pulled a key out of his pocket. I watched, fascinated, as he unlocked the door. "Do you have a key to the whole island?" I asked, only half joking.

He smiled. "It was a safety measure for Virgil all those years ago. In case he forgot his key. But since we remained friends, I just kept it." He motioned me inside. "Go on."

I wasn't sure what I was expecting when I stepped inside—something akin to a cheap motel room, perhaps—but whatever it was, it wasn't this. The room was one giant art studio. Each wall was a different mural, each depicting an animal of some sort—a wolf, a dog, a cat, an elephant. Even the ceiling was painted. Easels stood around the room, each one holding a painting. Some looked finished, others were in progress. Paints, brushes, and other paraphernalia covered a long table. The room smelled of paint and incense, fading now, but captured since the windows and doors had been shut tight.

I turned in a slow circle, taking it all in. The cottage was really only two rooms, plus another door I assumed led to a bathroom. But mostly what I noticed were that these paintings weren't like the ones on his wall at home. I had seen paintings like these before. I stepped over to one of the paintings on the easel and studied it. It was a pit bull with the most soulful eyes I'd ever seen looking right into mine, set against a background of pinks and purples. The details were amazing, down to the different-color fur around each eye. It almost reminded me of . . .

Holy crap. It couldn't be.

I glanced behind me at Leopard Man, who watched me intently. "This is Virgil's studio?" I confirmed.

He nodded.

"And Virgil didn't use his own name when he painted," I said. I was getting a tingly feeling all over that I couldn't ignore.

Leopard Man said nothing.

I moved from painting to painting, but wasn't finding what I wanted to see. It wasn't until I moved to the murals and crouched down on the floor that I found what I was looking for. At the very bottom of each was the signature: Salvato.

I sat back on my heels, my head spinning. "Salvato? Virgil Proust is Salvato? How? Why? How did I not know this?"

Leopard Man came and sat on the floor next to me, running his fingers lightly over a painting of a cat tumbling in the grass, butterfly over his head. "He was only Salvato near certain people," he said. "Very few, actually. It was difficult, with his wife."

I frowned. "What did she have to do with his work?"

He regarded me with a touch of amusement. "She didn't like animals. You said so yourself," he pointed out. "It had become a phobia of sorts. And she was never quite supportive of his love for the arts anyway. She much preferred his professor persona. So he developed an alter ego as he got more invested in this line of work, and kept a small studio at home where he painted seascapes and other nature-related things. And then his career got bigger and bigger, especially once Best Friends discovered him. By then he'd kept it from her for so long that it made no sense to reveal it. She'd already begun showing signs of early-onset dementia."

I had no idea what to say. I was overcome with sadness

at this news, because it meant the great Salvato was gone and the animals had lost an ally. And it also showed me I'd been completely, utterly wrong about Virgil Proust, and I felt awful about it. And about his death.

"There's more," Leopard Man said after a moment. He rose and pulled me to my feet, steering me toward the little door that I thought led to a bathroom. But when he pulled it open, I saw it was a whole other room.

I'd thought I'd had all the surprises I could take for the day, but when I stepped into the smaller studio, there were at least ten finished paintings positioned around. There was also cat paraphernalia. Litter boxes. Giant crates. Food bowls. I stepped over to the paintings, zeroing in on a painting of a fluffy black cat with a tipped ear. I'd recognize that face anywhere. It was Toby, from the Sea Spray colony. I moved to the next one and recognized the giant tiger cat I'd started calling Gus. The one I hadn't seen for a few days and been so worried about.

"What is this? He was painting the cats from his neighborhood? But how did he . . ."

"Virgil was helping Katrina," Leopard Man said. "He notified her about the colony and was supplying funds for her to care for the cats. The funds you thought I was supplying," he said with a wink. "And he was trying to keep June from interfering. Then when Katrina needed more space to house the cats while they were getting fixed, he let her keep them here while they recovered from the surgeries. He actually helped trap a few of them. While they were here, he decided to paint them for a new collection."

"A new collection? Of the ferals?" I moved to each of the paintings, tracing each detail. His depiction of them was brilliant—you would never guess they weren't house cats posing for their favorite human. "And he *trapped* them? Again, how did I not know any of this?"

Leopard Man nodded. He looked sad too. "He really

felt for them. And the whole dynamic was terribly hard for him."

"He tipped off Katrina about the poison petition," I said. "When it was raised at the meeting. That's how she knew."

Leopard Man nodded, and I could see his jaw tightening. "He told me about that. It's a disturbed mind that would suggest that option."

I agreed. I stared at the pictures a little longer, then suddenly realized where I'd seen this street name before. I pulled out my phone and checked my notes, where I'd copied down the address I'd found in Katrina's calendar. "What number is this house?"

"Five twenty-five."

Bingo. So Katrina's relationship with Virgil had been innocent. And I was a jerk. I turned to Leopard Man. "Who else knew about this?"

Leopard Man shrugged. "Not many. Me, because he trusted me. Dr. Kelly. They were friends also."

I remembered Dr. Kelly's reaction when I'd gone to his office asking about Virgil. Now I knew why. He hadn't wanted to be put in a position to reveal his friend's secret either.

"Why didn't you tell me?" But as soon as I asked the question, I knew what he was going to say.

"It wasn't my story to tell," he said simply. "But since people may have the wrong idea about his relationship with Katrina, it's not the time to keep more secrets. Hopefully we can find the real killer and get him the justice he deserves."

Chapter 43

My head was spinning when I dropped Leopard Man back off at the library. I still wasn't sure if everything I'd just learned had anything to do with Virgil's murder— unless someone had killed him because they knew he was fighting *for* the cats instead of against. Which would've pointed me right back to June, but I knew now it couldn't have been her.

But it did make me think of Whitney and her boyfriend— Paul the art agent, aka Dominick the Donkey. This knowledge of Virgil's real career changed things. While Virgil may have been donating his profits to animal causes, Paul still had to be getting a good payout from representing him. Which would give him no reason to kill him . . . unless something had happened to jeopardize that relationship. What if they'd had a falling out recently? Or Virgil had fired Paul? Had Whitney caused a problem because of the whole June thing? Without Virgil as a client, Paul could stand to lose a lot of money. I had no idea how I would find that out, but I knew I had to start with Whitney.

At least I could now offer up a half-dozen good reasons why it wouldn't have been Katrina, instead of my current *Because I know she would never do that*. It also meant I'd been way out of line accusing her of having an affair with him, and I needed to figure out what to do to fix that.

So I wasn't really in the mood to be accosted by Val and Ethan when I walked in the front door. They were waiting for me, and they looked serious enough that I got nervous.

"Maddie. Sit. We need to talk."

My heart sped up. "What's wrong? Is Grandpa okay?"

"He's fine. We just need to talk to you."

I sank into a chair, searching first her face, then Ethan's, for a clue to what this was about. I couldn't take any more bad news, and I tried to keep my mind from wandering there on its own. "What's going on?"

"I don't mean to butt in like this," Val said. "But I can't watch this any longer. You're cranky all the time and it's driving me crazy, for one thing. For another, well, I can't sit back and watch you throw this away."

"Throw what away?" I asked, exasperated. I turned to Ethan. "Can you translate please? And get to the point a little faster?"

"It's Lucas," Ethan said. Leave it to him to cut to the chase.

Oh, for Pete's sake. Who had time for this right now? I had a murder to solve. "Forget it." I started to get up, but Val blocked me from standing. "Jeez. Are you planning to tie me to the chair next?" I asked. I couldn't help but be annoyed with her. I knew I was conveniently forgetting how I'd forced her to leave her house and come stay with Grandpa and me when everything went to crap with Cole, but that was different.

"If I have to. Look. Lucas called me and asked if we could talk."

"He what?" I glared at her. "You went?"

"We both did." Val stuck her chin up defiantly.

"You too?" I looked at Ethan in disbelief.

He shrugged. "Val asked me to go. And I'm glad I did, Maddie. You need to cut the guy some slack. Seriously."

"What is with you two? And what is it with him? This isn't okay to broadcast around the whole island." I was getting angrier by the minute. He had no business involving all these people to try to get me to talk to him again. Not even just *people. Family.* Where were his carrier pigeons during his Houdini act, when no messages were being sent?

"We're not the whole island. We're your family," Val said pointedly. "And we care about you. Of course we wouldn't push you to talk to him if we thought he was playing us, or if it was bad for you. I really think this whole thing was just a bad misunderstanding and he would like the opportunity to explain."

"Yeah. You're absolutely right. You're my family. So you'll forgive me if this seems odd."

"He thought that if we were open to listening—" Ethan cleared his throat and fell silent when I shot him a look.

"So he told you what happened. Or at least what he said happened."

Val nodded. "The high-level version."

"So?" I spread my arms. "What happened?"

She shook her head. "Not our story to tell."

"Second time I've heard that today," I muttered. "Right. Well, that's convenient." I shoved back my chair and rose. "I have things to do, if you'll excuse me."

"Maddie. Can you stop being so stubborn?" Val asked, exasperated. "I wouldn't bother if I thought he was lying, or if he had an ulterior motive. He misses you. He knows things got crazy, and he wants to explain. That's all."

I still wasn't convinced. I so didn't want to be *that girl.* The one who got treated poorly but eagerly went back for more if there was a good explanation to go along with it. Especially since I'd been that girl too many times to count already.

"I'll think about it," I said. "Anything else?"

Val and Ethan exchanged a glance.

"No," Val said. "Nothing else."

"Great." I turned to go, then looked back. "Thanks for trying. Really. And I will think about it."

"I hope so," Val said.

I left the room and went upstairs, blinking the tears back. I so wanted to call Lucas right then and hear his story. I so wanted his story to be a good one. But what if it wasn't? What if I ended up not being able to trust him again . . . ever? That would be a crappy restart to a relationship.

It was all so complicated. And I had bigger fish to fry at the moment.

Chapter 44

I had to go feed the cats and check the traps Adele had put out a few hours ago anyway—she'd left me a message while I'd been with Leopard Man—so I used that as my excuse to go to Whitney's house that night. It was also an excuse to not be home with Val staring at me waiting to see if I'd called Lucas yet. I did call Grandpa, but he usually went to play cards with his friends on Saturday and his phone was off. I left him a message about where I was going just in case, then headed out in Grandma's car.

When I got to the neighborhood, it was quiet. We'd had a little more snow last night and the woods were white and virtually undisturbed. I filled the bowls and put out some wet food in the shelters. I spotted a few pairs of cat eyes watching from behind some trees, but no one was in the traps. I closed them up and headed back out to the street.

Lights were on at Whitney's. I went out and took care of the cat stuff in the shed before I went to the door, adding water to the heated bowl and leaving extra food out. While I was there, I took a casual sweep around with my flashlight. I'd been in here many times, but never paid much attention to what she had stored in here.

There wasn't much. A lawn mower and a weed whacker. Some gardening tools. No creepy matching gnomes.

I turned and left, leaving the door cracked so the cats could get in and out, and went to the front door. I wasn't sure if this was the smartest plan, but I was fresh out of plans. And if Paul had represented Virgil, Whitney had to know the truth about Virgil's real feelings about the cats. Unless she'd been upset with him for not doing anything about June. I really was having trouble sorting out what any of that meant, but I knew I had to talk to her.

She answered on the first ring. Her wild red hair was tamed by a green scarf, and her face was scrubbed clean of makeup. When she saw it was me, she visibly relaxed. "Maddie! Hi, sweetie. Come in." She kissed my cheek, then stepped back and clasped my hands. "You're not upset with me, are you?"

"Upset? Why?" I asked.

"Ah, well. Because I've been a bit of a liar." She motioned me inside and closed the door. "My leg and all."

"Whitney. Whatever is going on there, it's really not my business."

"But it's not right. I know that. But my ex-husband was completely at fault for what happened, and to add insult to injury he was trying to deny me health-care coverage as part of our divorce. It was dragging out and I needed to make sure I had insurance. I was very upset and I took it to the extreme. Can you forgive me?"

"Of course," I said, still not sure what I was forgiving her for. She wasn't committing insurance fraud on *me*. "Listen. I need to talk to you though. It's about Virgil."

Whitney took a breath. "I wondered when you'd come. Do you want to sit?"

I shook my head, choosing to stay at the door just in case. "Is Paul here?"

"No. He had a meeting in Boston tonight."

I looked her straight in the eye. "I know about Virgil's alter ego. And that Paul represented him," I said.

She nodded slowly. "I figured as much."

"Why did you pretend to hate him?"

"Because he didn't want anyone to know about his other career and how successful he'd become. June wouldn't have liked it," she said, making a face. "Why that man put up with her. . . . Anyway. He liked the anonymity too. He was very modest and didn't want attention for helping animals. He just wanted to help them. It became very awkward for him when I started dating Paul. He did think about changing agents, but I swore I'd never tell anyone. And I kept my promise."

I watched her carefully, trying to gauge if she was telling the truth. "But you were over there yelling at them. We saw you."

"I was yelling at June," she corrected.

"Where did you meet Paul?" I asked.

"At a fundraising event in Boston last year. It was for animals." She smiled wryly. "Virgil sent him."

I leaned against the door, still trying to process how very wrong I'd been about Virgil Proust. And not that it should change how I felt about his death—no one deserved to die that way regardless of their beliefs—but it seemed like a greater loss than ever when I looked at all he'd been doing for the animals.

"So was Paul still representing him? Nothing had changed?"

Whitney frowned. "Of course not. They were friends and business associates. Why?" It seemed to dawn on her as she was saying it. "Oh, Maddie. You thought Paul or I . . . I can't believe you would think that." She looked so disappointed, I felt even worse.

"No, Whitney, please. I was reaching. Trying to think of anything that made sense," I admitted. "And when I realized your leg was actually not damaged, I started wondering why you would fake that. It was an awful thing to even consider, and I'm so sorry."

We stared at each other for interminable seconds. I waited for her to throw me out, but instead, she started to giggle. I watched in fascination as the giggles turned into laughter until she was nearly bent over holding her stomach she was laughing so hard.

I had no idea what was so funny and was starting to wonder if the stress of all this might have gotten to her when she straightened up and wiped her eyes, regaining control.

"I'm sorry. That was really funny, though. I love that you think we're that devious. Paul will think it's funny too. Not that any of this is funny," she hastened to add. "Besides, the night Virgil died, Paul was off-island. At a meeting in Boston with his art cronies. And I was"—she winced a little—"at Blue Heaven. It was tango night. I got home right before I saw you, when all the police cars had shown up. I can definitely prove it."

Tango night. I resisted the urge to laugh too, at the ridiculousness of all of it. "I never believed Katrina did it anyway, but now that I know the truth about Virgil, it's even crazier anyone would think that. So I'm reaching."

She watched me, the remnants of laughter fading from her face. "When you put it that way," she said, "it is hard to fathom. Are you going to come sit? You're making me nervous standing by the door."

I followed her into the living room. "I wanted to be able to run if you and Paul decided to try to kill me if I had uncovered your crimes," I said, only half kidding.

"I don't know whether to laugh or cry at that," Whitney said. "So I guess I'll make some tea." She went to the stove to boil water.

"Thanks." I thought about my list at home and figured

it was worth asking. "What's up with Harvey? Do you know anything about him?"

"Harvey Hackett?" Whitney glanced at me.

I nodded, not wanting to give too much away.

She made a face and turned back to her task. "I find him spineless. Says whatever pleases the person in front of him at the moment."

"Really?"

"For sure. But too spineless to kill anyone, either."

"Harvey was the one who brought the cat problem to the Audubon board. And who started the poison petition."

Whitney's hands stilled. She turned to me slowly. "I'm sorry?"

I spread my hands wide. "It's true."

"But he . . . well, Monica loves the cats. She definitely wears the pants over there. Come to think of it, that's a common theme in this neighborhood," she mused.

"But what did he have to gain by lying about it and being against them?"

Whitney carried over two mugs of tea and sat down, handing me one. "That," she said, "could be the million-dollar question."

"Do you think Virgil threatened to tell Monica what he'd done?" I asked, taking the mug. "And maybe she wouldn't have let it slide?"

Whitney stared at me. "So you think Harvey killed Virgil?"

"I don't know what to think," I said. "But I'm running out of suspects, and Virgil did threaten him."

"Well if he did," Whitney said, "he would've had to sneak up on him and do it quick. Like I said, the man was spineless."

Chapter 45

The next afternoon I paused outside the grooming shop, peering inside. Lucas was in there—his Subaru was out front, so I'd already known that—and I was trying to decide about going in. I didn't see anyone else inside, which was good. I definitely didn't want an audience. I was more nervous about this than I'd been for our first real date, and I'd been pretty nervous then.

I hadn't called. I didn't want to give him a heads-up in case I chickened out or changed my mind. But it was time to clear the air. My visit to Whitney's yesterday had left me more frustrated than anything and made me realize I wasn't getting anywhere with the other puzzle in my life. Maybe if I cleared this up, I'd have more brainpower to spend on Virgil Proust. Whichever way this went.

Squaring my shoulders, I marched to the shop door and pulled it open. Lucas glanced up from where he'd been stocking some kind of shampoo on a shelf, and his eyes widened when he saw me.

"Maddie. Hi. What are you . . . I'm glad to see you."

"Hi," I said, nervously shifting my weight from foot to foot. "Sorry if this is a bad time."

"Not a bad time at all."

I glanced down as the dog I'd seen with Lucas on the street the other day trotted over to me. "Hi, Oliver," I said, bending down and offered my hand for him to sniff. He did, gingerly at first, then licked my fingers, looking up at me, tail wagging. I glanced up at Lucas. "If you have an appointment, I can come back."

Lucas shook his head slowly. "I'm not grooming him. He's mine."

"Oh." I shook off the way that made me feel. He'd gotten a dog and I hadn't even known about it. When had he had time to get a dog anyway?

"He's the reason I was gone," Lucas said.

My hand stilled on Oliver's head. I rose slowly. "What do you mean?"

He held up a finger, went to the door and turned the closed sign around, then locked it. "Let's go out back."

I followed him into the little room he used as a kitchen/ office, Oliver at my heels. He opened the fridge, pulled out a water, and offered it to me. I shook my head. He opened it and took a swig. I could tell he was having a hard time figuring out how to begin.

"So," I prompted, sitting down at the little table.

Lucas sat across from me. "Thank you for coming."

"Don't thank me yet. I just needed to know. So tell me."

He smiled, a little. "Fair enough. I did go to Boston for the gig and the conference. And the ferries did shut down."

I waved my hand. "I know all that."

"So while I was waiting for them to get up and running again, I got a phone call. From my ex."

I could feel my heart sink. This was one of the scenarios that had been running through my head. He'd never really told me why he'd come out to Daybreak, other than he loved islands and wanted to open his business here. He'd wanted a challenge, he said. But I'd made up other reasons, and of course one of them was that he'd had his heart broken and was looking to get far away from whoever broke it and have a fresh start.

And when he was gone, I imagined that she'd realized her mistake and called, begging him to come home and take her back. So of course, he had.

I didn't say any of this. Instead I said, "Your ex what? Wife? Girlfriend?"

"Girlfriend. I would've told you if I'd been married before, Maddie. Give me some credit. Anyway, she told me she was getting rid of Oliver." At the sound of his name, Oliver's tail started to thump again.

I blinked. "I don't understand."

"Oliver was our dog together. When we split, I wanted to take him but she—Amy—wouldn't let me. He was always more my dog, and I knew she just did it to hurt me, but she threatened to take me to court and everything if I didn't let her keep him." His eyes flashed as he spoke, though I don't think he realized it. "So I felt like I didn't have a choice. The only thing I asked her was if she could please call me if she ever couldn't keep him. She agreed."

"How long ago did you . . . break up?" I asked.

"Right before I came here. So two years or so. And I never heard from her. Until the night before I thought I was coming home from Boston. She called and said she was getting married and moving to Texas. And she couldn't take Oliver because her boyfriend's dog didn't like him." He grimaced. I could tell what he thought of that. Pretty much the same thing I would've thought of that. *Bye, honey, nice knowing you.*

"And she wanted you to come get him?"

Lucas nodded.

"Okay," I said. "Why did that have to be such a big secret?" I remembered Craig's words: *He was in jail, Maddie.*

"It didn't," Lucas admitted. "But I felt like it wasn't really the thing to tell you over the phone. That my ex-girlfriend had called and I'd dropped everything and run to Virginia. Since we were still . . . new, I didn't want to wreck things." He moved his shoulders in a miserable half shrug. "Not like I didn't anyway, but I had good intentions."

"I think you know me well enough by now to know that I would do anything for an animal, so I wouldn't have thought it was weird at all."

"Well, there's more. I'm sorry, this is kind of a hard story for me to tell . . ." He cleared his throat. "Amy isn't the most stable person in the world, and when I heard her on the phone I got the sense she wasn't telling me something. So I booked a flight out the next day, and when I showed up at her place, Oliver was already gone. Her boyfriend had dropped him off at a local shelter after she called me. So I asked if the boyfriend was home."

I winced. "Oh no. You didn't."

He nodded. "I did. Got in a fight with the guy. Got a couple of good punches in too. But the drama queen called the cops and I got hauled off for assault and battery. I accidentally slugged the cop too, so that didn't help."

My eyes widened. Lucas was not a violent guy. I'd never even seen him raise his voice. "God, Lucas. So what happened?"

"Like I said, I got hauled off to jail," he said, not meeting my eyes. "And the worst, most stupid part of all is that I lost my cell phone during this . . . altercation. I had no numbers to call anyone. And I only had one credit card with me, and it didn't have enough money on it to pay the twenty-five-hundred-dollar fine I got. They also sentenced me to ten days in jail. I guess I was lucky. They could've given me up to a year. First offense and all that."

"Lucas, why didn't you call a lawyer or call . . . information or something for Grandpa's house number? Or your family? Isn't your family down there?" I couldn't believe he'd let this get so out of hand. It sounded completely nuts. But if I was honest with myself, I could see exactly how one thing that went sideways could lead to another, and another—a total domino effect of insanity that no one could predict.

He sighed. "I used my one call to call the shelter where she said they'd dropped Oliver off at. But they had no dog that came in with that description."

I was feeling really, really bad. The whole time I'd been cursing Lucas, railing at myself for trusting him, and thinking mean, horrible thoughts about the whole situation, he'd been suffering. "I . . . can't believe you didn't try to call me," I said finally. "At any point. I could've helped."

He gave me a look. "You had a lot going on at the time. And I didn't want to freak you out. That's not the kind of thing you call a new girlfriend with. Plus, how many scams have you heard about where some guy calls you from somewhere else and asks for money for some sad story?"

That made me laugh, but I wasn't sure it was appropriate to laugh right then, so I pretended to have a coughing fit. "I think that's for like, fake men. You know, Russian bots or whatever."

"Still. Calling you for money was probably the last thing I would've thought of doing."

"Okay, well why didn't you call and ask for help with Oliver? And so what happened, anyway? Are you going to finish the story?"

"Yes. Right. So after I got out, I went straight to the shelter that I'd spoken to. I didn't know where else to go, and I wanted to see for myself that he wasn't there.

I didn't know if Amy had told me the wrong place on purpose, or if her boyfriend told *her* the wrong place—on purpose or otherwise."

"God. It had been a week. He could've been adopted." Or worse, but I didn't say that. I looked down at the pup, who was curled into a content ball at Lucas's feet. Pit bulls still got a bad rap, especially down south.

"I know. It was probably the worst experience of my life. And then thinking about how I'd surely screwed things up with you—" He shook his head. "But I didn't know what else to do besides try to go track him down. Otherwise I would go back and finish what I started with that piece of . . . anyway. So when I'd called the first time I'd told the woman on the phone what happened and she said she would keep her eye out. But when I went back, no one had seen him. I checked all the cages just to make sure. I was really bummed. Just as I was about to leave and start hunting him down through other shelters, this woman races in. She's one of the volunteers—she was there when I'd called the first time and heard the story. The woman on duty called her to see if she'd found out anything while I looked around for myself." He smiled that adorable half smile that had won my heart in the first place and still made it skip today. "And she apparently has contacts at a bunch of shelters. She'd been inquiring about Oliver because it really bothered her. When she heard I was there, she couldn't believe it because she had a lead, but they had no way of getting in touch with me—"

"Because you'd lost your cell phone," I finished.

He nodded. "And of course I couldn't go back to Amy's house to look for it or I'd get arrested again. So I had to go get another one when I got back." He reached into his pocket and held up the newest iPhone. "At least I got the new version, right? So anyway. This woman, Kristy, she had a friend who'd just taken in a foster. Older pittie, terrified of the shelter so someone took pity on him and took him home. He's only eight. Not so old, but . . . too old for that crap."

"Of course," I murmured. I'd barely noticed that I'd relocated myself to the floor next to Oliver and was stroking his soft fur. He rolled over, tail thumping, and offered me his belly. What a sweetie. "Why did she do that?" I asked. "Your ex?"

"Because she's heartless," he answered. "Like I said, she didn't care like I did. He was a trophy to her. A thing she used to get even with me for messing up her life. But Ollie was with me for a long time . . . through a lot of stuff. It nearly killed me to lose him."

"I bet. So you went to this foster home?" I prompted.

He nodded. "Kristy called the woman and she said to come right over. It was him. When I got there, he was so happy to see me." He reached down to rub Oliver's head. "And it made the whole debacle worth it."

"I'm sure," I said softly. I could feel my throat choking up with tears. He did exactly what I, or Katrina, or Adele, or any of us would have done. Maybe more. Going to jail must've been horrible. "I totally would've helped if you'd called," I said, looking up at him finally. "I wish you had. You should've just . . . trusted me." As I said the words, I was cringing inside. I'd been so ready to believe the worst about him. But in my defense, staying quiet and disappearing were never good things to do.

"I know. The longer it went on too, the harder it felt like it would be to call you," he said. "I figured after a certain point you wouldn't take my call. And you weren't exactly pleased to see me when I got back." He said it with no judgment, but I felt like a jerk just the same.

"I was really hurt," I said simply. "I thought you just took off. That you'd gotten sick of the island and, well, me, and just didn't want to come back."

He stared at me and I swore I saw his eyes welling up. "Maddie. That is the furthest thing from the truth. All I could think about was you, and how I'd explain this to you once I got back, and how much I wanted you to meet Ollie . . ." He trailed off and focused on his bottle of water. "Anyway, I don't expect this to change your mind or anything. I understand what I did was crappy. I'm just glad I got a chance to tell you the real story."

I stayed on the floor, still rubbing Ollie's tummy. Val and Ethan had been right. I should have heard him out sooner. I would've done exactly the same thing for JJ or, honestly, for any animal.

And the fact that he'd done it made me love him even more.

"Lucas," I said, getting to my feet.

"Yeah."

I went over and hugged him. "I'm glad you and Ollie are home. I really missed you."

Chapter 46

When I left the grooming salon a little while later, I felt transformed. Like a giant weight had been lifted off my chest and I could breathe again. We'd spent a long time talking after he'd told me his story—about Ollie, about what happened, about us.

Lucas hadn't abandoned me. And even better, he'd been doing something really noble and sweet. I felt a thousand percent better as I drove to Sea Spray to check the traps. Adele had sent me a text reminding me that she'd set them and could I please go check on them. So I did, feeling like I was floating on air.

When I got to the neighborhood, there were a bunch of cars parked out on the street, many of them in front of the Barneses' house. There was also a U-Haul parked in front of the Prousts'. What was going on there? Lilah would know. I made a mental note to stop by on my way out.

But when I got into the woods, I saw we'd hit the jackpot. Two of the three traps had cats in them. And even better, they weren't cats we'd already trapped and fixed. "Score," I said out loud. Although this meant I had to call Mick Ellory.

I brought the first trap out to my car and loaded it inside, then went back to get the second one. As I stooped to pick it up, I caught a glimpse of something out of the corner of my eye. Something pink, moving up ahead. I stood up slowly, my hand going for my phone, and began moving slowly toward it.

As I got closer, I realized it was a hat. And the person wearing it was dragging a giant tarp.

The adrenaline in my body kicked up a notch. "Hey," I called out.

The person froze, then got up and started to run in the opposite direction. I couldn't see her face, but it clearly was a woman. A woman in pretty-good shape, given how fast she took off. I didn't give it much thought—and clearly not good thought—before taking off after her. I had to know what she was doing out here. Was this the person who'd vandalized the cat houses? Stolen the decorations? Killed Virgil?

I wasn't much of a runner, but snow still covered the paths in the woods and it wasn't long before the chick in the pink hat tripped on roots or something and went down. She was up in a flash and almost took off again, but I took a dive and grabbed her by the leg. She went down again in a slippery, snowy pile of leaves and flailed around, delivering a kick to my jaw with her free leg that stunned me, but I was able to hold on. Finally she stopped fighting me and flipped over. We each tried to catch our breath.

I immediately recognized the face glaring at me. "Avery?" Avery Evans. Our former volunteer. But what on earth?

Avery shoved at her hat, which had slid down over her forehead. "Are you crazy? You could've broken my leg."

"Are *you* crazy? What are you even doing out here? You quit, remember?"

"I *know*," she responded, as if *I* were the idiot here. "I was just . . . taking care of some business."

"Business, huh? Let's go see what kind of business." I got up and dragged her up with me. She swiped furiously at her wet jeans, then let out a cry of dismay.

"My nails! I just got them done." She held up a hand with two broken fingernails. "Look what you did."

"Send me the bill. Let's go." I shoved her ahead of me. "So it was you who trashed the cat house? I know you were upset about what happened out here, but did you really need to take it out on the cats? Not cool, Avery."

Avery turned to give me another look of death. "I have no idea what you're talking about. I was taking it out on them, not the cats."

"Them? Who?"

"The idiots who live around here." She waved an impatient hand at the houses bordering the woods. "Bunch of jerks."

We'd reached the tarp. There could've been a dead body in it as big and full as it was. I sincerely hoped there was not. I'd had my fill of dead bodies. "What were you taking out on them? What's in there?"

She said nothing.

I gave her a little shake. "Open it."

"I plead the fifth," she said defiantly.

I rolled my eyes. "We're not in court, genius." I bent down and unhooked the bungee cords holding the tarp closed. And there was no part of me that was surprised when Santas, kissing balls, candy canes, and other Christmas decorations tumbled out.

"Avery." I reached up and rubbed my temples, trying to ward off the headache building there. "Are you kidding me? *You* were stealing their stupid decorations? And I was out here saying our volunteers had nothing to do with any of it?"

"What?" She crossed her arms defiantly over her chest. "Those people were jerks from the minute we came out here."

"That doesn't mean you get to steal their stuff. It makes all of us look bad." I unrolled the tarp even further and toed through the rest of the stuff.

And recoiled when I recognized a gnome just like the one used to bash Virgil's head in. I looked up at her. "What house did you get *that* from?"

"You really think I remember which cheesy decoration was from which house?"

I got up and went right in her face. "Drop the attitude. Someone's dead, and a friend of ours—well, a friend of mine—is about to take the fall for it. So you better start remembering."

The reminder about Katrina seemed to sober her. "I got it from that house," she said, pointing at the Barneses'.

I frowned. "You're sure?"

She nodded. "It was in the back, so it was easy to snatch."

"What were you planning to do with this stuff?"

Avery looked at the ground and toed at the snow. "I was going to dump it on their lawn. I parked over there"—she pointed behind her to the street that ran parallel to Sea Spray Lane on the other side of the woods—"and I dragged it through the woods. I was going to leave everything there in a pile once it got dark. I was tired of having the stuff in my trunk."

Great plan. "Where's the sleigh?"

"What sleigh?"

"The fancy sleigh from the Barneses' front lawn." Edie Barnes' handmade sleigh, the last thing to be stolen. Or at least the last reported thing.

"I didn't take a sleigh. Besides, it wasn't stolen. I saw that crazy lady who owns it pulling it out to her garage."

I frowned. "What do you mean?"

"I saw that woman. The one who lives there"—she pointed at Edie's house—"putting the sleigh in her garage. Isn't it hers?"

"You saw Edie putting the sleigh in her own garage?"

"Seriously, Maddie? I just said it twice. *Yes.*"

"When?"

"The night . . ." Her voice trailed off. "The night the cops were all out here because that guy died."

Chapter 47

I marched Avery back to get the poor cat still waiting in the trap, then brought them both out to my car, which was parked in Whitney's driveway. I put the cat in the backseat with the other one and Avery in the front and called Mick Ellory.

Thankfully, he answered.

"Sergeant, it's Maddie James," I said formally. "Sorry to bother you but I have a couple of cats that need a place to stay from Sea Spray. Can I bring them over?"

"I'm a little tied up right now," he said. "Can it be later on?"

"I guess, but I also have another issue—"

"Maddie, I have to go," he said. "Bring them by later. Around six." And he disconnected.

I gave the silent phone in my hand a dirty look, then tried Craig. No answer.

I turned to Avery. "Stay here. Do not leave this car or I'll call the cops on you. Got it?"

She crossed her arms sullenly across her chest. "Fine."

I slipped back into the woods through the Hacketts' again, but I wasn't going back to the cat area. I was curious now.

Avery said the gnome belonged to the Barneses. She also said she'd seen Edie putting her sleigh in her garage. Had Avery been mistaken? Why would Edie hide her own sleigh and then go to the trouble of reporting it stolen? Maybe she'd gotten a new one and that's what Avery saw? But that didn't make sense either. Why wouldn't she have put it back out with the other decorations?

I slipped into the Barneses' backyard. The house looked dark. Hopefully they were out. But Trey was already on my bad list, and my spidey sense about him had kicked up a few notches. I crept over to the garage. It was attached to the house, but hopefully not visible since the windows I was peeking in were farthest from the house. I wished I had a light, but I knew that would've called a lot more attention to myself.

I couldn't see much except a black Jaguar. But there was stuff piled up in there. And a tall object covered by a tarp, much like the one Avery had used. Frustrated, I jiggled the knob on the side door.

It opened.

Holding my breath, I paused and looked to see if anyone was around or if any lights had gone on inside. Nothing moved around me. Next door, the Prousts' house was quiet. The U-Haul was gone and it didn't look like anyone was home.

I stepped into the garage, staying low, and looked around. It was dusty and smelled like gasoline, which wasn't surprising. I saw a snowblower in the corner. I stepped past it and tugged at the tarp. It wasn't tied down because it came right off.

And then I just stared. Avery had been right. Edie's sleigh was standing up in the corner of the garage, and had been covered by a tarp.

Why had she pretended her own sleigh had been stolen?

A noise behind me caused me to jump. As I started to

turn around, something went around my neck. As I instinctively reached up to pull it away, it tightened. A cord of some sort, and it was biting into my neck. I tried to work my fingers under it and pull it loose, but it was too tight and my head was starting to spin. Gasping for air, I flailed and kicked at whoever was behind me, still trying to pull off the thing choking me.

"I believe your grandfather would call this burglary," a voice I vaguely recognized as belonging to Edie Barnes crowed triumphantly in my ear. "And of course I had to defend myself."

I felt like my whole body was starting to float away. My legs were shaking and I could barely stand up. I knew I wasn't getting enough oxygen and it was really likely this crazy woman was going to kill me. Just when I'd gotten things fixed with Lucas too.

That was the last thought floating through my mind before I felt myself sliding to the floor. Then, suddenly, blissfully, the pressure came off my neck. I heard a cry and a thud behind me but I couldn't really process it. I was on the ground myself, choking and trying to shake the stars from my eyes. When my vision cleared, I saw Avery standing over Edie with a rake. On the floor, Edie moaned.

Avery panicked and it looked like she was going to hit her again.

"No!" I jumped up, my voice hoarse, seeing stars again. But I knew the last thing I needed was someone else bludgeoned to death.

"She was trying to kill you! With Christmas lights!" Avery kicked at the abandoned string of lights on the ground.

I rubbed at my throat. "She sure was. What are you doing here?" I croaked, but I was thankful she'd come. Edie had been a few seconds away from seriously snuffing my life out.

"You were taking so long I figured you were over here poking around. I told you she hid her own sleigh." She waved at it triumphantly, then pointed outside as sirens wailed. "I called the cops. But hey, one thing?"

I looked at her expectantly.

"You gonna tell them about the other decorations?"

I smiled. "Your secret is safe with me."

Chapter 48

The next few hours after the cops arrived—and not just Turtle Point cops, but Daybreak Harbor cops including Mick Ellory and Craig—were a blur. Grandpa showed up too, of course, insisting I go to the hospital, but I fought him on that one. We settled on the EMTs checking me out completely. I just wanted this cleared up and to move on with our lives.

Avery and I had no trouble getting the cops to believe our story. In fact, they were all way ahead of us. The reason Mick Ellory hadn't been available when I'd called was because he and a few other cops—including Craig—were working with multiple agencies including the DEA to get Trey Barnes, who apparently was a big-time drug dealer. Unfortunately, his friends getting busted on New Year's Eve had put him on alert and he'd snuck off the island soon after. Edie was staying shut on that one, although the cops didn't believe she really knew the extent of what her husband was doing. But there was apparently a full-blown manhunt for this guy out on the mainland, Grandpa told me a while later, because they believed he was one of the major suppliers of meth on the East Coast.

"Wow," I said. It still hurt to talk, so I didn't offer much more than that. I was still sitting on the stretcher in the ambulance, where they had the heat blasting for me. The EMTs proclaimed that I would live, although my throat would be pretty bruised for a while. They put ice packs on it and offered me pain meds, which I'd declined. My voice was starting to come back, though.

"But there's more, Maddie. She confessed."

"To the murder?" My eyes widened. "Edie? I thought Trey . . ."

Grandpa shook his head slowly. "Seems Virgil witnessed one of Trey's drug drops—he was using Edie's handmade Christmas sleigh to hide his drugs, and his buyers would pick them up late at night—and confronted Trey about it. Edie heard them fighting, but they didn't know it. Virgil told Trey to get off his street for good or he was calling the cops, and Trey agreed." Grandpa looked grim. "Apparently Edie didn't want him to leave. She snuck out after Virgil walked home. Followed him into his yard and killed him. Then she hid the sleigh so the cops wouldn't find any traces of drugs accidentally if they came sniffing around. No pun intended."

I lay back and thought about that. How desperate did someone have to be to keep a marriage intact to go that far? The whole thing just seemed incredibly sad to me.

Grandpa squeezed my hand. "What were you thinking, snooping around at their house alone? It's a good thing that girl thought to come find you."

"Yeah. Where is Avery?" We still had a tarp full of decorations to get rid of.

"Over there. Just finishing giving her statement." He pointed.

Avery's dad had come to collect her. When she was done, they both came over to me. "I'm glad you're okay," she said.

I smiled at her. "I'm glad you didn't listen to me and stay in the car."

She laughed. "Thanks for . . . everything."

I nodded. "I'll call you tomorrow about the other thing."

Her dad looked at her. "What other thing?"

"Uh," Avery said. "I think I'm going to help out with the cats again." She looked at me, pleading for cover.

I nodded. "That's right. Call me and we'll get you back on the schedule," I said.

After they left, I looked at Grandpa. "Can we go now? I really just want to go to bed."

He looked at the EMT babysitting me. The guy shrugged. "She seems fine to me, and if she doesn't want to go to the hospital there's nothing else I can do."

"I'm not going to the hospital," I confirmed.

"Then you're free to go."

I gave him back his ice pack and Grandpa helped me out of the ambulance. The police had taken Edie away, and there were only a few cop cars left as they finished sweeping the scene. As we were getting into his truck, a car careened onto the street, slamming to a stop right behind us. Katrina.

She jumped out and raced over to us, throwing her arms around me. "Mick just called me. Oh my God. Are you okay, Maddie?"

She was hugging me so tight I couldn't breathe again. When I finally dislodged myself I nodded. "I'm fine. And Edie confessed to killing Virgil."

"I know. They dropped the charges. I'm free," she said, but her smile still looked sad. I knew she was feeling the loss of Virgil. I was too, especially as I processed who he really was. "And it's all thanks to you. I owe you."

"I'm just glad you're speaking to me again. I'm so sorry, Katrina. I never meant to hurt you. I'm sorry I thought you and Virgil—"

She waved it off. "It's okay, Maddie. Really. I would've probably thought the same thing. And I should've told you about Virgil helping out, but I knew you'd get all excited and accidentally tell someone. It's just as much my bad. Besides"—she glanced at Grandpa—"I'm seeing Mick."

My mouth dropped open. "Ellory?"

She nodded. "I have been for a while. I just kept it quiet because, well, we work together. He's really a good guy. He totally believed in me. And, he was doing a bunch of stuff for the animals while I was sidelined even though McAuliffe told him not to."

That made Grandpa laugh. "So he's a keeper," he said.

"Definitely," Katrina confirmed.

"If you're happy, I'm happy," I said. "So we're good?"

Katrina squeezed my hand. "We're good."

"And Avery is back on the job. I think."

"Oh, boy. I'm not sure if that's good," she said. "But we'll figure that out tomorrow. Now that I have a tomorrow to look forward to."

Chapter 49

"All in favor of allowing the feral cats to continue to live in peace in the neighborhood?" Whitney asked.

We were at the regularly scheduled meeting of the Sea Spray Neighborhood Association—my mom, Katrina, Mick Ellory, Lucas, who had insisted on coming with us, and me. Instead of a vote to poison the cats, the neighbors were voting on an official movement to "leave them the heck alone," as Whitney put it. Additionally, Whitney and Paul had appointed themselves the cats' official caretakers. Which would be easier now, given Whitney's miraculous recovery—her leg was no longer an issue.

But with the Barneses out of the picture—Trey had been apprehended in New York a few days after he fled Daybreak Island and was awaiting federal drug charges, and Edie was in jail for murder—and June Proust moving to Florida to be with her son, who would need to care for her, the major resistance had waned and people were eager to turn their attention to something else. People had even gotten their stolen Christmas decorations back, thanks to an anonymous Samaritan (Craig) who had deposited them in June Proust's yard under cover of darkness. I only owed him a million favors for that one. Although I might be able to avoid that since I'd been the reason he and Jade got back together. After our chat on New Year's Eve, she decided to give him another chance. Anyway, I then tipped off the cops that Edie had mentioned something about taking them there before she'd nearly strangled me to death. So everyone was happy about that too.

Conspicuously absent from the meeting were the Hacketts. I'd heard a rumor—from Lilah Gilmore, of course—that the Hacketts had separated. Monica had, surprisingly, been the one to move out with the kids. Lilah told me Monica had never liked the neighborhood anyway.

The vote passed unanimously.

When we left the meeting, I hugged my mother. "Thank you for all your help with this."

"Oh, honey. I was happy to." She kissed my cheek. "I'm so glad it worked out. Now you can focus your attention on your place. And your cute boyfriend."

I reddened. Lucas pretended not to hear her, but he was smiling. He had barely left my side the past week after my ordeal, and he and Ollie had basically moved into Grandpa's house too. Ollie loved the cats. So far, they were tolerating him.

Good thing Val had only pretended to throw his stuff in the dumpster when I'd been so angry.

He slung his arm around my shoulders now. "Dinner to celebrate?"

"I would love to." I looked at Katrina and Ellory. "Join us?"

Ellory raised his eyebrows. "Did Maddie James just invite me to dinner?"

I rolled my eyes. "If you're going to be a wise guy, I can rescind my invite."

"The two of you better figure out how to play nice,"

Katrina warned, but she was smiling too. I hadn't ever seen her so happy, and that made me actually like Mick Ellory. Who knew?

"I can be nice. So long as she stays out of my investigations," Mick said.

I didn't think he was entirely kidding, but I let it pass. I didn't want to think about investigations of any kind for a really long time. "It's a deal," I said, hiding my crossed fingers behind my back, then grabbed Lucas's hand and squeezed, admiring my new bracelet as I did so. I'd finally gotten around to opening the gift Lucas had brought me. He'd gotten a gorgeous silver custom-made charm bracelet, with three charms so far: one of JJ, one of the cat café sign, and one of a microphone, because I loved to sing. It reminded me of our first date.

He'd promised there were more on the way.

I was really looking forward to spring, and to new beginnings.

Don't miss the next enjoyable installment in Cate Conte's
Cat Café mystery series:

CLAWS FOR ALARM

Coming soon from St. Martin's Paperbacks!